THE PRIME SUSPECT

"Cloris Fennow hated the fact that she had new competition in town, and was very upset that the Garbers hired Trudy instead of her to work the Witches Ball, but she swears she was nowhere near the Garber house when Trudy died," Sergio continued.

"Where was she?" Hayley asked.

"Home," Sergio said.

Bruce raised an eyebrow. "Alone?"

Sergio nodded. "Yes."

"That's what I call a flimsy alibi," Hayley scoffed. "Did she have anything to say about poisoning poor Trudy so she would get sick and be unable to work the Witches Ball?"

"No, because we have no concrete proof Cloris was the one responsible for making Trudy sick, so it's just a suspicion at this point," Sergio said.

Hayley was not satisfied at all.

She was now determined to prove that Cloris Fennow had targeted Trudy by poisoning her, and then, when that didn't work, tampering with her propane tank and trapping her inside her own truck with the express purpose of killing her competition . . .

Books by Lee Hollis

Hayley Powell Mysteries
DEATH OF A KITCHEN DIVA
DEATH OF A COUNTRY FRIED REDNECK
DEATH OF A COUPON CLIPPER
DEATH OF A CHOCOHOLIC
DEATH OF A CHRISTMAS CATERER
DEATH OF A CUPCAKE QUEEN
DEATH OF A BACON HEIRESS
DEATH OF A PUMPKIN CARVER
DEATH OF A LOBSTER LOVER
DEATH OF A COOKBOOK AUTHOR
DEATH OF A WEDDING CAKE BAKER
DEATH OF A BLUEBERRY TART
DEATH OF A WICKED WITCH

Collections
EGGNOG MURDER
(with Leslie Meier and Barbara Ross)
YULE LOG MURDER
(with Leslie Meier and Barbara Ross)
HAUNTED HOUSE MURDER
(with Leslie Meier and Barbara Ross)

Poppy Harmon Mysteries
POPPY HARMON INVESTIGATES
POPPY HARMON AND THE HUNG JURY

Maya & Sandra Mysteries
MURDER AT THE PTA

Published by Kensington Publishing Corporation

DEATH of a WICKED WITCH

Lee Hollis

KENSINGTON BOOKS
www.kensingtonbooks.com

KENSINGTON BOOKS are published by

Kensington Publishing Corp.
119 West 40th Street
New York, NY 10018

To the extent that the image or images on the cover of this book depict a person or persons, such person or persons are merely models, and are not intended to portray any character or characters featured in the book.

This book is a work of fiction. Names, characters, places, and incidents either are products of the author's imagination or are used fictitiously. Any resemblance to actual persons, living or dead, events, or locales is entirely coincidental.

All Kensington titles, imprints, and distributed lines are available at special quantity discounts for bulk purchases for sales promotion, premiums, fund-raising, and educational or institutional use.

Special book excerpts or customized printings can also be created to fit specific needs. For details, write or phone the office of the Kensington Sales Manager: Kensington Publishing Corp., 119 West 40th Street, New York, NY 10018. Attn. Sales Department. Phone: 1-800-221-2647.

First Kensington Books Mass Market Paperback Printing: August 2020
ISBN-13: 978-1-4967-2495-3
ISBN-10: 1-4967-2495-X

ISBN-13: 978-1-4967-2496-0 (ebook)
ISBN-10: 1-4967-2496-8 (ebook)

10 9 8 7 6 5 4 3 2 1

Printed in the United States of America

Chapter 1

"Wicked 'Wiches," Hayley said, reading the business card that had just been handed to her. She glanced up at the pretty woman with long curly blond hair wearing a pink halter top and studded jean jacket, who stood in front of her desk at the *Island Times* office, a large carryall tote bag slung over her shoulder. "What kind of business is this?"

"Food truck," the woman said, smiling.

Hayley's face lit up. "I've always dreamed that one day we'd get another food truck in town! We've only had one for the longest time! Are you planning to be open all winter? Because I'll tell you, we are desperate around here for someplace to get a decent lunch during the winter! Practically every restaurant closes down once the summer tourists leave!"

"Well, I'm going to give it a go, but I guess it depends on how much business I get. But I'll try to stay open at least through the New Year."

"I'm sure you'll do just fine, especially once word gets around. Now, do you want to place an ad?"

The woman nodded. "Yes, I want to raise awareness as soon as possible and be up and going before Halloween. I was hoping to get an ad in for tomorrow."

"Unfortunately we're about to go to press with tomorrow's paper so I'm not sure I can get it in on time, but I certainly will make sure it's in Friday's edition."

"That will be fine. I scribbled down what I'd like to say on the back of the card."

Hayley turned over the card and read the woman's ad copy. *Wicked 'Wiches . . . Our Subs Are Pure Magic.* "Cute, but it doesn't say where people can find you."

"That's because I'm still waiting on my permit to set up shop down on the town pier. In the meantime, I'm just going to go where there is enough space to park my truck until someone kicks me out."

"I promise the police won't make you move if you give them a few of your wicked 'wiches on the house. I know the chief personally. He's my brother-in-law."

"It's always good to know people in high places," the woman said before extending a hand. "I'm Trudy Lancaster."

Hayley shook it. "Hayley Powell. Pleasure to meet you, Trudy. So tell me, besides delicious sandwiches, what else do you serve?"

"I've got a full working grill so I also do hamburgers, hot dogs, French fries, all the comfort food staples, but my specialty subs are my best sellers. I have a Tokyo Sub with roast beef and honey wasabi mayo, a Texas Turkey with barbecue sauce and grilled onions, my Hawaiian's popular with ham and cheese, pineapple and teriyaki sauce . . ."

"My mouth is watering already," Hayley moaned.

Trudy leaned over Hayley's desk and gave her a conspiratorial wink. "Tell you what, Hayley. You work *your* magic to get my ad in for tomorrow, and I'll go out to my truck and bring you back my top-selling jalapeño cheddar chicken meatball sandwich."

Hayley's eyes nearly popped out of her head. She quickly checked the clock on the wall. "Deal. Done. Go. I have, like, two minutes to make it."

Trudy turned and hightailed it out of the office as Hayley furiously tapped the keyboard of her desktop computer. By the time Trudy returned with a delectable-smelling savory sub wrapped in yellow paper, Hayley had successfully managed to place Trudy's advertisement.

Hayley eagerly reached out for the sandwich and Trudy playfully withheld it from her. "Did you make it?"

"With about two seconds to spare!" Hayley said, grabbing the sandwich and gleefully unwrapping it. "It smells wonderful!"

Trudy folded her arms, anxiously waiting for Hayley to try her creation.

After taking a big bite, Hayley moaned orgasmically. "Oh, Trudy . . . Oh . . . Wow . . ."

"Glad you like it," Trudy said, beaming.

Hayley chewed and swallowed and then wiped the sides of her mouth with a napkin Trudy had provided with the sandwich. "I have a strong feeling we're going to be fast friends."

"Good, because my husband and I just moved to town a few days ago and we barely know anyone."

"Well, I know pretty much everybody in town so I can change that. What brought you to Bar Harbor?"

"My husband, Ted, is a minister and he's been hired to take over at the Congregational church."

"I had heard rumors Reverend Staples was thinking about retiring, but I never thought he would get around to actually doing it."

"Ted is going to observe him for a few weeks before he officially takes the reins," Trudy said, watching happily as Hayley took another big bite of her sandwich, closing her eyes and moaning some more.

Hayley tried to speak, but her mouth was so full she couldn't, and she had to wait until she could chew enough to swallow again. "I'm sure you and Ted have a lot to do having just moved here, but once you get settled, maybe we can plan a dinner with you, Ted, me and my husband, Bruce—"

Trudy's eyes lit up. "How about tomorrow night?"

"That soon?"

"Like I said, we don't know anybody and I'm starved for good wine and good conversation."

"Well, I can guarantee good wine. As for the conversation, you'll just have to wait and see how Bruce and I do."

Sal Moretti barreled into the front office from the back bullpen, his nose sniffing, and bellowed, "What's that smell?"

"Sal, this is Trudy Lancaster. She and her husband—"

Sal ignored her and zeroed in on the sandwich lying on Hayley's desk. "What is that?"

"A sandwich," Hayley said, smiling at Trudy.

Sal rolled his eyes. "Yes, I know that, Hayley, but where did it come from?"

Hayley gestured toward Trudy. "Trudy brought it in. She just moved to town and she owns a food truck."

Sal's face brightened just as Hayley's had at this welcome news. "Where is it?"

"Parked right outside," Hayley said, chuckling.

Sal pushed past Trudy and looked out the window. "I've been wishing for years we'd get another food truck in town besides that rude Cloris Fennow's with her stale bread."

"See, Trudy?" Hayley said, grinning. "Your husband may be the new minister, but you're the one who is answering everyone's prayers."

Sal reached for his wallet in the back pocket of his pants and pulled out a twenty. "Do you make Italian grinders?"

Trudy nodded. "With my very own homemade Italian dressing."

"With extra pepperoncinis?" Sal asked, almost drooling.

"Coming right up!"

Sal pumped her hand and finally offered her a smile. "Sal Moretti, nice to meet you."

"Trudy Lancaster."

"Now make it quick, Trudy," Sal said, back to his usual gruff self. "I have to leave here by five to interview a town council member and I don't want to be rushed eating my sub."

Sal turned his back on them and marched back to his office without saying another word.

Hayley shrugged. "I swear he will grow on you. Eventually."

Chapter 2

If Hayley thought she had an immediate connection with Trudy Lancaster when they had met at the *Island Times* office a day earlier, it paled in comparison to Bruce's instant bonding with Trudy's husband, Ted. Ted was tall, lanky, and handsome in an offbeat sort of way, probably gawky as a kid, but had grown nicely into his looks. She was also surprised that he was in his mid-forties since Trudy was at the very least a decade younger. But the couple seemed to fit perfectly well together and Hayley found both of them utterly charming.

From the moment Bruce and Ted shook hands as they met in the parking lot of Mama DiMatteo's restaurant at the top of Rodick Street, the two men found themselves immersed in a lively discussion involving a variety of topics including politics, sports, and the best rock bands of the 1970s and '80s, with Bruce arguing the merits of Fleetwood Mac and Ted defending the legacy of the harder-edged Led Zeppelin.

Hayley and Trudy exchanged smiles and chose to take a backseat to the conversation in order to allow these two new buddies to get to know each other. As Hayley took the last few bites of her garlic-crusted haddock and helped herself to a tasting of Bruce's scallops in a coral vodka sauce, she decided she had heard enough about the genius of Robert Plant, having been more a child of the 1990s herself and a devotee of the Red Hot Chili Peppers. She gently steered the conversation toward a more neutral subject and inquired about the event that had brought the Lancasters to Bar Harbor in the first place: the impending retirement of Reverend Staples.

"I honestly never thought he'd retire," Hayley commented.

"Yeah, he loves performing in front of a crowd too much," Bruce said, smirking. "Which is why I was so surprised Lindsey Buckingham didn't join Fleetwood Mac on their last tour . . ."

"Bruce, enough about Fleetwood Mac! I want to talk about something else!" Hayley cried.

Ted set down his dessert menu and leaned forward. "Well, this stays between the four of us . . ."

"My wife *lives* for conversations that start like that," Bruce said.

Hayley playfully whacked him on the shoulder with her own dessert menu. "Let the man speak, Bruce."

Ted laughed and then continued. "I've only been at the church a few days, and as I have slowly gotten to know Reverend Staples and his wife, Edie, I get the distinct impression that it is the reverend who is pushing the whole retirement thing. Edie doesn't seem too happy about leaving the church."

"Of course not. She loves the power of the pulpit

and feeling important. Once Reverend Staples gives that up, they'll probably never get it back," Hayley said, grabbing the stem of her wine glass for a sip of Chardonnay.

Bruce turned to Hayley. "Since when have you become such a gossip?"

Hayley had just taken a gulp and nearly choked on her wine. She set the glass down and stared at Bruce, dumbfounded. "Do you have *any* idea who you married?"

Bruce patted her hand. "Yes, I was being sarcastic."

She resisted the urge to slap him with the dessert menu again. "She's probably also not looking forward to living on a fixed income."

The waitress arrived and the two couples decided they were too full from their meals for a dessert each, and so Trudy suggested they share a tiramisu and a crème brûlée. An idea they all jumped at, and so the waitress scooted off to the kitchen to put in the order.

Trudy waited until the waitress was out of earshot before resuming their private conversation. "Well, personally I'm not a big fan of Edie's."

"Come on, you've only known her for a few days," Ted said.

"I know, but I get the feeling she doesn't like me. When I stopped by to bring you all sandwiches on your first day, she was actually kind of cold to me," Trudy said.

Hayley raised an eyebrow. "Really? Usually if Edie doesn't warm to somebody, she makes a point of covering her true feelings by being fake nice."

"With me, she didn't even bother doing that. She was downright rude. Reverend Staples told me she loves salmon so I made her this delicious wild salmon sub with provolone and a roasted garlic sauce, and trust me, it's awesome, but when I gave it to her she didn't even thank me, and as far as I know, she never ate it. She tossed it aside and wouldn't even look at me," Trudy said.

"That's strange," Hayley said.

"Not really," Ted said with a shrug. "She resents Trudy."

"Why?" Bruce asked.

Trudy sat up in her chair, surprised. "Yes, Ted. Tell us why."

Ted smiled at his wife. "Because you're younger and prettier, and she caught the reverend checking out your backside as you left the church on the first day we all met," Ted said.

"Ted, that's not true!" Trudy wailed.

"Yes, it is," Ted said. "I saw him do it myself, and so did Edie. She knows her husband finds you sexy, and so now she considers you a threat."

Trudy blushed and shook her head, not wanting to discuss Edie's jealousy of her any further. Mercifully the waitress arrived with two plates and set the tiramisu and crème brûlée down in front of them. The foursome grabbed their dessert forks and excitedly dove in, ceasing all conversation as they shoveled in bites of the sweets with various moans of pleasure.

"Excuse me, we hate to interrupt your dinner, but we thought we'd stop by and say hello on our way out," a woman's voice said.

Hayley looked up to see a local couple, Mark and Mary Garber, standing next to their table. Hayley could see Bruce tense a bit because he found Mary rather loud and abrasive, but Hayley liked her. The Garbers had moved to town about eight or nine years ago. Mary worked at the bank and Mark was a contractor. Mary was in her mid-thirties, Mark a few years younger, and they tried hard to fit in, hosting happy hours on their deck, throwing holiday parties, getting involved as much as they could in the community by attending every fund-raiser and public event. Mary's determination to become a central part of the Bar Harbor social scene had initially met with middling success. But finally, after years of trying, she had hit pay dirt. Three years prior, Mark and Mary had hosted a Halloween party at their house called the Witches Ball where all the women were encouraged to come dressed as witches. The men had a much more relaxed dress code and could show up in any type of costume they chose. Mary likened it to the reverse Oscars where most of the men arrived in black tuxedos whereas the women were free to express their fashion creativity by working the red carpet in wild and colorful designer dresses. At the Garber house on Halloween, the men were the real standouts. The Witches Ball quickly caught on, and was now an annual staple that everyone looked forward to attending. Mary had met her goal. She had established a local tradition, cementing her place in the Bar Harbor cultural scene.

"How was your dinner?" Bruce asked.

Mark opened his mouth to speak but Mary cut him off before he had the chance. "Mark had the crab spinach-stuffed shells, which he liked. I had the pan-browned gnocchi, but frankly, the ones I make at home taste better."

"Mark, Mary, have you met the Lancasters?" Hayley asked, gesturing to their dining companions.

Mark shook Ted's hand. "Mark Garber."

"Ted Lancaster. Pleasure, Mark," Ted said. "This is my wife, Trudy."

Mark turned to Trudy and held out his hand but suddenly stopped short. His mouth dropped open and he just stared at her to the point where it began to get a little uncomfortable. It was obvious Reverend Staples wasn't the only one who found Trudy Lancaster breathtakingly attractive.

Finally, in an effort to ease the tension, Trudy reached out and took his hand. "Nice to meet you, Mark."

He didn't say anything.

He just kept his eyes glued on her.

Mary, annoyed, nudged her husband. "Close your mouth, Mark. You'll catch flies."

Mark finally snapped out of his haze and nodded to Trudy. "Sorry. Nice to meet you too."

Mary stepped in front of Mark. "Since my rude husband has forgotten I'm even here, I'm Mary Garber, the invisible wife."

They all laughed, pretending the moment had not been so excruciatingly awkward.

Mary turned to Trudy. "You're the woman with the food truck Wicked 'Wiches, am I right?"

"Yes, that's me," Trudy said with a warm smile.

Mary clapped her hands. "Oh, good! When I saw your ad in today's *Island Times*, I had this eureka moment. I'm sure you've heard about my annual Halloween party, the Witches Ball!"

It wasn't really a question. She just assumed the whole world knew about her soiree in the age of social media. Ted and Trudy just stared at her blankly, not sure how to respond.

"I was just about to tell them about it," Hayley chimed in, trying to be helpful.

"Oh, good. Well, needless to say, I'd love for you to come. Mark and I are always looking to make new friends," Mary cooed happily to the Lancasters before putting on a more serious face and zeroing in on Trudy. "But given the name of your food truck and the theme of my party, I thought we might be able to help each other out. Would you be interested in parking outside my house and serving your subs to the guests at my party? It would be a terrific way to promote your business and I will pay whatever you think is fair!"

Trudy's face lit up. "Of course!"

"If you have a card, I can call you in the morning to get a quote for the whole evening."

Trudy reached into her bag that was hanging on her chair and quickly produced a card, handing it to Mary.

"We won't bother you anymore. Enjoy your dessert," Mary said with a smile that quickly shot downward into a frown as she turned to her husband. "Let's go, Mark."

Mark had finally managed to pry his eyes off Trudy and had them now fixed onto the floor. He nodded and obediently followed his wife out.

Ted leaned over and put an arm around his beautiful wife. "How about that? Not even in town a week, and you already have your first catering gig."

Trudy beamed. "I think I'm really going to like living in Bar Harbor."

Hayley could not have been happier for her new friend.

Chapter 3

When Hayley stirred awake in her bed, it was still pitch black outside. She checked the digital alarm clock on her nightstand. Ten minutes to four in the morning. She wasn't sure what had awakened her, but she did know that whatever it was had interrupted a crazy dream she was having where she was lying in a hammock somewhere in the English countryside with Prince Harry, who was feeding her strawberries. She made a mental note not to share what she remembered about the dream to Bruce.

Hayley grabbed her pillow and turned over in bed to try and fall back to sleep and pick up where she had left off with Prince Harry when she felt something scraping against her big toe, which was exposed outside the fluffy white goose-down comforter. She sat up and stared at a furry little thing perched at the foot of the bed. It was her dog, Leroy, who had been licking her toe.

"What are you doing up, little man?" Hayley whispered, not wanting to wake up Bruce.

Leroy's tongue hung out of his mouth and he panted expectantly. He answered her with a discomfited whine.

Hayley didn't need a doggie translator to know what he was trying to say. She sighed. "I just took you out before bed."

Hayley reluctantly threw off the covers and crawled out of bed, pulling on some ratty gray sweats and sliding her feet into some furry slippers. Leroy excitedly jumped down onto the floor and scurried out of the bedroom and down the stairs. Hayley tiptoed across the room, but stopped suddenly when she noticed that there wasn't a big lump where Bruce was supposed to be. His side of the bed was empty.

Curious, Hayley stepped out into the hallway, wondering if Bruce had gotten out of bed to use the bathroom and that's what had jolted her out of her Prince Harry dream. But the bathroom door was wide open and the light was off. She made her way down the stairs to the kitchen to meet Leroy at the back door, his tail wagging, anxious to get out into the yard in order to take care of his business.

Hayley went to open the door when she suddenly noticed someone standing on the deck, his back to the house, looking up at the bright, shiny half moon. It was Bruce. She silently watched him for a few moments, utterly confusing Leroy, who was wondering why he wasn't outside yet, and that's when she saw puffs of smoke wafting into the night-light from the side of the house.

She reached for the knob and yanked the door open. Leroy shot out, obviously in a code-red situation, and the sudden ruckus startled Bruce, who spun around, dropping a lit cigarette that had been wedged between two fingers. The butt hit the wooden porch, and Bruce hurriedly stomped it out before the burning ash started a fire.

Hayley's mouth dropped open in shock. "Bruce!"

"I know, I know, please, Hayley, no lectures tonight."

"When did you start smoking again?"

"I don't know. Two, maybe three months ago. I don't really remember exactly when I started."

"But you were doing so well. How long has it been?"

"I quit cold turkey just about nine years ago."

"What happened?"

Bruce shrugged. "I've been under a lot of stress lately, and feeling a bit overwhelmed, and one day I was sitting in my office, and I had this craving I just couldn't shake, so I got in my car and drove over to the Big Apple and bought a pack, and just started up again."

"Well, the only recent big change in your life has been marrying me . . . Oh God!" Hayley cried.

Bruce chuckled. "It's not you, Hayley."

"Then what?"

"It's Sal. He's been riding me hard at work lately."

"Why?"

Bruce absentmindedly pulled a half pack of cigarettes from the pocket of his sweatpants and reached for one, but then realizing Hayley was still watching, decided against lighting it and stuffed it back inside the pack.

He looked up at Hayley gravely. "Circulation's been down. The paper's not doing as well as it should be. So Sal's been putting the pressure on me to cover more stories."

"Well, there are only so many crimes in Bar Harbor you can write about."

"Exactly. He wants me to expand my coverage. To

go outside the county, follow stories in Bangor, Waterville, Augusta, all the way down to Portland."

"I don't understand. All of those places have their own newspapers."

"I know, but he wants me to be more competitive, make more of a name for myself. Funny thing is, down in Boston I was doing just that. But I didn't like the constant stress and cutthroat competition of big-city reporting, which is a big reason why I moved back home and got a gig here at the local small-time paper."

"Bruce, why haven't you told me this before?"

"I didn't want to stress you out too."

"You should have said something. And you don't have to worry about me starting to smoke! I find it totally disgusting!"

"Believe me, I'm aware of that fact. Look, we all handle our problems in different ways, which is why when you're stressed you call Liddy and Mona to meet you at your brother's bar to decompress with a cocktail."

Hayley couldn't argue with him. He had a strong point. Everyone had their vices and so she decided to just blow past it. "So what are you going to do?"

Bruce shook his head solemnly. "I have no idea. But there are only so many hours in the day, my workload has basically more than doubled, and I've been feeling the heat. Sal keeps hinting that if I can't handle it, he'll find somebody younger and hungrier who can."

"Sal would *never* fire you," Hayley said.

"People always say that right before somebody gets fired."

He was right.

Hayley stepped forward and hugged him. He held her tightly and then kissed her gently on the forehead. She nuzzled her face in Bruce's chest as he stared back up at the beautiful moon, probably in an effort to keep himself from lighting up again.

"Don't worry. I'll figure it out," he muttered.

"Just do me a favor. I know you're going through a lot, but please try to quit again because—"

Bruce lovingly patted her back. "I know. Because we just got married and you want to have me around for a while."

Hayley hesitated before answering. "Yes."

Bruce pulled away and looked her straight in the eye. "Was that what you were going to say?"

Hayley nodded and said quickly, "Yes."

"You're lying. I can tell," Bruce said. "What were you *really* going to say?"

She hesitated again.

"Hayley . . ."

"I just hate kissing guys with smoker's breath."

Bruce laughed and then playfully kissed her all over her face as she feigned struggling to get him to stop just as Leroy scampered up the wooden steps, ready to go back inside.

Chapter 4

Hayley stood inside the terminal of the Hancock County Bar Harbor Airport mesmerized by the Cape Air Cessna 402 arriving from Boston that gently touched down on the runway. She could feel the excitement building inside her as she knew her daughter, Gemma, along with Gemma's boyfriend, Conner Gibson, were among the passengers onboard. Their originating flight from LaGuardia in New York had left late so there had been a question as to whether or not they would actually make their connection, but a small mechanical issue kept their Bar Harbor–bound flight grounded a few extra minutes, allowing them enough time to race from Terminal B to Gate 27 in Terminal C, according to a text from Gemma once she was strapped in her seat and the plane was ready for takeoff.

Sure enough, as the door opened, the stairs were lowered, and the nine passengers began to debark; first off was Gemma, looking healthy and radiant, followed by Conner. It was a windy afternoon and Gemma's silky blond hair was blowing in all kinds of directions as Conner took her hand and they quickly made their way inside.

Hayley headed to baggage claim, where she had agreed to meet up with them. Gemma spotted her first and ran over to the conveyor belt where her mother eagerly waited for them.

"I honestly didn't think we were going to make it!" Gemma cried, hugging her mother tightly.

"You look beautiful," Hayley marveled as she stepped back to get a good look at her gorgeous daughter.

Gemma shyly patted down her windswept hair. "No, I don't. I look awful. It's been such a long day."

Conner put an arm around her. "She's terrible at accepting compliments. I've practically given up trying."

"You're looking good too, Conner," Hayley said with a welcoming smile.

Conner was an actor, but not the scraggly, greasy-haired method type, more the impossibly handsome, put-together, could be in a toothpaste commercial type. Gemma would always joke that he was prettier than she was. Conner would wince every time because he wanted to be taken seriously as an actor not a model. Hayley had once reminded him that both Ashton Kutcher and Channing Tatum had started out as male models.

Gemma glanced down at the conveyor belt that hadn't started up yet. "I'll bet anything our luggage didn't make it. We barely got to the gate in time ourselves."

"I know they didn't make it because if they had put all the suitcases you brought in the cargo hold, the plane never would have gotten off the ground," Conner said with a wry smile.

Gemma playfully swatted Conner on the arm with her handbag and turned back to her mother. "Have you talked to Dustin?"

Hayley's heart sank. "No. Why?"

She never liked hearing that question, mostly because whenever Gemma asked it, that meant she had been in contact with her brother and he had confided some kind of bad news to her, like he was two months behind on his rent in LA, or had failed a class at art school, or crashed the junky used car he had just bought to get himself around the city. Hayley braced herself for the worst.

"Everything's fine, Mom. He's just got a girlfriend," Gemma said.

Hayley breathed a huge sigh of relief. "Oh, thank God. I can deal with that."

"He's being very cagey and is not telling me too much about her, but from what I have been able to get out of him so far, she's in his animation class and liked one of his drawings, and so now he's totally in love. He posted an adorable picture of the two of them at the beach on Facebook."

Hayley frowned. "I didn't see it. I think he blocked me so I can't see what he's been up to. His worst nightmare is if I post a comment like, 'What are you doing at the beach? Why aren't you in class?'"

"That's very possible," Gemma said, laughing. "How's Bruce?"

"Bruce is Bruce, steady as he goes, reliable, I couldn't be happier. Except for the fact he's smoking again."

Gemma crinkled her nose. "Oh no. You'll need to break him of that."

"Already working on it," Hayley said, nodding.

The baggage claim conveyor belt whirred to life and the checked suitcases and boxes began to arrive through the rubber curtain on the carousel. Conner pointed out three Ralph Lauren Signature Logo Series suitcases moving steadily along toward them.

"It's a miracle! Look, they made it!" Conner said, circling around the conveyor belt to retrieve them.

Hayley turned to Gemma. "Work good?"

Gemma nodded. "Yes, Cyndi keeps telling me how indispensable I am so at least I feel as if I have a little job security . . . for now, anyway. I have no illusions about the cable TV business."

Gemma had started out serving hors d'oeuvres at high-end parties for a catering company called Cyndi's Yummy Catering while working her way through culinary school in New York. But not long after she started, she was plucked out of the army of revolving cater waiters to be the personal assistant for the company's founder, Cyndi Reed, who had recently become a bona fide Food Network star with her own show, a series of cookbooks, and a massive social media presence. That was six months ago, and in that time, Gemma had quickly moved up the ladder to the point where she was now making cameo appearances on Cyndi's Food Network show as her personal sous-chef. Hayley and Bruce had hosted a watch party at the house on the night Gemma had made her first appearance on her boss's titular show, *Cyndi's Cravings*. Hayley could not have been more proud of her daughter's fast-growing success.

Hayley noticed Conner struggling with the three suitcases and grabbed Gemma's arm and guided her toward him. "Come on, I think he could use our help."

By the time they loaded up the trunk and backseat with their luggage, and Hayley was driving them across the Trenton Bridge onto Mount Desert Island and home to Bar Harbor, Hayley realized that she had been so curious about how Gemma's job was going, she had failed to inquire about Conner's own career.

"How have you been doing workwise, Conner? I'm sorry I didn't get to come to New York and see you in that show you did on Broadway a few months ago."

"*Fortune and Men's Eyes,*" Conner said, rolling his eyes. "It was a revival of an old play from the 1960s about the degradation and brutality of prison life."

Hayley raised an eyebrow.

Conner noticed and chuckled, "Yeah, it's as fun as it sounds."

Gemma piped in, helpfully adding, "Conner actually played the shower scene naked and he looked phenomenal!"

"Having nice abs isn't going to win me an Obie."

Gemma noticed Hayley looking at her, confused, and explained, "Off Broadway Theatre Awards."

"Ah, thank you," Hayley said, smiling, as she gripped the wheel and fixed her eyes back on the road.

Conner scowled. "It wasn't Off-Broadway. It was off-off-Broadway, practically in Jersey."

"Well, I still would have loved to have seen you act on stage," Hayley said, glancing at the rearview mirror to see him frowning in the backseat.

"It's a really dark play and I was way too old to be playing the lead, but it didn't matter anyway, because something like six people showed up on opening night," Conner said.

"I was one of them and you were wonderful in it," Gemma said, turning around in the passenger's seat and smiling at him, trying her best to be supportive.

Conner stared out the window. "Gemma's career is skyrocketing, but I seem to be stuck in the same place I was two years ago."

"That's not true," Gemma scoffed, swishing back around and looking at Hayley. "He had a really good role on *Law & Order: SVU* and got to play a scene with Ice T."

"It was one line. I was a bartender and Ice T came in looking for the owner, and all I had to say was . . ." Conner cleared his throat and adopted a detached tone. "'He's not here.' That was it."

"But you delivered it really, really well," Gemma said with an encouraging smile.

Hayley felt sorry for Conner, who continued staring blankly out the window. It had to be hard for him to see Gemma excelling in her chosen profession while he felt as if he was wallowing. "I'm sure it's just a matter of time before you get your big break, Conner."

He didn't answer her. Instead, he just offered her a half smile and then looked back out the window, lost in thought.

Gemma clammed up after that, deciding not to push the conversation any further, and Hayley could plainly see that this frustration on Conner's part regarding his career was having a serious effect on their relationship.

Chapter 5

It had been Hayley's idea, when Gemma announced that she and Conner would be visiting Bar Harbor on Halloween and would be in town for the Garbers' Witches Ball, that she and Gemma should go as a pair of iconic witches from the 1939 classic film *The Wizard of Oz*. With her cascading, silky blond hair that she had clearly inherited from her father's side of the family, Gemma was the obvious choice as Glinda the Good Witch, leaving Hayley to slap on some green makeup and a crooked black hat and try out her full-on Margaret Hamilton–inspired evil laugh as the Wicked Witch of the West. Gemma had instantly jumped at the idea, and the two of them got to work assembling their costumes.

Luckily, Liddy still had her frilly white dress from her disastrous ill-fated wedding day over a year ago boxed up and shoved in a corner in her attic. She was more than happy for Gemma to take it off her hands, and she certainly didn't care that it needed to be altered and hemmed to Gemma's exact size. They still needed a magic wand and a cheap tiara to complete the look, though. As for Hayley, she had already ordered some green water-based face and body paint from Amazon, ironed the black cape and dress she had worn to last year's ball, and had found a crooked black hat at a yard sale the previous spring. On her list remained a broom to carry around, and so she and Gemma stopped into the local hardware store to find one. Hayley wanted a broom with a wooden handle and quickly settled on one she liked. She held it out to Gemma.

"What do you think?"

Gemma, who appeared to be lost in thought, didn't answer her at first.

Hayley tried again. "Gemma?"

Gemma turned to her mother. "What?"

"Are you okay? You've been quiet all morning."

"No, I'm fine."

Hayley knew her daughter well enough to know she wasn't being completely honest, but she didn't have to say anything because Gemma could easily read her mother's skeptical face.

"I've just had a lot on my mind lately."

"Would you like to tell me about it?"

"Not really. I'm hungry. Can we get lunch somewhere?"

Gemma knew her mother's weakness was food, and so when she wanted to change the subject, that's where she would usually steer the conversation.

Hayley decided to drop it for now. "Sure, I know the perfect place we can go."

After paying for the broom and walking back to the car, Hayley had barely strapped her seat belt on when Gemma suddenly blurted out, "I'm thinking of breaking up with Conner!"

Hayley gripped the wheel and slowly turned to her

daughter, mouth agape. "I certainly didn't see that one coming."

"I love him, I do, or at least I think I do. I don't know anymore . . ."

"What's changed?"

Gemma shrugged. "Nothing, really. I mean, we get along great, and I know he's been down lately because his career hasn't turned out the way he had hoped it would, at least not yet, and I don't think he resents me because I've been kind of on an upswing career-wise, but sometimes when I talk about working for Cyndi, he gets really quiet and I can sense he's frustrated."

"It can be hard on a relationship when one person is succeeding and the other is struggling, but that's something that can be worked on . . ."

"I guess so, I just feel we've been in a rut for a while now and I don't know how to get out of it. I just wish I felt more confident that we can go the distance, you know, make a future together . . ."

"How does Conner feel?"

Gemma thought about it for a moment, and then nodded. "I'm sure he feels the same way. He has to . . ."

Hayley shifted the car in reverse and backed out of the hardware store's gravel parking lot. "Well, whatever you decide, I support you one hundred percent."

"Thanks, Mom . . ." Gemma whispered, staring absently out the window.

Hayley left her daughter to ruminate until they pulled up behind Trudy Lancaster's food truck, Wicked 'Wiches.

Suddenly Gemma snapped out of her reverie and bolted upright, excited. "When did Bar Harbor get a new food truck?"

"It hasn't even been a week. Her gourmet subs are amazing. Trust me, I've sampled most of the menu."

They hopped out of the car and walked to the window where Trudy was slapping together an Italian Combo for a balding, potbellied, middle-aged lobsterman with a scraggly beard, still in his waders from hauling traps all morning.

Gemma grabbed a paper menu off the pile that was set out on the counter and held down by a rock to keep them from blowing away in a sudden gust of wind.

After serving the lobsterman, who gratefully took a giant bite of the sub as he ambled away, Trudy happily waved at Hayley. “Good seeing you, Hayley.”

“Trudy, this is my daughter, Gemma,” Hayley said.

Trudy smiled. “I’ve heard a lot about you, Gemma. Welcome home.”

Gemma’s eyes were glued to the menu. “Thank you. I want one of everything.”

“May I recommend today’s special? It’s a bacon cheddar grilled cheese with sweet mustard,” Trudy said, pointing to a chalkboard listing her off-the-menu items of the day. “It comes with waffle fries.”

“Please, you had me at bacon,” Hayley said with a laugh. “I’ll take one.”

“Make it two,” Gemma said.

Trudy disappeared from the window and got to work filling their order. As Gemma continued perusing the menu, Hayley noticed another food truck, this one called Burger She Wrote, pull into an empty parking space directly across the street. Hayley recognized the fifty-something woman with her wild, unkempt gray hair, jumping out of the driver’s seat and hustling across the street, failing to even look both ways and nearly getting mowed down by a passing pickup truck with its horn blaring. She could hear the truck driver shouting out his open window, “Get out of the street, idiot!”

The woman, Cloris Fennow, ignored him as she

marched up to the Wicked 'Wiches truck, ignoring Hayley and Gemma. She violently pounded on the counter just below the service window.

At first, Trudy didn't hear her over the strips of bacon sizzling on her grill, but after a few more attempts at slamming her fist, Cloris finally got her attention.

Trudy poked her head out the window, somewhat annoyed.

"May I help you?" Trudy asked.

"Do you have a permit to park here?" Cloris Fennow shouted.

"As a matter of fact, I do," Trudy said.

"May I see it, please?" Cloris demanded.

"Are you the police?" Trudy asked calmly.

"I most certainly am not!" Cloris huffed.

"Then I don't have to show you anything," Trudy said with a pleasant smile. "Now if you would like to order something, you'll have to wait a few minutes." And then she disappeared back inside her truck to resume preparing Hayley and Gemma's lunch.

Cloris reared back, thoroughly aghast and insulted, and twisted around to Hayley and Gemma. "I don't know how she expects to do well in this town if she's going to be so rude to the locals!"

Cloris stared at Hayley and Gemma, as if expecting them to agree with her, but they didn't. Hayley had never been a fan of Cloris Fennow. She liked that she was a bit of an oddball, opinionated, and creative with the name of her food truck, the only one in town up until now. But Cloris was also paranoid, abrasive, and basically unpleasant to be around, and so that was why Hayley made it a habit of avoiding buying lunch from her despite the fact that others in town had readily attested to the fact that Cloris made a decent hamburger, despite Sal's opinion of her stale buns.

But as the only game in town, Cloris didn't feel the need to actually be nice to her customers. However, now that she had some real competition in the form of the pretty, young, and talented Trudy Lancaster, Cloris was going to be forced into making more of an effort.

And that cold, hard fact did not sit well with her.

In fact, it made her downright livid.

"I don't see how this woman can just blow into town with her big ugly truck and try to run me out of business!" Cloris cried, her face red and puffy. "Did you hear the Garbers passed me over this year in favor of this *stranger*? I mean honestly, what do we know about her?"

Hayley decided not to point out that the Garbers had never hired Cloris Fennow to cater one of their Witches Balls because, quite frankly, nobody in town could stand her, least of all the Garbers themselves.

"She has no history here!" Cloris wailed, stomping her foot.

Trudy set out a plastic tray with two delectable-looking grilled cheese and bacon sandwiches and a generous pile of waffle fries on the side of each paper plate.

Ignoring Cloris, Gemma picked up the tray and looked giddily at the sandwiches. "Oh my God, Trudy, they look absolutely delicious!"

This innocent comment just enraged Cloris even further. She stomped her foot again and wagged a crooked finger at Trudy, who did not seem the least bit perturbed by her business rival's childish temper tantrum.

"You better watch yourself, lady, because I can play rough if I have to!" Cloris warned.

"Is that supposed to scare me?" Trudy asked with a dismissive chuckle.

"Mark my words, you will rue the day you decided to come to Bar Harbor and set up shop in *my* territory!"

Cloris raced back across the street, again not looking where she was going, nearly getting hit by a passing Volvo, horn blaring. She climbed into her Burger She Wrote truck and roared away, nearly sideswiping two Cub Scouts who were in the middle of the crosswalk in front of her.

Trudy, who possessed a remarkable sense of calm, glanced down at Hayley and Gemma, who were already diving into their sandwiches, and asked, "Should I be nervous?"

Hayley shook her head, mouth full. Once she swallowed, she finally answered. "Cloris Fennow is just a big talker, kind of a crank. Believe me, there's no need to worry."

Gemma, her mouth also full, nodded in agreement.

Both of them could not have been more wrong.

Chapter 6

"I wish you wouldn't speak to me like that," Ted Lancaster said as he wandered toward the Wicked 'Wiches food truck, his phone clamped to his ear, grimacing.

Hayley and Gemma, who were finishing up eating their sandwiches, eyed him as he approached, declining to greet him as he was too engaged in what appeared to be a very difficult, prickly conversation with someone. He did nod to them in acknowledgment as he continued talking. "Listen, I understand where you're coming from, but at some point you're going to have to make an effort to—" He paused. "Hello?" And then he sighed and stuffed the phone in his back pocket, frustrated.

Trudy leaned out of the window of her truck. "Was that who I think it was?"

"Yes, I'm afraid so," Ted growled. "Sometimes she can be so . . . so . . . thickheaded and impossible."

"Just like her father," Trudy joked, winking at her husband before glancing over at Hayley and Gemma, who were standing awkwardly nearby and chewing the last bites of their subs. "Ted's daughter, Alyssa."

Hayley and Gemma both nodded, choosing to remain silent, not anxious to overstep their bounds and ask too many questions. But, fortunately, Trudy was in a chatty mood.

"She's been having a rough time of it ever since Ted divorced her mom and married *moi*."

"How old is she?" Gemma asked.

"Twenty-one," Ted answered gruffly, obviously replaying the conversation with his daughter over again in his head.

"She's a senior at Boston College, studying Education. She wants to be a teacher," Trudy said.

"Not anymore. She just told me she's dropping out and moving to New York to sing in a rock band, if you can believe it. She's in her final semester, with enough credits to graduate in a few months, and now she's throwing it all away on a whim!"

"Wow, is that why she called?" Trudy asked.

"Yes, and to remind me what a terrible father I am," Ted grumbled.

Hayley and Gemma crumpled up the paper plates and tossed them in the trash can next to the food truck and were about to sneak away when Trudy drew them back into the uncomfortable conversation again.

"There has been a lot of tension ever since I came onto the scene. A lot of it has to do with the age difference between Ted and me. Alyssa has made it quite clear that she hates the fact I'm closer to her age than I am to Ted's."

"Look, I know how awful it is when your parents get divorced," Gemma said softly, glancing furtively at Hayley. "But you can't force them to stay together, and you certainly can't control who they fall in love with."

Ted didn't appear to be listening because he was too lost in his own thoughts. "She's doing this just to get a rise out of me. She wants to get me angry because *she's* so angry."

"Ted, maybe her going to New York is a good thing. If she wants to be a performer, that's the place to be," Trudy said.

"Have you *heard* her sing? I say this with love because I'm her father, but she *stinks*!"

"Ted!" Trudy cried.

"It's true! No, this is her way of punishing me."

Before Hayley and Gemma could finally make their escape, Trudy was talking to them again. "I feel terrible I haven't been able to forge a positive relationship with her, and Lord knows I've tried. She just doesn't want to have anything to do with me."

"It's her problem, not yours, honey," Ted said, gazing lovingly at his wife. "You've made a herculean effort to become her friend. She's just acting like a spoiled brat."

"Well, we better get going," Hayley said, grabbing Gemma by the arm to quickly steer her away.

"Wait," Trudy said. She disappeared inside her truck and then reemerged with a paper bag that she handed to Ted. "Did you walk here, honey?"

Ted nodded. "Yeah, when Alyssa called I figured it would be safer if we didn't talk while I was behind the wheel of a car."

Trudy turned back to Hayley and Gemma. "Ted's picking up lunch for himself and the Reverend and Mrs. Staples over at the church. I was wondering if you wouldn't mind dropping him off on your way home."

"Not at all," Hayley said. "We'd be happy to."

"Thanks," Ted said, taking the bag from his wife

and looking up at her. "You did remember no olives on Edie's veggie sub?"

"Yes," Trudy sighed. "She reminded me five times when she called to place the order."

When Hayley, Gemma, and Ted piled into Hayley's car for the five-minute drive to the Congregational church, Ted dropped any further references to his troubled daughter, Alyssa, and focused on how much he was looking forward to taking over ministerial duties from Reverend Staples. Hayley couldn't agree more given her own complicated history with the mercurial reverend. She was eagerly anticipating some new blood at the church.

As Hayley pulled her Kia into the church's gravel parking lot, she and Gemma were both stunned by the sight of a monstrous RV parked parallel to the backside of the church building.

Reverend Staples, who was just stepping out of the brand-new, pristine, shiny vehicle, spotted them immediately and waved frantically at them to get out of the car and join him.

Ted, who was sitting in the backseat, leaned forward and said, "I don't think there is any way you are going to get out of a tour."

Hayley shifted the gear into park. "I'm actually curious."

They all jumped out of the Kia as Reverend Staples hurried over to them, excitedly huffing and puffing.

"So, what do you think?" he asked expectantly.

"It looks really nice," Gemma said.

"It's a 2020 Coachman Mirada 32SS," Reverend Staples said, beaming proudly. "She's such a beauty. And she better be because she cost us half our retirement savings!"

Hayley could only imagine what the reverend's nettlesome and stingy wife, Edie, had thought about that.

"She's thirty-four feet and ten inches long," Reverend Staples boasted, leading them over and rapping on the side of the RV with his knuckles. "Exterior is champagne glass with partial paint."

Hayley and Gemma nodded, pretending to have some idea as to what he was talking about.

"And she's fully loaded. Come inside!" Reverend Staples said, clambering up the steps.

They all dutifully followed. Once inside, they found Edie sitting at the dinette table, scowling as she paid bills from a checkbook.

"Hi, Edie, we're here for the tour," Hayley said, smiling.

Edie grunted, obviously not at all sold on her husband's self-proclaimed magnificent purchase.

Reverend Staples didn't seem to notice his wife's less than enthusiastic demeanor and prattled on. "It's got a king-size bed, full-wall slide, fireplace, hardwood cabinet doors, and a solid-surface kitchen countertop." He pounded on it with his fist for good measure. "And we went with the deluxe package that features stainless-steel appliances, a WiFi ranger, exterior speakers—oh, and a power drop-down bunk in case we have guests."

"Have you thought about where you're going to go first?" Gemma asked.

"We're heading north to Niagara Falls as we make our way west. I've never seen Mount Rushmore in South Dakota and the Black Hills, I'm partial to the canyons and alpine rivers in Wyoming and Utah, Vegas is a must, and then when we hit California and dip our toes in the Pacific, we'll turn around and head south because Edie has always dreamed of touring the old plantation homes of New Orleans. Isn't that right, dear?"

"I can't wait," Edie said, scowling. "I just envisioned us flying there and staying in a nice hotel in the French quarter, like the Hotel Monteleone where my sister and her family stayed, not in some RV park outside of town."

"Oh, you'll love it!" Reverend Staples insisted, obviously turning a blind eye to what his wife wanted in his dream retirement scenario.

"Whatever you say, dear," Edie said, forcing a smile.

Hayley had known Edie Staples long enough to know that this simmering and so-far-unspoken conflict between her and her still oblivious husband would eventually come to a boil. She could only imagine what kind of knock-down, drag-out fights were going to erupt in this surprisingly spacious RV as the couple slowly made their way from sea to shining sea. She just hadn't expected those fights would start before the Coachman had even left the parking lot.

Chapter 7

After dropping Gemma off at the house, Hayley stopped by the office to finish writing and filing her column for the next edition of the paper and attending to a few office managerial duties that she had neglected all week. She wanted an empty inbox by the time she went home for the evening, and just barely managed to get everything done by five o'clock. She popped her head into Bruce's office after shutting down her computer and packing up for the day. He was slumped over his desk, staring into space, lost in another world.

"Working late?"

He didn't answer at first, but then he peered up at Hayley hovering in the doorway and gave her a tired smile. "No, I'm coming right behind you. I just have to wrap up this column. You have no idea how challenging it is to make a bike theft sound exciting. It's not even an expensive one either. The owner wasn't too upset it got stolen because he's been wanting to buy a new one anyway."

Hayley chuckled. "I'm sure if anyone can make it a page-turner, you can, honey."

"Whatever happened to the good old days of just reporting the facts?"

"Everyone wants to hear a good story. Any thoughts on dinner?"

"I don't want you and Gemma making a fuss and putting on a fancy spread," Bruce said. "I'll take us all out. Talk to the kids and see what they feel like."

"Okay, see you at home," Hayley said, blowing him a kiss. She could tell from the worry lines on Bruce's forehead that Sal's recent demands to juice up his column were getting to him. She could only hope that sales would eventually improve and the pressure would finally subside, at least a little bit.

Hayley got in her car and drove straight home, forgoing her usual stop at the Shop 'n Save since she would mercifully not be cooking tonight.

When she pulled into the driveway of the house, she was surprised to see the garage door wide open. Inside, Conner was foraging around, opening plastic bins that had been stacked in a corner. He pulled out a giant furry spider and held it up excitedly as Hayley hopped out of her Kia.

"This is awesome!" Conner yelled, holding it over his head.

"Gemma's dad bought that thing years ago. He was always a huge fan of Halloween. You hang it from the roof and when people come up on the porch, there is a sensor that sends it hurtling down on this webby thing to scare them!"

"Does it still work?"

"I think so. It may need some batteries."

Conner set the spider down and stepped out into the driveway to join her. "I also found some cool-looking skeletons I could put up there as well that you can see from the street as you're driving by. Do you have a ladder?"

"There's one in the garage, opposite corner, but wait until Bruce gets home so he can help you," Hayley said, heading inside.

Conner dashed back into the garage.

Hayley entered the kitchen through the back door to find Gemma almost finished carving a jack-o'-lantern. Hayley couldn't help but smile as she instantly recognized the face of Harry Potter. Ever since Gemma was a little girl, she had made it an annual tradition to carve her pumpkin into the likeness of her favorite literary character, and she still paid homage to him every Halloween to this day. Gemma was attaching the round glasses to his face as Hayley leaned down to inspect her work.

"You really outdid yourself this year," Hayley said.

"You think so? I feel like I'm losing my touch. The older I've gotten, the more I seem to just want to get it done, like I totally rushed doing his nose. That's more of a Lord Voldemort nose rather than a Harry Potter nose. Anyway, I'm not going to worry about it. I should get dinner started."

"You can relax. Bruce is taking us out tonight," Hayley said.

"Oh, that's nice of him," Gemma said before turning to look out the window where Conner had just set a metal ladder against the side of the house. "What's he doing?"

"He discovered a box of your father's old Halloween decorations and got inspired," Hayley said.

Conner climbed the ladder, the giant furry spider underneath one arm, past the window.

Hayley leaned against the sink, concerned. "I told

him to wait for Bruce to get home so he could help him, but he's too excited."

Gemma opened the window and called out to Conner, who they could now hear stomping across the roof above them. "Conner, why don't you wait until Bruce gets home to do that?"

"Don't worry! I got this!" he called down.

"Well, be careful!" Gemma said, shaking her head and closing the window. "He can be so stubborn."

"Have you talked to him yet?"

"No," Gemma sighed. "I haven't been able to find the right moment. He's really having a good time here and I don't want to ruin it. I'll probably wait until we're back in New York."

Gemma jumped, startled at the sight of the giant furry spider bobbing up and down in front of the kitchen window in front of them as Conner worked to attach it to the roof.

Hayley couldn't help but laugh.

"He's like a big kid," Gemma said, smiling. But then the smile faded and she became more serious. "I just hate the idea of hurting him."

Hayley put a comforting arm around her daughter's shoulders. "Well, you don't have to do anything tonight. Let's just go out, the four of us, and have a nice dinner."

"Where's Bruce taking us?"

"You can ask him yourself. He just pulled in," Hayley said as Bruce's car rolled to a stop in the driveway behind her parked Kia.

Before Bruce had the chance to even step out of his car, suddenly they heard a man scream, some stumbling sounds on the roof, and then Conner's body fell from the sky, landing hard on the hood of Bruce's car.

Island Food & Spirits

BY

HAYLEY POWELL

There are two things that I have loved for as long as I can remember: Halloween and sandwiches. And not necessarily in that order. Well, you can imagine how excited I was when a new food truck called Wicked 'Wiches (as in sandwiches) rolled into town in early October just a few weeks shy of my favorite holiday. And let me tell you, the awesome assortment of subs and wraps and paninis on the menu did not disappoint!

Of course as I am known to do, I immediately raced home after trying a few and attempted to recreate them in my own kitchen, especially with that new husband of mine who, like me, loves to eat. It's really our secret to a successful marriage: matching appetites!

What we don't share is a love of Halloween. Truth be told, Bruce hates it. Every year he complains about the town going to H-E-double hockey sticks! Kids running around throwing eggs and spraying shaving cream and generally on a mission to scare people. Not to mention all the dentist bills people have to pay when their kids get cavities from all that sugary candy! Bruce gets so grumpy this time of year I call him Halloween Scrooge.

This all might have something to do with an episode that happened a few years ago when Bruce accompanied me to the annual Cross House of Horrors, a makeshift haunted house sponsored by a now sadly deceased local resident, master of horror novelist Norman Cross. The haunted house, open in early October through Halloween, was, to put it mildly, a fright fest with college kids hired to play monsters, evil spirits, and movie serial killers.

Well, suffice it to say, Bruce, who scares rather easily, did not enjoy the heart-stopping experience at all. And since I was the one who had dragged him there, the blame was placed squarely on my shoulders.

So last Halloween, when Bruce and I had officially begun dating, I had one of those lightbulb moments. I came up with the idea of treating Bruce to a Haunted Hayride. Now I know what you're all thinking: Hayley, why on earth would you subject your poor husband-to-be to something like that knowing how much he hates to be scared? Well, here's the thing. The Haunted Hayride, which was organized and run by the Southwest Fire Department, was what you would call "family friendly," which means it was designed for children of *all* ages. I knew there would be nothing too spine-chilling that might put a strain on Bruce's heart.

Bruce balked at first, but after quickly explaining how he would be among five-year-olds, and with the bribe of bringing some homemade Italian subs and a thermos of cocktails to enjoy after the ride, Bruce finally got on board.

Literally.

After standing in a long line of people to purchase tickets, we were escorted to a large wooden wagon decked out with hay-bale seats, spiderwebs, and hanging lanterns. The wagon was hitched up to a tractor trailer driven by a headless horseman. Nothing too frightening. Bruce even laughed at the headless horseman and said he might go as one next year. I was ecstatic he was finally getting into the Halloween spirit.

As the tractor lurched forward, Bruce grabbed my hand and appeared slightly nervous as we headed toward an opening in the woods dimly lit by eerily glowing lanterns. I leaned in and whispered in Bruce's ear, "Don't worry. It's all going to be very G-rated, nothing too spooky. Maybe a cardboard cutout of Casper the Friendly Ghost."

My first clue that something was amiss was when I looked around at everyone else in the wagon and didn't see any small children, just adults and a few raucous teenagers. I turned to the woman sitting on my other side and casually mentioned that I found it strange that there weren't more kids on such a family friendly ride. The woman laughed and noted, "What parent in their right mind would bring a child on this ride tonight of all nights?" When I asked what she meant, the woman informed me that tonight was the special "Adults-Only" ride. You had to be at least sixteen years old to come on board because the scares in store were too dark and horrifying for little kids. She excitedly added, "And I've heard this year is the most hair-raising ride yet!"

I wanted to grab Bruce and jump out of the wagon, but it was too late. We were already deep inside the dark woods. Suddenly ear-splitting screams and eerie music were blasting out of speakers strategically placed around us. Then, bloodthirsty zombies surrounded the wagon, moaning and clawing at us. Bruce's eyes popped open and he screamed like a little girl, which I found adorable, but refrained from commenting on in this rather tense moment. I felt so guilty. Bruce squeezed my hand so hard he cut off my circulation!

Thankfully, the zombies finally receded and we continued on our way. We came upon a docile-looking family roasting marshmallows over a campfire. The wagon slowed and we were able to watch the peaceful, serene scene until suddenly out of nowhere a marauding band of chain-saw-wielding lumberjacks came out of hiding and chased the family around before turning their attention toward us. The lumberjacks suddenly ran up behind the wagon, which was now racing to escape. I thought Bruce was going to faint. In fact, he may have actually passed out for a moment, or maybe he was just frozen in a state of shock. But then, as a lumberjack barreled up along the side of the wagon, waving his chain saw inches from Bruce, he was wide-awake, waving his arms, and screaming again!

When the last of the killer lumberjacks had run back into the darkness of the woods, I finally had the time to explain my unfortunate mistake to Bruce. Suffice it to say, he was not happy about it, and even the promise of gorging on my delicious subs and washing them down with a few strong cocktails when this terrible nightmare was over did not seem to brighten his mood in the least.

The rest of the frights were a little less gruesome: a scary ghost, knife-wielding goblins, a cackling witch. Not for kids, but Bruce wouldn't have to start taking heart medicine.

Mercifully, the wagon finally came to a jarring halt. I thought the ride might be over, but unfortunately it wasn't because hundreds of furry, fuzzy, gross black spiders suddenly dropped from the sky and fell all around us, onto the wagon, and worst of all on top of our heads. Everyone in the back of the wagon screamed and brushed the terrifying spiders away! It took me a few panicked moments to realize that the spiders were just a lot of fake rubber spiders on strings descending from the trees while others were being thrown at us by people hiding in the woods.

Unfortunately, poor Bruce, who has a crippling fear of spiders, had seen enough. He pushed me out of the way, leaped over the side of the wagon, and hightailed it out of there. I wasn't sure if Bruce was running away from me or the spiders.

I knew that would be the last time I would

ever get Bruce Linney to join me on a Haunted Hayride. But with that said, I had a whole year to butter him up with my delicious Italian subs and sandwiches so I wasn't going to count him out just yet.

Speaking of subs, this Italian sub is a great addition to any party, and topped off with a mouth-watering Maple Bourbon Cocktail on a chilly October evening, well, let's just say, it's scary good!

MAPLE BOURBON COCKTAIL

INGREDIENTS
2 ounces bourbon
1 ounce pure maple syrup
½ ounce fresh-squeezed lemon
Pinch of ground cinnamon

In a cocktail glass, add your bourbon and maple syrup and stir until combined.

Add the lemon juice, pinch of cinnamon, and ice cubes, and then stir and enjoy!

Italian Sub

Ingredients

1 pound of deli ham
1 small onion, sliced
1 tomato, sliced
1 green pepper, sliced
8 slices white American deli cheese
Dill pickles
Salt and pepper to taste
Olive oil
Red wine vinegar
4 Italian sub rolls

Cut your rolls in half, but not completely through. Layer your cheese and ham on each of your rolls. Top with pickles, tomatoes, onion, and green pepper.

Drizzle with olive oil and vinegar, and sprinkle with salt and pepper.

And don't forget to serve with some crunchy potato chips!

Chapter 8

By the time Conner had rolled off the hood of Bruce's car and landed facedown on the ground, moaning, Bruce had already jumped out of the driver's seat, and was kneeling at his side as Hayley and Gemma came flying out the back door to see if Conner was all right.

Bruce gently touched his back. "You okay there, buddy?"

Conner didn't answer at first because the wind had been knocked out of him, but soon he managed to nod his head a bit, and then gasp, "Yes, but could you help me stand up, please?"

"No!" Gemma cried. "He may have broken a bone or something and moving him could make it worse!"

Conner pressed the palms of his hands on the ground and rolled over on his back so he was facing up and smiled at Gemma. "It's okay, Gemma. I'm fine." He then held out his hand, which Bruce grasped, and slowly, Bruce carefully helped to lift him up onto his feet. Conner slowly dusted himself off. "Seriously, I don't think anything's broken."

He took a step and winced in pain.

"I think we should take you to a doctor and get you checked out," Hayley urged.

Conner shook his head. "No, please. It was just a shock falling like that. I only have a few scrapes and bruises. Seriously, if I honestly felt there was something wrong, I'd go straight to the hospital."

They all stared at him skeptically, but Conner was insistent. He did agree to postpone finishing the rooftop decorations until a later time, and also promised not to proceed without Bruce present to keep watch and catch him if he happened to fall again. He wanted to forget this whole clumsy accident happened and just go to dinner as planned. He limped inside the house to change his shirt, again dismissing a slightly sprained ankle and begging them all to relax.

When he reemerged, his foot appeared to already be better. They piled into Bruce's car, no one wanting to bring up the now heavily dented front hood, a result of Conner's fall. They drove to McKay's on Main Street, which was one of the few restaurants in town still open after the tourist season had died down after Labor Day. They were sipping on cocktails and wine and munching on pretzels and beer cheese, perusing the menu, deciding on their entrees, when Hayley noticed Conner wincing again.

"Conner, what is it?" Hayley asked.

"Nothing, I'm good," Conner lied, keeping his eyes glued to the menu, not wanting to make an issue out of what was bothering him. "The Tempura Tuna Tacos sound delicious."

Gemma slapped her menu down on the table. "You're obviously in pain! What's wrong?"

Conner sighed. "My shoulder's a little sore, that's all."

They all focused on his left side, where he had landed on the hood of the car. The swelling on his arm and shoulder looked as if it might burst through his shirt, like Bruce Banner when he got angry and transformed into the Incredible Hulk.

"That's it," Gemma said as she stood up from the table. "We're going to the emergency room."

"Can we just wait and see if the swelling goes down? If it hasn't by the morning, I'll go see a doctor," Conner begged.

Gemma reached over and rolled up the sleeve of his shirt. His arm was turning purple. "We're going right now. Come on!"

Conner knew he was not going to win this one. He shook his head, annoyed and frustrated, and they all stood up to leave as Bruce handed Hayley the key to his car. "You take him. I'll pay for our drinks and meet you over there."

Luckily, the hospital was only a few blocks away.

By the time Hayley and Gemma had parked the car and escorted Conner into the ER, his arm had only gotten worse.

Nurse Tilly, a perky RN with a bright demeanor and infectious smile, was manning the reception desk. She took one look at Conner and jumped on the phone to get a doctor on call to get down to exam room three where she told Conner to wait. Gemma never left his side and the two disappeared down the hall led by another nurse. Hayley remained in the ER and was joined by Bruce a few minutes later.

After forty-five minutes had passed, and Hayley and Bruce had gorged on just about every processed snack the vending machine had to offer, Gemma finally emerged from the exam room and crossed over to them.

"He dislocated his shoulder."

"Oh no!" Hayley cried.

"They fixed it and the doctor says it should heal in about six to eight weeks. He just needs to wear a sling to keep it immobilized so he doesn't injure it again. It could have been a lot worse."

"Well, that's a relief," Hayley said.

"He should be out in a few minutes. Is it too late to go back to the restaurant? I'm starving," Gemma said.

Bruce checked his watch. "I think we can get in under the wire before the kitchen closes."

Suddenly, a man burst through the doors into the emergency room yelling, "Please, my wife is very sick! I need help!"

Nurse Tilly quickly grabbed the phone on her desk to call for some assistance.

They all spun around to see Ted Lancaster, sweat running down his cheeks, a panicked look on his face. Trudy was in his arms, her eyes closed, her face a ghostly white.

Hayley was the first to rush over to them. "Ted, what's happened to her?"

Ted gasped, out of breath. "I don't know. One minute she was fine, and then the next she had a fever and chills and was vomiting! I rushed her here as fast as I could, but by the time we got here, she was too weak to even walk by herself."

Two orderlies showed up with a gurney and Ted gently set his wife down on it. They quickly whisked Trudy away, leaving her distraught husband behind.

Hayley had managed to get a look at Trudy as they wheeled her off. She was barely conscious and gasping for air, as if she was having trouble breathing.

Something was seriously wrong with her.

Chapter 9

Hayley was not about to leave Ted Lancaster alone to wander around the emergency room waiting area, lost and distressed after the ER staff had rushed his wife off to be examined by a doctor. She told Bruce to take Gemma and Conner to get some food and she would meet them all home later once she got word that Trudy's condition had hopefully improved.

Bruce didn't like the idea of leaving her behind, but Hayley was insistent and determined to remain with Ted, who she felt needed a friend right now. Bruce finally agreed, and with Gemma doting on her injured boyfriend, who was now sporting a white sling, the three of them filed out to try and get back to McKay's before closing time.

Hayley sat down next to Ted, who was slumped over in a chair, head down, his hands covering his face. She put a comforting arm around him. "Can I get you anything, Ted?"

He shook his head and mumbled that he was fine.

Hayley sat back and sighed. She had just seen Trudy

earlier that day and she had appeared healthy, robust, and energetic. What possibly could have happened to her since then that had made her so gravely ill? She wondered if she should try to lightly question Ted, but decided against engaging him at this time because he was so obviously physically and emotionally distraught. Instead, they sat in silence, Hayley keeping a hand resting gently on Ted's back so he would know that she was there for him if he needed her.

After nearly ninety minutes passed, and the last few patients in the waiting area were taken into the exam rooms by a nurse, leaving only Hayley and Ted and Nurse Tilly, who was behind the reception desk, a doctor solemnly walked out in a white coat, carrying a clipboard. Hayley didn't know him. He was rather short and stout with thick, heavy eyeglasses and a scruffy beard.

"Mr. Lancaster?" the doctor asked gruffly.

Ted shot up to his feet and raced over to the doctor. "Yes, I'm Ted Lancaster. How's my wife?"

"Resting comfortably now," he said, glancing at some notes he had scribbled down on a piece of paper attached to the clipboard. "She was showing symptoms of severe food poisoning and so we pumped her stomach and got rid of all the contents. Her fever went down. She's still very weak but doing much better."

Ted looked at the doctor, confused. "Food poisoning?"

He nodded. "As far as we can tell. We're still waiting on the toxicology report to prove it. Do you know what she had to eat today?"

"No, I didn't see her until I got home from the church where I work. We hadn't had dinner yet, and she was already feeling sick when I saw her," Ted said.

"I'm sure we'll figure out the culprit," the doctor

said, distracted. "She's in room two-eleven if you'd like to go see her. I have another patient I need to attend to."

The doctor brusquely pushed past Ted, hardly a candidate to win Best Bedside Manner.

Ted called after him, "Thank you, Doctor . . . I didn't get your name!"

But the doctor was already gone.

Hayley stood up and crossed over to join Ted. "Would you mind if I came with you?"

Ted turned and seemed to notice her for the first time. "No, of course not, Hayley. I'm sure she'll be happy to see you."

They took the elevator up to the second floor and found Trudy in a corner room, lying in bed with her eyes closed. There was another bed next to hers in the bland, sterile semiprivate room but it was not currently occupied. A pitcher of water and a plastic cup had been set out for her on the Formica table attached to her bed.

"I need to go down to the gift shop to buy some flowers so we can spruce up this room at some point," Hayley said softly.

Trudy slowly opened her eyes and smiled at the sight of her husband and Hayley.

Ted leaned over and grasped her hand. "How are you feeling, honey?"

"Better," she whispered, her lips dry and chapped.

"The doctor said you suffered a bad bout of food poisoning. What on earth did you eat today?" Ted asked, squeezing her hand before lifting it up to kiss it.

Trudy grimaced. "A candy apple."

"Well, who can resist eating a candy apple? It's Halloween," Hayley said, laughing.

Trudy tried sitting up in bed but she was too weak. She slowly leaned back, resting her head on the lumpy pillow, and with her jaw clenched, managed to spit out, "It was from Cloris Fennow."

"*What?*" Hayley gasped.

"Who's Cloris Fennow?" Ted asked, perplexed.

"She owns a rival food truck called Burger She Wrote," Hayley explained. "And she's made no secret of the fact that she is supremely unhappy that Trudy has arrived in town and become her chief competition."

Ted blinked, aghast. "Well, that's the craziest thing I've ever heard! Do you honestly believe she's evil enough to try and *poison* my wife?"

Trudy nodded. "She came back a while after you left today, Hayley, with a peace offering, one of her self-described 'world-famous candy apples.' She apologized for her behavior earlier and explained that she had overreacted and was embarrassed about it, and just wanted to let me know that she had no ill feelings toward me. I wasn't going to eat the apple, but she waited around and wouldn't leave until I at least tasted it . . ." Trudy stopped, took a deep breath, and exhaled.

Ted kissed her hand again. "Don't speak anymore, honey. This can wait until you get your strength back."

But Trudy was determined to continue. She waited a few moments, staring at the ceiling, gathering her thoughts, and then went on. "I took a few bites, and that finally seemed to satisfy her, and so she left. Not long after that, I started to feel feverish, and my stomach ached and it just kept getting worse and worse . . ."

"You poor thing," Hayley said in a hushed tone.

"I know it was her. And I know why she did it. She wanted to make me sick, or worse, so she could swoop in and take over at the Garbers' Witches Ball with her own truck."

Ted grabbed his phone from the back pocket of his

jeans. "I'm going to call the police and have her arrested."

"We should probably wait until the toxicology report comes back so we know for sure Trudy was poisoned," Hayley suggested quietly.

"I don't want to wait!" Ted howled. "She tried *killing* my wife!"

Trudy weakly tugged on her husband's shirtsleeve. "No, Ted. Hayley is right. I don't want to make any accusations until we know for certain . . ."

Ted quickly became docile again at the sound of his wife's soothing voice and put his phone back in his pocket. "Okay, sweetheart, whatever you want."

"You haven't eaten anything all night, Ted," Trudy said. "Why don't you go down to the cafeteria and get yourself a sandwich or something?"

"I'm not leaving your side," Ted said emphatically.

"I want you to go, Ted, please, you must be starving. Hayley will stay here with me until you come back."

Ted was only interested in pleasing his wife, and so he nodded to Hayley, and reluctantly walked out of the room.

Hayley sat down in a chair next to the bed and smiled at Trudy. "You had us pretty scared there for a while."

Before Trudy had time to respond, Reverend Staples swept into the room, out of breath, looking alarmed. "Trudy, my dear, how are you?"

Hayley noticed Trudy stiffen slightly. "Reverend Staples, what are you doing here?"

"I was on the floor visiting one of my congregation, Vera Smallidge. She's here having her gall bladder removed . . ."

Vera Smallidge was a devout churchgoer and could always be counted on to drop a fifty-dollar bill in the collection plate every Sunday, so of course she had

VIP status, with one benefit being a friendly visit from the good reverend whenever she was under the weather or suffered any kind of malady.

"I was literally on my way out when Nurse Tilly told me you were here," Reverend Staples said as he crossed the room to Trudy's bedside.

"I'll leave you two alone . . ." Hayley said, starting to get up.

Trudy shot her a pleading look, begging her with her eyes to stay put. "No, Hayley, you don't have to go . . ." she whispered, almost desperately. "*Please* stay."

Hayley immediately picked up on the cue and sat back down, smiling at Reverend Staples, who didn't seem at all happy she had chosen to remain there.

Reverend Staples reached over with his bony, wrinkled hand and gently stroked Trudy's hair. "Tilly told me you might have eaten something that made you ill?"

Hayley studied the reverend's face, which was so full of affection and devotion as he continued stroking Trudy's hair like he would his own wife. It was odd and disconcerting and Hayley felt like she was intruding on a deeply personal moment, except for the fact that Trudy's expression betrayed a sense of revulsion at the reverend's touch. It was obvious he was making her exceedingly uncomfortable. She seemed to want to recoil and push his hand away, but she was weak and probably did not want to offend her husband's superior, at least for the time being.

Hayley was transfixed by Reverend Staples's behavior, mostly because she had never seen him act this way around anyone, least of all his own wife, Edie. It was as if he had a boyish crush on Trudy, who was frankly less than half his age, and he seemed to have completely forgotten that Hayley was in the room to witness it.

"What can I do to make you feel better?" Reverend Staples asked, hovering over Trudy, still stroking her hair and holding her hand. Trudy just stared up at him, either too weak or too apprehensive to rebuff his laser-like focus.

It was downright creepy.

Hayley was just about to intervene and rescue Trudy when Ted returned, carrying a paper sack of food. He was surprised to see the reverend at his wife's bedside. "Oh, hello, Reverend. I didn't expect to see you here."

"I was just leaving," Reverend Staples said, a smile slapped quickly on his face to hide his disappointment that Trudy's husband had soured their time together. "You know how to reach me if you need anything. I'm here for you . . ."

He let the words linger before deciding it might be better to add, "Me and Edie, of course."

And then he stalked out of the room.

Ted didn't seem to pick up on the tension or icky behavior on the reverend's part, but Hayley certainly did, and she found it utterly disturbing that Reverend Staples appeared to be so obsessed and obviously in love with his successor's wife.

Chapter 10

After some reassurance from the short, bearded doctor they met earlier that Trudy would make a full recovery, Hayley finally headed home. It was already past ten at night, and she was hoping to get to bed right away.

When she pulled into the driveway, she noticed all the lights upstairs were off, and when she entered the kitchen and was greeted by an excited Leroy jumping up and down with his tail wagging, she could hear someone in the living room watching an opinion show on a cable news channel. After grabbing a doggie treat from the cupboard and tossing it to Leroy, Hayley wandered down the hall to find Conner slouched in one of the recliners, relaxing in sweatpants and a T-shirt. He clutched a half-empty bottle of water in his free arm, the one not in a sling.

He sat upright, startled, when Hayley suddenly appeared as if he had not heard her come into the house. "How is she?"

"Doing better." Hayley sighed. "They say she has to stay overnight for observation, but the doctor thinks he'll be able to release her sometime tomorrow."

"What a scare," Conner said, shaking his head.

Hayley nodded, still not quite believing that someone—as in Cloris Fennow—would deliberately poison her chief food truck competitor.

It just didn't seem real.

Cloris was many things, but a poisoner?

"You heading up to bed?" Conner asked before taking a swig of his bottled water.

"After I take Leroy out for a quick walk around the block."

Leroy's ears perked up at the mention of his name.

"Mind if I join you?" Conner asked.

The question surprised Hayley. Not that she didn't want him coming along, she just realized that she had never really been alone with Conner, or had any kind of meaningful conversation without Gemma present.

"No, of course not. Glad to have the company," Hayley said.

Conner jumped out of the recliner and bounded into the kitchen to grab his sneakers, which he had left near the back door. Leroy was running around in circles now, unable to contain himself as it became clear there was a lot of activity happening that indicated they were going out. When Hayley grabbed his leash from the hook next to the laundry room, he nearly took flight he was so beside himself with excitement. It took Conner a few minutes to get his shoes on as he only had the use of one good arm. After struggling a bit, Hayley decided to help him out by kneeling down and tying his laces.

A few minutes later, they were strolling down the sidewalk side by side, Leroy a few feet ahead, straining to break into a run but held back by his leash.

Hayley glanced at Conner, who was keeping stride next to her, an intense look on his face, which was illuminated by the streetlamp they were walking past. Hayley knew he had something on his mind, but she waited for him to speak first.

After about half a block, Conner cleared his throat, kept his eyes fixed on the road ahead, and said quietly, "There's something I've been wanting to talk to you about."

"Okay . . ." Hayley said tentatively, still clueless as to what might be coming.

"I've been thinking about this a lot lately, and I didn't want to move ahead with anything until I had your blessing . . ."

Hayley didn't respond. She was thoroughly confused. But then he just came out with it.

"I want to marry your daughter."

The shock of his words caused Hayley to drop the leash and Leroy bolted ahead of them, the tags on his collar jangling in the night breeze.

"Leroy, get back here!" Hayley cried.

Leroy ignored her and kept running.

"Leroy!"

Finally, Leroy stopped and sniffed some grass on a lawn, allowing them to catch up to him and get a hold of the leash that he had been dragging along behind him.

"I take it you didn't expect that," Conner said with a wry smile.

"To be honest, no, I didn't."

"Do you think it's too soon?"

Hayley shook her head, still stunned. "No . . . I . . ."

"I've already spoken with her father."

"You called Danny?"

"Yes, to formerly ask for her hand in marriage."

Hayley had not realized just how old-fashioned Conner was. Asking permission from both parents before proposing seemed like a throwback to another era.

"Luckily he got on board right away and granted me his permission. But he also strongly suggested I run it past you as well."

"Wise advice," Hayley said, chuckling.

They walked in silence for a few more seconds. Hayley's mind was reeling. How could Gemma and Conner be on such different pages? How could he not on some level suspect Gemma's general dissatisfaction with the relationship? How could one person be on the verge of ending it while the other one was on the verge of making it official?

Conner winced, his shoulder causing him some pain and discomfort. Then he scratched his chin nervously, furtively looking at Hayley, trying to judge her feelings about this major decision.

For Hayley's part, she was just trying to stay calm and not do or say anything that would break her daughter's confidence and upset the situation.

"So . . . ?" Conner finally asked.

Hayley thought long and hard before finally responding. "If Gemma wants to marry you, then you have my full support."

Not exactly a glowing endorsement, but it would have to do in a pinch.

Conner breathed an audible sigh of relief. "Great. Now I just hope she says yes."

Hayley tried giving him an encouraging smile, but it was hardly genuine since she was now full of dread. Gemma was going to be blindsided by a marriage proposal, and Hayley was now in the uncomfortable position of having to decide whether or not she should at least warn her daughter that one was coming her way at breakneck speed.

Chapter 11

"Bruce, are you awake?" Hayley whispered, poking her husband lightly on his bare arm. He was lying on his side, facing away from her in their bed.

Hayley waited a few seconds, and when she didn't get an answer, she asked again, this time a bit louder. "Bruce, are you awake?"

Still no response.

Frustrated, she shook him and he snorted and tried rolling away from her. "Bruce!"

"What?" Bruce mumbled into his pillow.

"Are you awake?"

Bruce sighed, turned over, and yawned. "Uh, yeah, I am now. What time is it?"

"A little after two," Hayley said, glancing at the digital clock on her nightstand.

"Does the dog have to go out?"

"No, I took care of that earlier when I got home from the hospital, but that's what I want to talk to you about. I've been sitting here, wide-awake, thinking and worrying about what I should do."

"About the dog?"

"No! Conner! He told me he is going to ask Gemma to marry him!"

This finally stirred some interest in Bruce. He rubbed his eyes and sat up in bed. "Oh . . . damn . . ."

"Gemma told me shortly after she got here that she is thinking of breaking up with him, but he is completely oblivious to her true feelings because the poor guy just told me he is on the verge of proposing!"

"I'll say," Bruce said. "Are you going to give her a heads-up?"

"I don't know, that's what I've been up all night trying to decide. What do you think?"

Bruce leaned back on the headboard, scratched his chest hair, mulled it over for a few seconds, and then said matter-of-factly, "I think you should stay out of it. Good night." And then he dropped back down on his side and yanked the covers over his head.

Hayley considered his opinion for a few moments, and then turning to Bruce, said, "I think I would want to know."

Silence from Bruce.

And so Hayley shook him again. "Bruce?"

She could hear him groaning under the covers, but that didn't stop her from continuing the conversation. "Gemma told me in no uncertain terms that she was having serious doubts about her relationship, and in a sense, her confiding in me gives me a license to tell her anything I might know, don't you agree?"

Bruce slowly sat up again. "If I agree with you, will you let me go back to sleep, please?"

"I want you to be honest with me."

Bruce's head slumped down as he tried to come up with a way to end this discussion and get back to sleep. Finally, he turned and looked directly at his wife. "I already told you what I think. Stay out of it. This is between Gemma and Conner. Let the guy propose and allow Gemma to give an honest, unrehearsed answer without you getting involved. That's my official opinion, but because I'm really tired and I want to get a few hours of sleep before I have to be up to go to work, I'm willing right here and now to just tow the party line and tell you that you should do what your gut tells you. And if that means warning Gemma, then that's what you should do. And if it somehow backfires, and Conner gets upset at you for spilling the beans, or Gemma gets upset at you for meddling, then I promise not to say 'I told you so.' Now, I've said my piece, I'm going to lie back down and close my eyes, and I'm going to have faith that you will finally stop talking and I can drift back to Dreamland."

He leaned over and kissed her lightly on the lips. He waited for her to speak again, but she mercifully refrained. When he was reasonably certain she was done chatting with him, shaking, and poking him, he smiled and disappeared back down underneath the covers.

Hayley stared at the lump next to her.

He was probably right.

She should just keep her mouth shut.

But this was huge.

This was a marriage proposal.

And she didn't want Gemma to be caught blindsided.

But given that, all Hayley knew at this point was that she would undoubtedly be up and wide-awake for the rest of the night, debating about what she should do while occasionally pinching closed the nostrils on her husband's nose when he inevitably snored too loudly and distracted her.

Chapter 12

Hayley had been up most of the night, but finally around five in the morning, she dozed off and didn't wake up again until after nine. Bruce had already left for work, and as she walked down the stairs, she saw Conner propped up on the couch, his arm in his sling, watching an old black-and-white James Cagney movie on Turner Classic Movies.

"Good morning, Conner."

"Morning, Hayley," he said, eyes glued to the TV set. Cagney at the moment was shoving a grapefruit into Mae Clarke's face. Hayley tried to remember the name of the movie—perhaps *White Heat* or *Public Enemy*, two of his best gangster films. She loved Cagney. "Where's Gemma?"

"She took Leroy to hike around Eagle Lake. She'll be back in a couple of hours."

"How's your arm?"

"Still sore," Conner groaned. "But doing better. Are you off to work?"

"No, I took the day off to help Edie Staples set up

for the reception they're hosting at the church for all the Emerson Conners school kids marching in the Halloween parade. I baked some cookies to take with me because, well, Edie's baking skills are a bit sketchy, and I want the kids to at least have some edible sweets to eat with their fruit punch."

"You mean those Halloween cookies that were in the four tins on the kitchen counter?"

"Yes, did you eat them all?" Hayley asked, folding her arms, and staring sternly at him.

Conner vigorously shook his head. "No, just a few, I mean there are still three whole tins left!"

"There were twenty cookies in each tin!"

"Yes, and they were so delicious! Now I know where Gemma gets her incredible culinary talents from!"

"Don't bother trying to butter me up. I'll make some more for you when I get home. Now I have to jump in the shower and get going." Hayley downed a quick cup of coffee from the coffeemaker in the kitchen, and was heading back up the stairs again, when she stopped halfway and called down into the living room, "Did you talk to Gemma?"

There was a long pause before he answered, "No, I'm still waiting for the right time."

She hurried up the rest of the steps, relieved to know there was still a little time to intervene if she decided to do so against Bruce's advice.

After showering and dressing and offering to make Conner breakfast, which he politely declined, Hayley loaded up her car with the three remaining tins of cookies and drove straight to the Congregational church. She hoped to find Ted Lancaster there so she could get an update on Trudy and find out when she would be released from the hospital.

When she pulled into the church parking lot and

stopped next to the Staples' brand-new RV, she noticed Trudy Lancaster's food truck parked outside on the street in front of the church.

Edie emerged from the RV with a tray of brownies that she carried while wearing black-and-white-checkered oven mitts.

Hayley hopped out of her car. "Hi, Edie, sorry I'm a little late. I didn't sleep very well last night."

"No problem. We still have plenty of time before the kids get here. The parade isn't even halfway down Cottage Street yet," Edie said. "I was just warming up some brownies in the RV. The kitchen is so small I can hardly move in there. I don't see how I am ever going to prepare any kind of decent meal under those conditions!"

"Well, I'm sure you'll want to experience the local cuisine as you drive across country and won't need to cook all the time."

"I have serious food allergies so I can't see how that will work out," Edie complained.

Edie was obviously not looking forward at all to their long-awaited retirement plans. It appeared as if she would be a lot happier just staying home.

Hayley stacked the three tins of cookies in her arms and joined Edie, who was balancing the tray of brownies with one arm as she slammed the door to the RV shut with the other. Then she turned and noticed Hayley with the tins. "Oh, Hayley, I told you not to bake anything. I made plenty of treats for the kids as well as their parents and teachers."

"I know, I just wanted to contribute a little something. Why should you have to do all the work?" Hayley said, as she glanced at Edie's rock-hard and no doubt tasteless batch of brownies. "After I help you set up, I may swing by the hospital and visit with Trudy to see how she's doing."

"There's no need," Edie said as they walked toward the church entrance. "She was released this morning and she's here, right inside with Ted. She's got her coloring back and is feeling much better. She says she's determined to have her food truck open for the Garbers' Witches Ball tonight."

"Oh, that's such a relief," Hayley said.

They entered through a side door where several long cardboard tables had been set up with Halloween-themed paper tablecloths. A big fruit punch bowl and stacks of plastic cups were on one table while plates of decorated cookies in shapes of ghosts, witches, Frankenstein monsters, and pumpkins were lined up on the other, evenly spread out with military-style precision. There was even a large cake in the shape of a haunted house on a third table. Hayley set her own cookies down as Edie went searching for a knife to try and cut her tray of brownies into squares.

Ted strolled in from a side office.

"Hayley, thanks again for staying so long with Trudy last night," he said, smiling.

"I'm so happy to hear she's feeling better."

Ted nodded. "It was a rough night, but by this morning, she was back to her old self—a little weak, maybe, but raring to go. She wants to be well prepared for her catering gig tonight."

"Do you think it's a good idea for her to be working so hard so soon after a such a serious bout of food poisoning?"

"Of course not, but she won't listen to me."

"Where is she?"

"She went outside to her truck to finish making

sandwiches for the kids when they arrive. Reverend Staples just went out there to volunteer to be her sous-chef."

Hayley stiffened. "Oh? He's out there too?"

Ted noticed her sudden change in demeanor. "Yes. Is everything all right?"

"Oh, yes, everything's fine," Hayley fibbed. She did not like the idea of Reverend Staples out in the truck alone with Trudy, especially after witnessing how inappropriately he had behaved in the hospital room. "Maybe she could use my help too."

At that moment, Edie flew out of a tiny kitchen off the reception room. "I can't find a knife to save my life! Now where's my husband? I have a whole box of Halloween decorations he needs to tape on the walls!"

"He's outside. I'll go get him," Hayley said.

"Don't bother. I'll do it. I'm sure Trudy has a knife out there I can borrow to cut the brownies," Edie said, hustling out into the main room, past the altar and down through the pews toward the exit. Hayley chased after her. She had a sickening feeling something bad was about to happen.

And she was right.

Hayley managed to catch up to Edie outside just as she hurried down the stone steps of the church and saw, through the open window of Trudy Lancaster's food truck, her husband groping Trudy and trying to kiss her while Trudy's scrunched-up face displayed a horrified look of disgust as she tried desperately to squirm out of his tight grasp.

"Dear Lord, what are you doing to that poor woman?" Edie cried, her eyes nearly popping out of her head.

Reverend Staples suddenly froze in place, allowing Trudy to slip out of his embrace. A few seconds later, Trudy barreled out of her food truck carrying a large tin pan filled with turkey, roast beef, and chicken salad sandwiches. She raced past Edie and Hayley, hoping to find shelter from Hurricane Edie inside the church.

Hayley intercepted her. “Trudy, let me take those sandwiches. You shouldn’t be carrying that so soon after your illness.”

Trudy looked at her, instantly picking up on Hayley’s desire to escape with her.

“Thanks, Hayley,” Trudy said, shoving the pan at Hayley while keeping one eye on Edie, who was apoplectic, eyes blazing, as she glared at her husband cowering inside the food truck. He was now a bundle of nerves, clearly afraid to come out of the truck and face his enraged wife.

Hayley and Trudy flew back inside the church, a house of worship, where hopefully they would be protected from the wrath of Edie Staples. There was no doubt in Hayley’s mind that at that moment Edie was furiously chewing out her handsy husband. And even though Reverend Staples was technically a man of the cloth, in his wife’s own mind at this point, he was more like the devil himself.

Chapter 13

The last thing Hayley expected to happen to her on Halloween was to end up waist deep in a sea of loud, unruly children dressed as witches and ghosts and goblins and ghoulies, not to mention assorted Marvel and DC superheroes and even one Spongebob Squarepants. She hurriedly filled plastic cups with fruit punch to hand out to the rowdy little kids that weren't tall enough to pour their own. She ran around with plates of cookies, handing them out, at one point having to pull apart a wizard from Harry Potter and a chimpanzee from one of the *Planet of the Apes* movies who were fighting over the last oatmeal chocolate chip cookie.

It was a madhouse.

The parents and teachers were too busy gossiping with one another to look after their screaming kids, who were now experiencing the upper reaches of a sugar high post-parade. So all of the supervision was left to Hayley, who had basically been abandoned by all the other adults in the room.

Just as the parade had looped around to Mount Desert Street and the kids started to arrive for the after-parade party at the church, Ted had taken Trudy home to get some much-needed rest before her big catering gig at the Garbers' party later that evening.

Shortly after catching her husband making an unwanted pass at Trudy, Edie had gone home, sending word through her husband that she was suddenly afflicted with a massive headache and needed to take some medicine and lie down in the quiet of her own home.

Alone.

As for Reverend Staples, after informing Hayley that she was basically on her own to wrangle the hyperactive rug rats, he retreated inside his office to hide with the door locked, too embarrassed to come out.

When Hayley needed someone to mix up a fresh bowl of fruit punch, which was getting dangerously low, she knocked on the reverend's office door, but he didn't even bother to answer her. Hayley then had to fight her way into the tiny church kitchen and do it herself.

After an hour and a half, the crowd began to thin out, and when there were just a few stragglers left, Hayley finally had time to commence cleanup. She washed all the bowls and trays and wiped down the tables and folded them up along with the twenty chairs that had been set up, and returned everything to the storage closet.

Some day off, Hayley thought.

But it was finally over, and she was about to treat herself to a burger and onion rings at Jordan's Restaurant when her phone buzzed.

It was Mark Garber.

She answered his call. "Hi, Mark! Ready for the big night?"

"Hayley, I need your help," Mark wailed, skipping any pleasantries.

"What's wrong? What's happened now?"

"I don't have a costume for tonight. Mary has been after me for weeks to get something good, and I've just kept putting it off and putting it off, thinking I would come up with something at the last minute. But now it's the last minute and I still don't have one!"

"Why are you calling *me*?"

"Because you're very creative and your kids always used to have the best costumes in the Halloween parade, and I just need someone to help me so Mary doesn't yell at me for not putting enough thought into what I show up in tonight—"

"I'm not sure what I can do, Mark—"

"Can you meet me at the drugstore? They still have a few masks and things left and I know you'll pick just the right one. Please, I can meet you there in five minutes."

"You want me to come *now*?"

"The party starts in a few hours. I'm in a code-red situation, Hayley, I'm begging you . . ."

"Fine, you head over there and I'll be there shortly," Hayley said, and hung up. She crossed to Reverend Staples's office door and rapped on it. "I'm leaving now, Reverend. I left the reception room just as I found it."

She wasn't sure if she heard him say something or not, but after a few seconds of silence, Hayley sighed and hurried out the side door to her car.

When she arrived at the Cottage Street drugstore—which had a whole aisle devoted to Halloween trinkets, toys, and costumes—she found Mark Garber standing in the middle of the aisle, staring at a shelf full of masks, utterly confused and noncommittal. When he sensed Hayley approaching, he smiled at her and sighed. "Thank God you came! I'm at a total loss . . ."

Hayley touched his arm and reassured him, "Stop worrying. We'll find you something."

After a few seconds of perusing the left over choices that had been thoroughly picked over, Hayley zeroed in on a mask in a damaged package, stuffed in the back of the shelf in front of another box of the same mask. There were only two of this particular mask left in stock. Hayley knew this was the right one and turned to Mark. "Do you have some coveralls?"

"Yeah, I think so," he said with a nod.

"How about a black jacket and black boots?"

"Yes, for sure."

Hayley reached in, grabbed the half-crushed box with its torn plastic cover and handed it to Mark. "We're done."

He stared at the mask inside the box. "Creepy. Who is it?"

Hayley's mouth dropped open. "You never saw *Halloween*? Or the dozen sequels and reboots that followed?"

"No, I'm not much of a movie person. I mostly watch sports," Mark admitted.

"It's Michael Myers, one of film's greatest serial killers. You'll be scary but everyone will know who you're supposed to be. Mary will love it."

"Okay," he said. He turned and grabbed the last remaining Michael Myers mask on the shelf to buy along with the one he already held in his hand.

"Why are you buying two?"

"For insurance. I don't want anyone else buying this last one and showing up at our party in the same costume."

"I think you're safe. It's only a few hours until the party. Save your money."

Mark hesitated, but then tossed the second box back on the shelf. "Maybe you're right. Thank you, Hayley, you're a lifesaver," Mark said, checking his watch and then scurrying to the counter.

Chapter 14

Hayley had to admit, she and Gemma rocked it as the *Wizard of Oz* witches at the Garbers' Annual Witches Ball. Gemma was luminous in her shimmering white gown and teased out blond hair punctuated with a glossy shiny tiara. She playfully waved her wand at the awed guests as Hayley chased behind her in her green pancake makeup, long crooked nose made of putty, and her black dress and hat. A few of the other guests even burst out in applause as they made their way inside to the party.

As for their significant others, Bruce and Conner had chosen to team up as the men from the original *Men in Black*, not the recent reboot with a man and a woman. They wore tailor-made black suits and ties as well as sunglasses to complete the look. They were very proud of the cool factor they felt they were generating.

Mary Garber, looking more like a Harry Potter wizard than a traditional witch with her purple flowing muumuu with moons and stars printed all over it, sashayed up to the foursome, clapping her hands. "Oh,

Hayley, you and Gemma outdid yourselves! You two look perfect!"

"Thank you, my child," Gemma cooed in a sing-songy voice that she had practiced by watching the scenes from *The Wizard of Oz* with Glinda the Good Witch over and over earlier in the day. Hayley just cackled, doing her best Margaret Hamilton impression, but falling a bit short, in her own opinion. Still, Mary seemed to love it. Mary then turned to the boys.

"Look who it is, the Blues Brothers!" Mary cried, clapping her hands again.

Bruce and Conner exchanged a disappointed look. Bruce turned back to Mary. "We're supposed to be the Men in Black."

"I never saw those movies. I don't like anything that has to do with aliens, but you look just like the Blues Brothers!"

Conner did not appreciate the misinterpretation of his costume choice and huffed, "Well, we're *not*. We're Men in Black!"

Mark Garber joined his wife's side, looking appropriately scary as Michael Meyers. He towered over them because he was wearing work boots with lifts to make him appear taller. He raised the mask Hayley had picked out for him. "Let me guess. The Blues Brothers!"

Conner sighed, giving up. "Okay, yes, fine, we're the Blues Brothers."

"I don't remember one of them having a broken arm," Mark said, looking at the sling Conner was wearing.

"They didn't," Conner tried to explain. "I fell off the roof."

"In which movie did one of the Men in Black fall off the roof?" Mary asked, blinking, utterly confused.

"No one fell off the roof!" Conner cried.

"Actually *you* did," Gemma reminded him.

"In real life, yes, this is a genuine injury, not part of the costume!" Conner yelled.

Trudy Lancaster, who also happened to be decked out in the same loose-fitting Wicked Witch of the West costume as Hayley, hustled up to her. She looked much healthier than the last time Hayley had seen her despite her painted green face. She had obviously regained her strength with each passing hour.

"I guess we should have consulted each other on our witch costumes," Hayley said, laughing. "Oh, well. Great minds think alike, I guess."

Trudy didn't crack a smile over the two of them wearing the same costume. She was too preoccupied and dead serious.

"Hayley," she said urgently in a hushed tone. "May I speak to you privately, please?"

"Yes, of course, Trudy," Hayley said. They stepped over to a corner of the room with very little traffic so they would not be overheard.

"You're looking so much better," Hayley said, relieved.

"I feel better," Trudy confirmed before adding, "Let's hope it lasts."

"Why? What's going on?"

"I have to get outside and fire up the grill in my truck, people are getting hungry, but I wanted you to know that the toxicology report came back."

"And?"

"The lab found traces of an insecticide in my system!"

"An insecticide? What kind of insecticide?"

"A pretty fatal one if enough is ingested. But I only

consumed a very small amount, enough to make me sick but not enough to kill me."

"But *how* . . . ?"

"You *know* how! It was that candy apple Cloris Fennow came around with. I knew she was acting suspicious when she showed up at my truck. She was perspiring and nervous and couldn't run away fast enough after I took the first bite of that apple!"

"Cloris? Are you absolutely sure?"

"Yes! I'm certain of it! The only trouble is, I can't prove it. I gave the doctor a list of all the food I had eaten that day before I started getting sick. I had a full breakfast, a power bar, a handful of almonds. I swear, if Ted hadn't gotten me to the hospital to get my stomach pumped, I'd still be bed-ridden. It's so obvious Cloris wanted me out of the picture! But unfortunately, there's no way of conclusively proving the insecticide came from eating her candy apple."

"Has Sergio seen the toxicology report yet?"

Sergio Alvarez, Hayley's brother-in-law, was the police chief.

Trudy nodded. "First person I talked to. He said he'll keep investigating to see if he can uncover more substantial evidence that points the finger at Cloris. Look, I better get outside and start making sandwiches before the guests storm my food truck."

"Good luck," Hayley said as Trudy lifted the hem of her witch's dress and hurried toward the front door and outside.

Hayley noticed Reverend Staples—who was, in her best estimation, dressed as one of the apostles from the Last Supper—trying to intercept Trudy. He managed to snare her upper arm and pull her over close to him, but Trudy rather directly and abruptly yanked her arm free, said something to him under her breath, and kept going out the door.

Off to her right, Hayley noticed that Edie Staples had also witnessed the brief, terse exchange between her husband and his object of affection.

And an incensed Edie had seen enough.

Downing the rest of her witch's brew cocktail consisting of chilled vodka, lemon and lime soda, pineapple juice, and—for color—green Jell-O, Edie slammed the glass down on the coffee table and started yelling.

"How dare you humiliate me like this, in front of our congregation, practically the entire town?"

The blood began draining from Reverend Staples's face as he made his way through the crowd, his mind no doubt racing over just how he was going to politely silence his wife short of muzzling her mouth with his hand.

Mary suddenly appeared at Hayley's side and sighed. "I knew someone would cause a scene. It happens every year."

"This one is shaping up to be one for the record books," Hayley whispered.

Edie stumbled a bit, then managed to balance herself, giving her husband the stink eye as he struggled to reach her. Before he could get to her, however, she whirled around to the crowd of guests, most of whom were frozen in place watching her with rapt attention as she unraveled right in front of them. "In case any of you have been living in a cave these past few weeks, my husband, the good Reverend Staples, the pillar of our community, the arbiter of morality and decency, is in *love* with another woman!"

Although the rumor mill had already been churning at a clipped speed, the announcement was shocking enough to illicit a few surprised gasps.

"That's right! Just in time for our retirement, my cheating husband has decided to chase after a woman *far* less than half his age! In fact, she could be his *granddaughter*!"

Reverend Staples finally managed to push his way across the room and get to his wife, clasping her hand and nearly twisting her arm behind her back like a cop would to frog-march a perp. "I'm sorry, everyone, Edie has had a little too much to drink, and isn't thinking clearly. She's quite mistaken—"

Edie scoffed. "I'm not an idiot! I know what's going on!"

Reverend Staples kept pushing his boozy, belligerent wife toward the door, but it only made her madder and more determined to embarrass him. "Look, everyone, this apostle has made such a fool of himself, he wants to leave the Last Supper early! Can you believe that? Our minister is standing up Jesus!"

Finally, mercifully, Reverend Staples was able to hustle his drunk, angry wife out of the party.

Mary Garber turned to Hayley and chuckled. "One for the record books, indeed."

Chapter 15

After Reverend and Mrs. Staples's hasty retreat from the Witches Ball, the festivities resumed without further incident, at least for a little while. Hayley chatted with a coven of witches, who by day worked as tellers at the First National Bank, then moved on to Nurse Tilly from the hospital who was ravishing in an all-white flowing sheer gown as Jadis the White Witch from *The Chronicles of Narnia.* Tilly was distracted by her boyfriend, Sam, a firefighter—not a real one, but dressed like one—who stepped on the hem of her dress, causing it to rip down the middle. After yelling at him, she dashed to the bathroom to see if she could fix it. Hayley gave Sam a sympathetic smile and excused herself in order to refill her witch's brew.

Liddy Crawford, local real estate maven and Hayley's best friend next to Mona Barnes, frantically ran up behind Hayley, and shouted, "Hayley, we have a situation!"

Hayley turned around, surprised to see Liddy decked out in the same Wicked Witch of the West costume, green makeup and all. Liddy's face fell. "Hayley! What were you thinking dressing up in the same costume as me? Why didn't you call and consult me?"

"Because frankly I never thought in a million years you'd come dressed as a Wicked Witch! I thought for sure you'd choose something more glamorous like Maleficent so people would compare you to Angelina Jolie!"

"Well, I didn't want to be predictable! Everyone expects me to look beautiful! I thought I'd go in a different direction!"

"You said something about a situation?"

"Yes! I saw that new food truck lady outside as I was arriving and she's *also* wearing the same costume as me, I mean *us*!"

"I know."

"You *knew* and you didn't tell me?"

"To be fair, I just saw her a few minutes ago, and didn't think I needed to put out a breaking news alert."

"This is a disaster! I'm so sorry you both have to go home and change!"

Hayley laughed in Liddy's frantic green face. "Forget it, Liddy. I know your goal in life is to stand out, but you're just going to have to deal with this situation."

"At least Trudy will be outside in her truck all night," Liddy muttered before looking at Hayley. "You know I love you, and you're my best friend in the whole wide world, but keep your distance tonight, okay?"

And then Liddy trundled off toward the bar.

Hayley scanned the crowd, smiling at all the clever and imaginative costumes on display, and also praying she wouldn't see anyone else channeling Margaret Hamilton. She spotted Gemma across the room, looking gorgeous as Glinda the Good Witch, holding court, entertaining a gaggle of admiring guests. Hayley marveled to herself at how self-assured and beautiful, how sharp and funny her once gangly, shy daughter had blossomed into as an adult. She was downright bursting with pride. Then, off to Gemma's right, she saw Conner, shifting uncomfortably, lost in thought, scratching his arm in the sling, as if working up the courage to propose to Gemma right here at the party.

Hayley took a step toward her daughter when a hand pulled her back and a man said, "You're not going to listen to a word I said, are you?"

Hayley spun around to see her handsome Man in Black smiling at her. "What are you talking about?"

"My advice, to just let things play out naturally. You can't do it. You're going to give Gemma a heads-up."

Hayley scoffed, "You think you know me so well! But you don't, Bruce! You don't know me nearly as well as you think you do because for the record, I was *not* going to do anything of the kind!"

Bruce nodded, still sporting that confident, knowing grin, which drove her absolutely crazy because she knew he was right. He handed her a cup of witch's brew. "I also know you're probably ready for another round so I took the liberty of getting you a fresh drink."

Hayley stared into the bottom of her empty cup and then tossed it into a nearby trash can. She snatched the drink from Bruce and scowled at him. "I never did like the Blues Brothers!"

Bruce laughed heartily as Hayley stormed off, crossing the room to where Gemma was just finishing a story about how she was working a fancy party in the Hamptons and accidentally released a springform pan filled with chocolate torte. It landed all over the hostess's ridiculously expensive designer dress.

As everyone laughed uproariously, Hayley gently pulled Gemma aside and whispered in her ear, "Can I talk to you outside?"

Gemma gave her a perplexed look. "Sure, Mom. Is everything all right?"

Hayley nodded. "Yes, I just need to tell you something."

Gemma suddenly appeared worried and Hayley touched her arm, and said reassuringly, "No one's died, I promise."

Hayley turned around and weaved her way through the crowd toward the front door. She heard Gemma say to her admirers, "Hold that thought. I'll be right back."

Once they were outside, Hayley led Gemma away from the house down on the lawn where they could have a modicum of privacy.

"Mom, you're making me nervous. What is it?" Gemma asked.

"I just thought you should know, so it doesn't come as a shock when it actually happens—" Hayley suddenly stopped, distracted.

"What? What?" Gemma cried.

But Hayley's attention was focused on something else entirely now. "What's going on over there?"

Gemma turned to see what her mother was gawking at. On the street in front of the house, a line of guests—women dressed as witches, men in various costumes including a *Stargate* soldier, a cowboy, a priest, and someone painted blue with a red vest and pantaloons, obviously going for the genie from *Aladdin*—all gathered around Trudy Lancaster's food truck.

"That's odd," Hayley said, leaving Gemma to wander over to the crowd. Gemma immediately followed after her, and as they reached the group milling around the truck, Hayley asked the genie, "What's going on?"

"The Garbers told us Wicked 'Wiches would be making us sandwiches all night, but she hasn't opened yet and we're all starving."

Hayley rapped on the metal security gate that had been rolled down in front of the serving window. "Trudy, there are a lot of hungry people out here!"

There was no answer from inside.

Hayley tried pounding on the gate again. "Trudy?"

Still nothing.

They couldn't hear any movement inside the truck. Hayley moved around to the back door and tried opening it but it was locked. She tried the driver's side door and it was locked too.

"Maybe she ran out of a condiment or something and went to the store to pick it up," Gemma suggested.

"Maybe . . ." Hayley said absently, starting to get worried.

The cowboy in line sniffed and said, "What's that smell?"

Hayley sniffed too and recoiled at a noxious odor.

One of the six witches stepped back, pinching her nose, "It smells like gas. I think it's coming from inside the truck."

Hayley started to panic. She banged on the metal gate one more time. "Trudy, are you in there? Are you all right?"

Gemma gasped, "Mom, if she's in there, we need to get her out!"

Hayley turned to the crowd. "Can somebody help me break the lock on the back door?"

The soldier stepped forward, brandishing a fake rifle, but it was made of strong metal and he used the butt of it to repeatedly hit the padlock that secured the two doors in the back. He tried several times to bust it open, but to no avail.

"Quick, break the window!"

The soldier raced around to the driver's side of the truck and raised the butt of the rifle, smashing it against the glass. After two tries, the glass shattered, allowing him to reach inside and unlock the door.

Hayley pushed past him, climbing into the truck where she was suddenly overcome with choking fumes. She covered her face with the long flowing sleeves of her costume, and managed to crawl into the back to the kitchen where she felt around for some kind of switch that would open the metal security gate covering the serving window. She was nearly overcome herself by the heavy fumes and suddenly felt light-headed, but finally located a key on the wall that she cranked quickly to the right. The heavy metal gate slowly began to squeak open and light from a nearby streetlamp flooded into the truck.

Hayley gasped, choking on gas fumes, still covering her nose and mouth, as her eyes fell upon Trudy Lancaster sprawled out on the floor of her food truck, dressed in the same costume as Hayley from *The Wizard of Oz*.

The *Stargate* soldier climbed into the truck behind Hayley and stared slack-jawed at the body. Unfortunately it was at that moment when he spoke aloud for everyone outside to hear the first thought to pop into his mind. "Ding-dong, the witch is dead."

Island Food & Spirits

BY

HAYLEY POWELL

I recently got together with my two BFFs Mona and Liddy at Liddy's house for one of our twice-monthly "catch-up dinners" where we all bring each other up to speed on the latest goings-on in our lives and, of course, all the latest gossip burning up town. It's always a fun, laugh-filled gathering, and I have to admit, Liddy outdid herself serving us Godiva Chocolate Martinis followed by some mouthwatering Slow Cooker Pulled Pork Cuban Sandwiches. I was so stuffed I could barely get up from the table once we finally decided to call it a night. Luckily, Liddy agreed to allow me to share both recipes with you this week!

Since we're right in the thick of October, the hot topic at this particular "catch-up dinner" was Halloween, and what we all would be wearing to the annual Witches Ball. Mona, who hates to dress up in a costume let alone a dress of any kind, had no intention of going and abstained from the conversation. But once we began reminiscing about Halloweens gone by, she deigned to rejoin the conversation. Especially when Liddy brought up one memorable Halloween memory I would just as soon forget!

It's no secret that Halloween has always been my ex-husband Danny's favorite holiday. It takes him back to the time when he was a kid. But let me tell you, it's not a very long trip since Danny has always had major maturity issues! Anyway, I should stay positive. Danny always loved playing a good Halloween trick to scare me, but he always seemed to be disappointed when he didn't get the reaction he expected. Mostly because I was usually ready for him to pull some kind of silly stunt and mentally prepared myself. But one year, Danny felt he had come up with a masterful plan to scare the living daylights out of me, and he was downright giddy as he set the wheels in motion.

Danny had a buddy, Al, who worked at the high school in the drama department doing makeup and special effects for all the theater productions, and so Danny bribed him with a six-pack of Michelob to come over to our house while I was at work on Halloween day, and use his stage makeup to turn Danny into a terrifying corpse worthy of an R-rated horror film! There was plenty of fake blood and gobs of flesh all over him, but the crowning glory was the fake organs and guts Al managed to attach to Danny's stomach so it looked like some marauding killer had essentially gutted him with a hunting knife! The idea was, Danny would lie down on the kitchen floor in a pool of blood, with all the gore and guts spilling out of him, and when I walked in and saw his cold, dead eyes staring up at me, it would scare the bejesus out of me! As I stood there screaming bloody murder, he'd pop up to his feet and yell in his typical charming tone, "Trick or Treat, babe!"

Well, lucky for me, Al's wife, Susan, got wind of this treacherous plot, and was so afraid I might die of fright she drove right over to the *Island Times* office and gave me a heads-up. I was mortified that our husbands were so willfully and blithely planning to scare me to death! After all, there are a few weak hearts in the family, so who could say if I was actually a time bomb walking around waiting for a little stress to set it off? Danny's little "harmless" prank might have literally killed me!

Susan and I decided to formulate our own plan. Susan went to her husband's theater prop box he kept in the basement and got one of the fake stage knives. You know, the kind of knife that retracts into the handle upon contact so it only looks like you're actually stabbing someone. Well, I was going to hide it in my utensil drawer so when I walked in and saw Danny lying dead on the floor, I would run and grab it, stand over Danny, profess my undying love and how I couldn't fathom carrying on without him, and then I would plunge the knife into my heart and sink to the floor, pretend to die, and wait for Danny's reaction. My husband was about to get a little taste of his own medicine.

Well, on Halloween after I got home from

work, I nervously walked up the deck steps and through the kitchen door at the allotted time I was supposed to discover "the body." I actually did gasp out loud at the sight of Danny lying on the floor, soaked in all that fake blood. It looked so real! I had to commend the bang-up job Al had done. I quickly tried channeling my best Meryl Streep, and let out a proper bloodcurdling scream. I rushed to Danny and kneeled down, wailing, "Why? Why? Why?" Danny's eyes were shut tight but I could almost see a smirk on his face as he listened to me loudly lamenting his death. I raced to the utensil drawer, found the correct knife (at least I hoped it was the correct one), and with great fanfare plunged it into my chest. Then, in full Oscar-worthy performance mode (at least in my mind), I dramatically sank to the floor and slowly died.

I had one eye open as I saw Danny trying to figure out what I had just done, but before either of us could sit up, an ear-splitting scream startled us both. I glanced over to see our elderly widow neighbor Ms. Millie standing in the doorway to the kitchen, eyes popped open, mouth ajar, staring at our "corpses." She must have heard my screaming and crying all the way next door and come over to investigate. Before I could assure her everything was fine, she clutched her heart and fainted dead away.

Danny, realizing his joke had taken an unexpected turn, tried getting up but slipped on the fake blood and fell back down again, landing hard on his butt. I crawled on my hands and knees over to Ms. Millie's prone body, praying she hadn't had a heart attack, and shook her, hoping to revive her.

That's about the time we heard sirens and two police cruisers screeching into our driveway. Apparently upon hearing my scream, a startled Ms. Millie had time to call 911 before racing across the street to see if we were still alive.

Thankfully, Ms. Millie was roused with some smelling salts, and I'm happy to say her heart was just fine. As for me and Danny, we just received a very stern warning from the police that perhaps it was in our best interest that we tone down our Halloween hijinks in the coming years.

That was one Halloween for the record books, or at least the police blotter!

As promised, here is how you can indulge in a chocolate martini and a slow-cooked Cuban sandwich that will warm up any chilly Halloween night. So when it comes to trick or treat, definitely choose these treats!

Godiva Chocolate Martini

Ingredients
2 ounces vanilla vodka
1.2 ounces crème de cacao
1 ounce Godiva chocolate liqueur
Optional: shaved chocolate

Use a chilled martini glass from the freezer.

Fill the cocktail shaker half full of ice.

Add the vanilla vodka, crème de cacao and Godiva chocolate liqueur to the cocktail shaker.

Shake well and strain into the chilled martini glass and top with shaved chocolate.

SLOW COOKER CUBAN SANDWICHES

INGREDIENTS

For the marinade and pork

4-pound pork shoulder
½ cup orange juice
¼ cup lime juice
4 garlic cloves, minced
2 teaspoons cumin
2 teaspoons dried oregano
½ teaspoon red pepper flakes
2 bay leaves
½ tablespoon kosher salt
½ tablespoon fresh ground black pepper
2 tablespoons olive oil

To build the sandwich

4 Cuban rolls (I use Italian rolls when I can't find Cuban)
12 slices of ham
16 slices Swiss cheese
8 long-sliced pickles

For the bread spread

4 tablespoons butter
½ teaspoon garlic powder

Cut your pork shoulder in 4 quarters and put in a large slow cooker.

Add the marinade ingredients and combine well.
Cover and cook on low for 6 to 8 hours until fork-tender and can be shredded.
Shred the meat using two forks.

In a small saucepan melt the butter and garlic powder and brush it on both sides of the bread.

To assemble your sandwich, spread mustard on the bottom of the bread, then layer 2 slices of Swiss cheese, 3 slices of ham, a nice helping of pulled pork, and 2 pickle slices, and top with 2 more slices of cheese and add top bun.

Place into a panini press until golden brown.

Note: I use a griddle and place my sandwich on it and then press a heavy cast-iron pan on top, brown one side, flip over and brown the other. When golden brown, it is done.

This makes enough pork for more sandwiches, and feel free to use as much ham, cheese, and pork that suits your preference.

Chapter 16

"According to the autopsy report, she died from acute carbon monoxide intoxication," Sergio Alvarez said before shoveling a forkful of Hayley's homemade lasagna into his mouth while sitting at her dining room table next to his husband, Randy, who was still working on his Caesar salad.

It had been two days since Hayley had discovered the body of Trudy Lancaster in her food truck, and her sudden death was all anyone in Bar Harbor was talking about.

Hayley would have been lying if she said that her dinner invitation to her brother and his police chief husband had been out of a desire for some quality family time together. No, she had a burning need to know what was going on with the investigation, and by promising Sergio that she would make his favorite dinner, a meat lasagna with Caesar salad and her buttery garlic bread—which he reliably used to sop up the remainder of the spicy marinara sauce on his plate—

there was little doubt in her mind that they would readily accept the invite and head right over at the usual time of six o'clock.

Hayley had politely waited until after they had finished their first glass of Pinot Noir and made most of their way through the salad course. In fact, when Sergio speared the last crouton on his plate and popped it into his mouth, Hayley had already shot up from the table and was using a spatula to cut the first generous piece of Sergio's usual three helpings of lasagna, delivering it to him and taking her seat back down at the table where everyone else—Bruce, Randy, Gemma, and Conner—were all still slowly eating their Caesar salad. She waited until Sergio had taken his first bite of the piping hot lasagna before casually asking what was going on with the Trudy Lancaster case, and that's when Sergio happily complied and freely offered the cause of death.

Everyone at the table now felt free to pepper Sergio with a series of follow-up questions.

"So was it an accident or suicide or foul play?" Gemma asked, curious.

Sergio shrugged. "We still don't know. Boy, Hayley, I have to say, you've really outdone yourself this time. Your lasagna is spicier than usual."

"I added a little crushed red pepper to the sauce to give it a little extra kick," Hayley said, quietly frustrated that Sergio seemed to want to change the subject.

Hayley opened her mouth to spew out a slew of questions related to the autopsy report when Conner interrupted her.

"Hayley, could you pass the garlic bread?"

Hayley turned to him, grimacing. He gave her an apologetic shrug and pointed to his arm in the sling, which prevented him from reaching across the table and grabbing the basket himself. She smiled and nodded, and then practically tossed the basket at him. He squinted, fearing it might hit him in the face, before catching it with his free hand and setting it back down on the table in front of him. He carefully chose a hunk and took a bite, chewing and savoring it.

"Was something wrong with the grill's propane tank?" Hayley asked.

"Hayley, I have to say, this is the *best* garlic bread I've ever tasted, and I spent a summer in Italy during my gap year between high school graduation and college," Conner said after swallowing.

"Thank you, Conner," Hayley said with a thin smile before turning back to Sergio. Before she could speak, however, Gemma opened her mouth first.

"I didn't know you took a gap year. Did you travel all over Europe or just Italy?"

Hayley dropped her fork, irritated, as the conversation seemed to have taken a sharp turn away from Trudy Lancaster.

"I spent most of it in Italy, I taught English at a middle school in Perugia."

"Where is that exactly?" Bruce asked, not helping at all.

"Central Italy. In the Umbria region." Conner said.

Hayley turned to see Sergio, almost done with his first serving of lasagna. She tried to get the dinner discussion back on track. "I just find it strange that Trudy's truck was locked up with the windows shut tight and the security gate down. I mean, she was there to serve the Garbers' guests. Why didn't she open the windows while she was preparing the food?"

"Beats me," Sergio said, shrugging with his mouth full.

"Perugia . . . Isn't that the area where the Amanda Knox murder case happened?" Randy asked.

Conner nodded. "Yes, the trial was still happening when I was there. Every day when I walked to the school, I would see the international press buzzing outside the courthouse. It was utter madness."

Hayley wanted to swat her brother with her napkin for changing the subject back to Italy and the sensational murder trial of an American college student convicted in 2009 of killing her roommate with the help of her Italian boyfriend at the time. After a yearlong trial, faulty evidence, and a corrupt prosecutor, the court reversed the conviction in 2011 and she was ultimately acquitted. But Hayley hardly wanted to spend the meal discussing a decade old scandal that was long over. Amanda Knox was back home in Seattle safe and sound. Trudy Lancaster's death was far more relevant and important, at least in the town of Bar Harbor and at this dinner table.

"Well, I'm sure Trudy Lancaster's death won't garner near as much attention," Hayley said, hoping to steer the conversation back to her preferred topic.

There was a lull in the conversation as Sergio finished his first serving of lasagna, sopping up the leftover sauce with the bread, while everyone else polished off the rest of their salads and sat expectantly waiting to be served their main course.

Finally, with Hayley's mind clearly elsewhere, Gemma stood up from the table. "You sit, Mom, I'll serve."

Snapping out of her thoughts, Hayley looked around to see everyone's empty plates. "Oh, I'm sorry, Gemma, no, I can do it."

Hayley grabbed Sergio's empty plate and raced into the kitchen. She cut the biggest piece for Sergio, and then filled the other five plates. Gemma followed her into the kitchen and began uncorking a fresh bottle of red wine to serve with the dinner. They didn't exchange a word. With all the hoopla and drama following her startling discovery of Trudy's body, Hayley had lost her opportunity to warn Gemma about Conner's intention to propose to her. Since all seemed relatively calm between her daughter and her boyfriend, she could only assume that Conner had not found the right moment yet, so there was still some time to talk to her, if she chose to do so. Bruce's strong advice to stay out of it was still haunting her so the one time they were alone and she had the chance to say something, she had let it pass. Now, she simply wanted to focus on what had happened to her new friend Trudy. She found her death disturbing and confusing and she needed to find answers.

Gemma assisted her mother with carrying all the plates to the table before returning to the kitchen to grab the wine and refill everyone's glasses.

Once they were all seated again and diving into their lasagna, Hayley was determined not to allow the conversation to drift back to Conner's lazy afternoons strolling the seaside or Amanda Knox's almost four years in an Italian prison. "So, you think something could have malfunctioned with the propane tank and filled the truck with gas, and Trudy was overcome by the fumes before she had the chance to get out?"

Sergio thought about her theory as he chewed a hunk of garlic bread and then nodded. "Yes, that's what I thought at first."

Hayley dropped her fork. "*At first*? What do you mean 'at first'?"

"There seems to be a glitch with the accidental death theory."

Bruce, who usually inhaled Hayley's lasagna at record speed, also put down his fork and stared at Sergio with renewed interest.

Sergio opened his mouth to speak.

But then Conner beat him to the punch. "I have a funny story that happened to me in Italy. I felt like such an ugly American—"

"Can it wait?" Hayley snapped.

"Mom!" Gemma admonished.

"I'm sorry," Hayley said to her daughter before turning to Conner and offering him an apologetic smile. "Forgive me, Conner, I was just really curious as to what Sergio was about to say."

Conner raised his free hand holding his fork, signaling his surrender, and quietly went back to eating his lasagna.

Hayley felt bad about lashing out, but she was on the edge of her seat. She spun back to Sergio. "You were saying something about 'at first'?"

"At first I thought it was an accident. But after talking to Ted, I'm not so sure."

"Why? What did he say?" Bruce asked, now as curious as Hayley.

"Ted insists there was a carbon monoxide detector inside the truck that would have gone off and warned Trudy if her kitchen was filling up with gas. But when we swept the food truck for any evidence of foul play, we found no sign of any detector."

"You think someone deliberately removed it?" Bruce asked.

"We're not sure. But Ted maintains he saw it there earlier in the day. But it was missing when we arrived on the scene. Still, that's not enough to classify the death as a homicide. Trudy could have removed it to replace the batteries and just forgot to put it back."

"Well, what about Cloris Fennow?" Hayley asked pointedly.

"I know all about Cloris," Sergio said. "I already questioned her. She admitted she wasn't happy about Trudy cockroach-ing on her territory . . ."

Conner stared at Sergio, puzzled.

Randy smiled and patted Sergio's arm. "Encroaching. Encroaching on her territory."

"What did I say?" Sergio asked.

"Cockroach-ing," Randy said.

"Isn't that the same thing?" Sergio asked.

Randy shook his head. "No, not really." He turned to Conner. "English is his second language."

Conner tried not to laugh.

"Anyway," Sergio continued. "Cloris Fennow hated the fact that she had new competition in town, and was very upset that the Garbers hired Trudy instead of her to work the Witches Ball, but she swears she was nowhere near the Garber house when Trudy died."

"Where was she?" Hayley asked.

"Home," Sergio said.

Bruce raised an eyebrow. "Alone?"

Sergio nodded. "Yes."

"That's what I call a flimsy alibi," Hayley scoffed.

"Did she have anything to say about poisoning poor Trudy so she would get sick and be unable to work the Witches Ball?"

"No, because we have no concrete proof Cloris was the one responsible for making Trudy sick, so it's just a suspicion at this point," Sergio said.

Hayley was not satisfied at all.

She was now determined to prove that Cloris Fennow had targeted her new friend by poisoning her, and then, when that didn't work, tampering with her propane tank and trapping her inside her own truck with the express purpose of killing her competition.

Sergio was done discussing the Trudy Lancaster case, and decided to redirect back to Conner and his ugly American in Italy story, which Hayley only half heard because she was so consumed with thoughts of proving Cloris Fennow's guilt, and just how she was going to do that.

After everyone was done eating and waited for Sergio to polish off his third helping, Gemma took charge clearing the plates and serving the spumoni ice cream cake from the freezer. By the time the third wine bottle was empty and the coffee pot was brewing, Bruce stood up from the table. "Sergio, could I speak to you privately?"

Hayley suddenly jolted out of her own thoughts and was now laser-focused on Bruce.

What was this all about?

"Sure," Sergio said. He wiped his mouth with a napkin and followed Bruce out of the room. They didn't just go into the living room to talk, which was still within earshot, they actually stepped outside onto the front porch, closing the door behind them.

Gemma glanced at her mother, wondering if she

knew what this could be about, but Hayley just shrugged and shook her head. She was dumbfounded.

What was so secretive that her newlywed husband could not speak freely in front of her? Hayley was suddenly very worried about what it was that he might be hiding from her.

Chapter 17

Hayley had to admit that the cheeseburger with its homemade tangy ketchup and grilled onions she had ordered from Cloris Fennow's food truck, Burger She Wrote, during her lunch hour was delicious. She had taken a bite and could not hide her look of pleasure from Cloris, who glared down at her from the truck's service window, waiting to gauge her reaction.

With her mouth full, Hayley nodded and managed to get out, "Tasty" as she chewed. Satisfied her only customer was happy, Cloris disappeared back inside her truck. Hayley was half done eating her burger when Cloris reappeared with a paper bag of seasoned curly fries and handed it down to her. "Oh, I didn't order these."

"They come with the burger," Cloris barked.

"Um, okay, thank you." With the last of her burger in one hand and a bag of fries in the other, Hayley leaned down and grabbed one of the fries with her teeth. She threw her head back so the curly fry fell into her open mouth and gasped with delight at the mouth-watering salty taste.

After swallowing, she smiled at Cloris. “These are remarkable.”

“It’s all in the seasoning,” Cloris said, puffed out and proud that Hayley, who had been such a vocal supporter of her late rival, Trudy Lancaster, was finally appreciating her obvious culinary talents.

Hayley was far less interested in building up Cloris’s confidence, however. That was not the reason she had driven around town until she spotted Cloris’s food truck parked outside the post office. No, she wanted to locate Cloris in order to pump her for information, perhaps even catch her in a lie, in order to prove that she was behind Trudy’s demise. And she had already spotted possible evidence that Cloris might not have been truthful with Sergio while she was busy grilling Hayley’s burger because just behind Cloris when she was peeling off a piece of cheddar cheese to top the burger with, Hayley could clearly see a traditional black witch costume hanging on a rack in the corner of the truck.

“I didn’t see you at the Witches Ball,” Hayley remarked as casually as possible.

“That’s because I wasn’t there,” Cloris barked. “Like I told the police chief, I stayed home.”

“Oh, I just assumed you were there because you have a witch costume hanging in your truck.”

Cloris paused, turned to look at the costume hanging on the rack, and then turned back, remaining silent for a few moments as she decided on just how she would respond.

Finally, she cleared her throat and said abruptly, “I had planned on going, but decided against it. It would have upset me too much to see Trudy Lancaster there making all the money I should have made catering that party."

"I see," Hayley said, studying Cloris and trying to assess if she was telling the truth or not.

"Thanks for reminding me. I need to return that costume to the rental shop. What a waste of twenty-five dollars." Cloris snorted as she disappeared again from the Burger She Wrote service window, only to reappear holding a candy apple on a stick. "Here, have a candy apple on the house."

Hayley stepped back, startled, which caused Cloris to wrinkle her nose and raise an eyebrow. "What's wrong?"

"Nothing," Hayley sputtered. "Is that the same kind of candy apple you gave Trudy?"

"Yeah, I like to make a few batches every year, but now that Halloween is over, I'm trying to get rid of them. Go ahead, take it."

"No, thank you," Hayley said abruptly.

There was no way she was going to risk ending up in the hospital the way Trudy did.

"You don't like candy apples?" Cloris said, scowling.

Hayley patted her stomach. "I'm just trying to cut down on sugar."

"Suit yourself," Cloris huffed, withdrawing her toffee-coated offering. Then she slammed down her security gate, locking it from the inside. She emerged from the back of the truck with the witch's costume in a paper shopping bag. "Lunch rush is over so I'm going to run a few errands."

"Will I see you at Trudy's memorial later this week?"

Cloris stared at her dumbfounded and then said,

"No, you won't. I'm many things, but a hypocrite is not one of them."

"I totally understand. It's probably what Trudy would have wanted anyway," Hayley said without thinking.

Cloris stared icily at her, trying to determine if what Hayley had just said was a direct insult, which of course it was.

Hayley braced herself for a verbal attack, but Cloris declined going on the offense, probably because Hayley was now a paying customer and quite possibly a new regular.

Instead, she just barked, "Whatever."

Cloris slammed the back doors of her truck shut and typed a code on a digital security panel, which automatically locked all the doors.

Hayley smiled to herself. Cloris hadn't bothered covering the panel with her hand so Hayley could not see the numbers she had pressed.

6-1-2-7-5.

Hayley repeated the numbers over in her mind several times trying to memorize them. If the opportunity presented itself at some point, she had just found a way to search the Burger She Wrote food truck for further evidence that might implicate Cloris Fennow in what Hayley was now becoming convinced was Trudy Lancaster's murder.

Chapter 18

The turnout for Trudy's memorial service at the Bar Harbor Congregational church was far larger than Hayley had expected given the short amount of time the Lancasters had been in town. But the tragic circumstances surrounding Trudy's death and the vociferous local support for the new minister drew a healthy crowd. By Hayley's estimation, there had to be upward of a hundred people filling the pews on that chilly, overcast early November Saturday afternoon.

Hayley and Bruce waited behind a group of people paying their respects to Trudy, whose coffin was set up near the front amidst an array of flower arrangements. Hayley was also surprised Ted had requested an open-casket service, but according to Reverend Staples, the grieving husband wanted everyone to be able to get one last look at his beautiful wife before they buried her.

When the mourners ahead of them had parted, leaving the way clear for Hayley and Bruce to step up to the coffin, Hayley took a deep breath and gripped

Bruce's hand tightly. She had seen many dead bodies in her life and so she never got apprehensive or nervous, but Bruce on the other hand, who ironically covered local crime, which required him on many occasions to gaze upon a corpse, was constantly filled with anxiety whenever he had to take even a quick peek. Bruce had spent the entire morning preparing, gearing himself up for the inevitable when Hayley broke the news that Ted was going with an open-casket service. Still, he wanted to be there to show his support for his new buddy Ted and what he was going through, so despite his instinct to blow it off, he had dutifully put on a suit and tie and bravely drove to the church with his wife.

Hayley noticed as they stepped up to the coffin that Bruce's eyes were squeezed shut. She smiled to herself, deciding not to force Bruce to look if he didn't want to. His back was turned to the congregation of mourners so it wasn't as if anyone would know he was avoiding looking at the deceased in repose.

Staring at Trudy, who looked gorgeous and peaceful, as if she was just taking a nap, Hayley's heart broke at the tragic loss. Trudy was such a vibrant, lovely young woman and Hayley had been looking forward to getting to know her better, convinced they were destined to be close friends. Trudy looked resplendent in a stylish yet demure dress she was wearing, a long-sleeved pink wrap dress, her favorite color according to Ted. What stood out most to Hayley, however, was a ruby teardrop birthstone pendant pinned to the dress.

"That's exquisite," Hayley said mostly to herself since Bruce's eyes were still shut.

"What?" Bruce whispered, refusing to even open one eye to see what she was talking about.

"The pendant she's wearing. It's stunning."

"It's her birthstone," a man said from behind them. Hayley turned to find Ted, his face pale and drawn, his shoulders slumped, physically exhausted from the gut-wrenching events of the last week. "Trudy was born in July. When she was twelve, her mother gave her a red ruby, which she had fashioned into that pendant. Trudy treasured it and wore it on very special occasions. I knew she would want to be buried with it."

Bruce turned away from the coffin and finally opened his eyes as he faced Ted and gave him a hug. "I am so, so sorry for your loss, Ted."

"Thanks, Bruce," Ted said, his voice cracking, trying to stay strong but finding it harder by the minute.

Hayley followed Bruce's lead and hugged Ted as well once Bruce took a step back. "If there is anything we can do—"

Before she had a chance to finish her thought, Ted was nodding and interrupting her. "There is absolutely something you both can do. You can help me prove that Trudy was murdered."

This took them both by surprise. Not that Ted suspected foul play, but that he was not even going to wait until after the memorial to discuss it. But his searing look of grim determination told Hayley that he was out of patience and wanted answers.

"The police are still investigating and so I'm sure we will know something soon . . ." Bruce said, gently placing a hand on Ted's arm.

"I'm sick of waiting around for them to tell me what I already know. I had just replaced the batteries in that carbon monoxide detector and had tested it myself on the morning Trudy died. It was there in the truck, I'd swear on my life. Somebody *deliberately* removed it before fiddling with the propane tank!"

Reverend Staples suddenly appeared, and said solemnly, "If you would be so kind and take your seats, we can get started."

Ted reacted, startled, a bit discombobulated by the reverend's presence, but he acquiesced to the request and nodded to Reverend Staples before whispering out of the side of his mouth to Hayley and Bruce, "We'll talk later."

Ted then took his seat in the front row of the pew. Hayley and Bruce walked back a few rows, settling in on the aisle across from Edie Staples, who was squeezed into a tight black dress and wearing a matching black hat, which was decorated with white tulips to apparently give it a little flair.

Reverend Staples signaled the doddering, bespectacled organist, who had been playing "Time to Say Goodbye" during the viewing, to finish up and she abruptly stopped, grabbing her bottle of water off the top of the organ and taking a swig.

Reverend Staples gripped the sides of the podium, cleared his throat and began. "I'd like to welcome you all here as we celebrate the life of a truly remarkable woman, Trudy Lancaster."

Hayley noticed the reverend's eyes welling up with tears.

"I was lucky enough to get to know Trudy during the few short weeks she was here in Bar Harbor. As many of you know, Trudy's husband, Ted, has been designated as my successor, and we have been working closely together during the transition to my retirement, and Trudy . . ." He choked up, tried clearing his throat again. "Trudy . . ."

Hayley glanced over to see Edie Staples rolling her eyes in annoyance.

"She . . . Well, you can see for yourselves what a beautiful, dare I say, dazzling woman she was . . ."

The mourners shifted uncomfortably in their seats as Reverend Staples's sermon threatened to cross the border into creepy terrain.

"When I first laid eyes on her, she literally took my breath away . . ."

Hayley turned to Bruce, whose eyes were glued to the floor as he said to Hayley out of the side of his mouth, "This is getting too weird."

Suddenly Reverend Staples finally lost it and broke down sobbing. "Trudy, I will miss you . . . we will all miss you so much!"

Everyone sat still, waiting for him to compose himself again, but two minutes passed and he was still a blubbering mess, unable to speak, constantly wiping his wet face with the sleeves of his purple peach-skin pulpit robe.

Finally, after what seemed like an eternity, someone heckled from the congregation, "For the love of God, get a hold of yourself!"

It was Edie Staples, who frankly had suffered enough. She stood up and pointed a crooked finger at her husband. "You're making a complete fool of yourself! Now buck up and get on with it!"

Reverend Staples nodded to his wife, trying his best to get his well of emotions under control. Finally, he managed to resume his sermon, mostly from the fear of further browbeating and pestering from his peeved spouse. The rest of the reverend's speech was actually quite moving and inspirational; it was clear he had spent quite a bit of time preparing it. But he wrapped it up pretty quickly. Hayley suspected he had cut it short due to his overwrought emotions that were now consuming him.

After inviting everyone to partake in the reception in the side room, featuring Edie's homemade baked goods, Reverend Staples disappeared into his office and apparently locked himself inside, never to be heard from again for the rest of the afternoon.

Edie put on a brave face as she ignored her husband's obvious affection for the deceased and focused on making sure everyone feasted on her dry, tasteless cakes and brownies. Hayley and Bruce tried locating Ted to once again offer their condolences but the handsome minister-in-training was already being descended upon by women who were mostly single, older, and made available by death or divorce, anxious to let the grieving widower know they wanted to be there for him in his time of need. Instead of waiting for him to have a free moment, Hayley and Bruce decided to slip out and head home.

Outside the church, they stopped at their car, which was parked toward the back of the packed gravel lot.

Bruce turned to Hayley. "Why didn't Sergio and Randy come today?"

"Randy's understaffed and could not get anyone to cover for him at the bar, and Sergio's busy trying to get Ted some answers about Trudy's death."

"Poor guy. What he must be going through . . ."

"Speaking of Sergio, are you ever going to tell me what you so urgently needed to speak to him about the other night?"

Bruce sighed. "Do I have to?"

"Now that we're married, it's kind of expected that we tell each other everything," Hayley said pointedly.

"Okay, fine. I wanted to tell him that on the night of the Witches Ball, when you were busy flitting around chatting with everybody, I stepped outside to get some air, and I saw someone dressed as a witch running away from Trudy's truck. I didn't think anything about it at the time since all of the women in the vicinity were dressed in witch costumes, but after you and Gemma found Trudy's body, I felt like I needed to share that information with Sergio."

"You saw the *killer*?" Hayley gasped. "And it was a *woman*?"

"No, I saw *someone*, not necessarily the killer, leaving the scene right before you discovered the body."

"Cloris Fennow! I bet my bottom dollar it was Cloris Fennow! She rented a witch costume! I saw it hanging in her truck, and her alibi's shaky!"

"Maybe, but you're going to need more evidence than that. Half the women in Bar Harbor have witch costumes," Bruce said emphatically. "I just thought Sergio should know."

"You did the right thing," Hayley said. "But what I don't understand is, why couldn't you just tell him that in front of me? Why be so mysterious and take him outside so I couldn't hear you?"

Bruce shuffled his feet, not wanting to reveal any more. But he knew Hayley well enough by now to know that keeping a secret from her would be impossible and make his life miserable.

"Bruce . . . ?"

"Okay, okay. I didn't want to say anything in front of you because the reason I went outside was because . . ."

"Yes?"

"Because I needed a smoke . . ."

"Oh, Bruce," Hayley wailed, disappointed.

"See? That's *exactly* why I took Sergio outside on the porch! I didn't want to have to see that look of judgment!"

"If you don't get a grip on this nasty habit, you'll get lung cancer and die and then where will you be?"

"Free from your nagging."

"Did you really just say that?"

"It just slipped out."

"Is that supposed to make it better?"

"I love you, Hayley."

"No, you are not going to try and wiggle out of this by saying 'I love you,' and then kissing me, and giving me those sad, cute puppy dog eyes until I start to melt and finally let you get away with it."

Bruce kissed her.

"No, it's not going to work."

He gave her the sad, cute puppy dog eyes.

"Nope. Not going to work."

But she couldn't help herself.

Especially when he kissed her again, this time with more passion.

"You have smoke breath," Hayley scoffed.

"No, I don't. I ate half a box of Tic Tacs. You're just trying to make me feel guilty."

"You're right. You're minty fresh. But we don't need any funeral attendees watching us make out in the parking lot of the church!"

"Good idea! I have a lot more planned for when we get home," Bruce said with a sly smile.

"Only if you promise to quit smoking!"

Chapter 19

Hayley stood in the middle of the aisle at the drugstore staring at all the selections of nicotine patches, gum, and coated lozenges. Which brand was the best? Should she start him out small, perhaps the four-milligram nicotine gum, or go big, like the twenty-one-milligram patch? She had one mission in mind, and that was to find the right solution to help Bruce finally kick his nasty smoking habit. She just wasn't sure how to go about it. After perusing her choices, Hayley grabbed the box with the twenty-one-milligram patches, which promised to help reduce nicotine withdrawal symptoms such as irritability, anxiety, depression, sleeplessness, and increased appetite and nicotine cravings. Whatever made Bruce easier to live with while he powered through this was fine by her.

She was halfway to the counter when she heard a familiar voice at the pharmacy window toward the back of the store. She veered right, heading in the opposite direction of the checkout counter, and spotted Edie Staples talking to the pharmacy employee in a white lab coat, a girl she didn't know, who stood behind a window, a helpful smile plastered on her face.

"I tried the Lexapro but it did nothing for me, and the Celexa elevated my heart rate too much and made me shaky and I had terrible insomnia, so I'm hoping this Zoloft finally does the trick," Edie said to the pharmacist, who glanced nervously toward Hayley, thinking she might be eavesdropping.

Which to be honest, she was.

Edie noticed the girl's wandering eyes and turned to see Hayley holding the box of nicotine patches. "Oh, good for you, Hayley, for trying to kick the habit."

"What?" Hayley asked, confused, before remembering the box she was holding. "Oh, I don't smoke. This is for Bruce."

"Well, good for him, then. I wish him all the luck in the world. Those patches never worked for me when I smoked. But then I went to a hypnotist in Portsmouth, and after just one session, I completely lost my craving! Can you believe that? He was a miracle worker!"

"I may need to get his number."

Edie held up a finger to Hayley. "Here, let me just pay for this. Don't go anywhere."

The pharmacist rang up the sale on her register. "That will be forty-six ninety-two, please, Mrs. Staples."

"Lord, and that's *with* insurance! When are those idiot politicians in Washington going to do something about drug prices?" Edie lamented as she handed over her credit card. "This is much more expensive than my last drug."

Hayley knew enough about Zoloft to know it was an antidepressant medication, and she was surprised that Edie Staples, who normally struck her as so upbeat and positive, was battling some kind of depression.

"Thank you, Mrs. Staples," the girl behind the counter chirped as she handed Edie back her card. "You have a wonderful day."

After signing the slip and sliding it back to the girl through the slot below the window, Edie grabbed her bag and receipt and marched over to Hayley.

"The hypnotist did wonders for my smoking habit but I'm afraid when it came to my erratic mood swings, he didn't help me at all on that front."

"I'm sorry to hear that, Edie," Hayley said as they strolled up to the front of the store where Hayley could pay for her nicotine patches at the regular checkout counter.

"Frankly, I've tried everything with dismal results," Edie said quietly, shaking her head. "Trudy Lancaster told me right before she died to try Zoloft. She claimed it worked wonders for her. Calmed her right down and got her through the day, so fingers crossed it does the same for me."

Hayley stopped suddenly. "Trudy was on antidepressants?"

"Yes, she was. And believe me, she needed them," Edie said with a derisive sneer.

"Why do you say that?"

Edie glanced around to make sure no one was loitering about listening to their conversation before leaning in to Hayley. "When the Lancasters first moved to town and didn't know anyone, the reverend and I tried to make them feel welcome by hosting them at our house for dinner their first few nights. The men had much to discuss about the goings-on at the church and the training period they were about to begin, and so Trudy and I spent a lot of time alone talking about our lives. Well, after a few glasses of wine on the second night, Trudy intimated that she and Ted did *not* have a storybook marriage."

"She *told* you that?"

Edie nodded conspiratorially, thrilled that she finally had someone to tell this juicy revelation. "I know it's shocking. On the outside, they looked like such the perfect couple. Both good-looking and personable, and he's a minister for heaven's sake! But apparently the handsome Reverend Ted can be moody and demanding and it was taking quite a toll on their marriage."

When Hayley noticed the short, stout male clerk behind the checkout counter staring at them, curious as to what they were so intensely discussing, Hayley gestured toward Edie to wait, and she stepped up to the counter and paid for her box of nicotine patches. Once they were outside safely out of the nosy clerk's earshot, Hayley and Edie immediately resumed their conversation.

"I had no idea Ted and Trudy were having problems," Hayley said, stunned. "We saw them socially a few times and never got that impression."

"Poor Trudy was an emotional mess. She also hinted that moving to Bar Harbor was a last-ditch attempt to save the marriage. If they couldn't make a go of it here, she was going to bring up the D word."

Divorce.

Hayley couldn't believe it.

Neither Ted nor Trudy had ever hinted at any marital discord. Not once.

Normally Hayley might question Edie's trustworthiness, but in this case, Hayley's instinct told her that Edie was not embellishing facts or making things up. It made perfect sense that the two women would have gotten to know each other since their husbands were working together, at least in the short run before Reverend Staples officially retired and they headed west in their RV.

"The sad thing is, Hayley, Trudy and I were on the road to becoming very close friends until my nitwit randy husband suddenly developed an unseemly obsession for the poor woman!"

"He did seem to like her an awful lot."

"That's the understatement of the year," Edie snorted. "After he started chasing her around like some girl-crazy teenager, she wisely chose to keep her distance from both of us, and so our blossoming friendship was sadly nipped in the bud."

"What do you think of Ted?" Hayley asked.

Edie frowned, not sure she should go there, but ultimately admitting, "I don't like him. I found him charming at first, maybe a little distant, but certainly personable. Once Trudy told me what was going on behind the scenes, I paid more careful attention to his personality and I did see flashes—nothing too obvious, but I could tell he could be controlling and easy to anger, but again, on the surface, he was quite lovely."

"Do you think based on your observations that he might be capable of—?"

"Oh, goodness, you mean do I think he killed his wife? I am hardly qualified to make that kind of assessment. Which is why I've told you all this."

"Me? Why?"

"Given your history in this town, and your track record of exposing people who have done terrible things, I'm hoping you might be able to unmask Ted Lancaster and reveal him to be the truly scary man I believe he might be."

Hayley was taken aback.

Edie Staples was asking her to prove Ted Lancaster was a cold-blooded killer who had no compunction about offing his wife by trapping her inside her food truck and gassing her to death.

And although her opinion of Edie Staples had always been a bit wobbly, Hayley was ready to accept the challenge.

Chapter 20

After leaving Edie, Hayley raced in her car over to the police station, swerving into an empty space in the parking lot across the street. As she dashed toward the nondescript brick building, her phone buzzed, and she glanced at the screen to see it was Gemma calling. She didn't answer, intending to call her right back just as soon as she found Sergio and related the information Edie Staples had just confided to her about the Lancasters.

As she hurried up the stone stairs, the door flew open and Sergio barreled out with Officer Earl close on his heels.

"Sergio, just the man I came to see!" Hayley said, awkwardly blocking his exit on the steps.

"Sorry, Hayley, I can't talk now!" he shouted, almost roughly pushing past her as he and Earl, who was already huffing and puffing from trying to keep up with his more athletic boss, rushed to the police cruiser parked in front of the station.

Hayley whipped around and chased after them. "But I have some important information regarding the Trudy Lancaster case!"

"It will have to wait," Sergio called back. "Joanna Liscomb was driving her son, Emory, home from soccer practice at the high school and just hit a Great Black Hawk with her car out on Eagle Lake Road!"

"Well, that doesn't sound like such a big emergency! This will only take a second!" Hayley cried.

"She killed it! It's a rare bird! The Maine Audubon Society is going to be up in arms, and I think we may have to report it to the Fish and Wildlife Service!"

Sergio unlocked the driver's side door of the cruiser with his remote as Officer Earl circled around to the other side and jumped in the passenger seat.

"What about Joanna and her son?"

Sergio stopped, turned to Hayley. "They're both fine. Her Ford Escape has a cracked windshield, though. But we need to get out there and make a report."

Hayley heard a pinging sound coming from her phone. Gemma had left a voice-mail message. She made a mental note to listen to it after she was done talking to Sergio.

Sergio slid behind the wheel of the cruiser and fired it up. Hayley rapped on the window. He grimaced, annoyed by her persistence, and pressed the button that lowered the driver's side window. "Hayley, I'm sorry, but we really have to go—"

"The Lancasters were having marital problems!" she blurted out. "Edie Staples told me. Apparently Trudy was depressed about it and was even taking medication."

Sergio nodded, indifferent. "Okay, thanks."

He then turned the wheel, steering the cruiser away

from the curb toward the street. Hayley found herself running alongside, her hand gripping the car door to keep up. "You don't sound very surprised."

"I'm not," he said, looking up at Hayley, who was now jogging next to him as the cruiser slowly moved down the street. "Now, will you let go so I can get to the scene of the accident?"

"I thought you'd at least be mildly curious. I mean, Ted is acting so broken up over losing Trudy, what if it's all an act? Don't you find that highly suspicious?"

"Yes, and I'm on it. I already knew they were having issues in their marriage," Sergio said.

"How? Did Edie already tell you?"

"No, I got my hands on some court papers. Trudy Lancaster filed for divorce from her husband on the day she died."

Hayley gasped, stunned.

Even Officer Earl raised an eyebrow, surprised. "No kidding?"

Sergio shot him a look to stay out of it.

"The *same* day?" Hayley said, wheezing.

"Yes, don't worry, Hayley, I'm taking this case seriously, now will you please let go? Joanna Liscomb is distraught enough over killing an endangered species and really needs my help right now."

Hayley released her grip on the car door and Sergio, without wanting to risk her trying to stop him again, sped off, rounding the corner onto Mount Desert Street and disappearing from view.

Hayley was left standing in the middle of the street, her mouth open in shock as she processed this revelation. Trudy was unhappy and wanted out of her marriage. Hayley had definitely not seen that coming. Trudy had gone to such great lengths along with Ted of presenting themselves as the picture-perfect happy couple to the community. Ted probably needed that stable image in order to ensure his smooth transition into his new role of minister at the Congregational church. What if Trudy threatened to ruin everything by leaving him? A nasty divorce would not have been a good look for the new clergyman in town. Ted appeared to be very good at presenting himself as the blissfully content husband. That obviously was an act. And it was entirely possible that he was also fully capable of acting the part of the now-grieving husband. After all, in a way, ministers are performers too.

Suddenly Hayley feared that Ted Lancaster might have gone to extreme lengths to stop the town from finding out that his marriage to Trudy was about to blow up in his face.

Hayley's phone buzzed again.

It was a text from Gemma.

I need to talk to you!

First a voicemail and now a text within the span of just a few minutes. Hayley was officially concerned something was wrong. She was about to listen to the voicemail when she received another text.

It's an emergency!

Hayley didn't bother listening to the voicemail. She immediately called her daughter back.

Gemma answered the call on the first ring. "Mom, where are you? I've been trying to reach you!"

"I know, I was busy. I'm sorry."

"The most terrible thing has happened!"

Hayley's heart sank. "Oh no. What?"

"Conner just proposed to me!"

Chapter 21

After speeding home and nearly swerving her Kia into a lamppost to avoid mowing down a black cat darting across the street, Hayley peeled into her driveway so fast she thought she might have left skid marks on the pavement. Rushing into the house, Hayley found Gemma in an agitated state, pacing back and forth in the living room. She dramatically threw her arms up in the air as her eyes fell upon her mother.

"What took you so long?"

"I got here in seven minutes flat! I nearly killed a black cat on the way, I was driving so fast! I guess I should be grateful I'm not Joanna Liscomb. At least I didn't hit a rare bird!"

"What on earth are you talking about, Mother?"

"Nothing! It doesn't matter! Where's Conner?"

"I sent him out to the store. I told him I'm making an authentic Bangladeshi beef curry, and needed cumin."

"That sounds delicious. Are you really making it?"

"No, I made it up in the moment to get him out of

the house so we could talk. I don't know what I'll do when he sits down at the table and I serve him leftover lasagna from the other night."

"We'll figure something out."

"I feel like I've been hit by a truck," Gemma wailed. "Just like that poor Great Black Hawk."

"Why do you keep talking about birds, Mother?"

"I'm sorry, I suddenly can't seem to get the image out of my head. Forget it. Tell me what happened with Conner."

"Conner wanted to go on a drive along the Park Loop Road and stop and take a few pictures of Thunder Hole, Bubble Rock, the Bass Harbor Head Lighthouse, the usual touristy stuff. You know how he fancies himself as some kind of talented photographer, although frankly, none of his photos would make the cut on a postcard, if you ask me . . ."

"Gemma . . ." Hayley whispered calmly.

Gemma grabbed her head with her hands. "I know, I'm getting off track! I always do that when I'm spiraling!"

"Take a deep breath," Hayley suggested.

Gemma nodded and did as instructed, inhaling, holding it, and then releasing it. It seemed to do the trick and she managed to continue. "We ended up on top of Cadillac Mountain so we could watch the sunset, and while we were sitting on a rock, holding hands, he just stood up, kneeled down before me holding a ring box, and asked me to do him the honor of marrying him!"

"Oh, dear . . ."

"It was such a shock! I was speechless! I couldn't say anything! Finally, he asked me if I would like to think about it, and I just nodded and had this weird smile on my face, which he took as me being happy. But I wasn't! My face was completely frozen, like I had just had a stroke, or suffered from Bell's palsy! I finally managed to get out that I suddenly had a headache, and so we walked back to the car and drove straight home. When we got here, I went straight to my room and had a nervous breakdown while he checked his emails down here. That's when I tried calling you. Mother, what am I going to do? This was totally out of the blue! I mean, I had absolutely no hint he was going to do this!"

"I know, and I am *so* sorry."

"What do you have to be sorry about?"

Hayley paused. Her gut instinct had been right. She should have said something to Gemma earlier. She had just gotten so distracted by the events surrounding Trudy Lancaster's untimely demise, frankly she had forgotten all about it.

"Mom?"

Now it was Hayley's turn to take a deep breath.

Gemma's eyes narrowed. "Is there something you're not telling me?"

"Yes, Gemma, I was going to warn you about this, but with everything that's been going on these past few days—"

"You *knew*?"

Hayley slowly nodded. "Conner came to me and let me know what he was planning. He had already called your father in Iowa and asked his permission."

"He *what*? Dad knew too? How could you two not warn me about something like this?"

"Conner wanted to surprise you. I-I wasn't sure if I should obey his wishes or get involved—"

"Of course you should have said something! Especially after what I told you about my conflicted feelings, and how I've been thinking of breaking it off!"

"I see that now in hindsight, and again, I am *so* sorry."

"He's going to be back any minute. How am I going to act like everything's normal now?"

"You can't. You have to be honest with him. It's best if you let him down sooner rather than later. He's a good guy and doesn't deserve to be strung along."

Hayley could see that Gemma's thoughts were roiling through her brain as she considered all her options. Finally, she sighed and turned to her mother. "You're right. I'll sit him down tomorrow and we'll have a real heart-to-heart. I just need some time to think about what I'm going to say."

Shortly thereafter, Conner returned with the cumin, eagerly expecting an authentic Bangladeshi beef curry. Luckily, Hayley had enough beef chuck in the freezer out in the garage that she could thaw in the microwave along with a fully stocked spice rack, including cinnamon sticks. So there was a good chance they could turn Gemma's little white lie into an actual meal if given at least two and a half hours. So when Bruce arrived just a few minutes later, Hayley parked him and Conner in front of the television with a six-pack of beer, and had them watch a *John Wick* movie starring Keanu Reeves on Netflix, which bought her and Gemma the time they would need to prepare the promised dinner.

The plan worked, and by nine they were dining on a tasteful beef curry as if they were at a little hideaway eatery on the Bay of Bengal amidst the lush greenery and twisty waterways in Southeast Asia instead of Hayley's dining room with its peeling wallpaper.

Later, when the two couples had retired to their

rooms, Hayley came up behind Bruce, who was standing in front of the bathroom mirror, shirtless and flossing his teeth, and held up the box of nicotine patches.

"Consider it an early birthday present," she said with a sympathetic smile as she set it down in front of him on the counter and opened it.

"Mine or yours?" he grumbled.

"Mine, definitely mine," she said, unwrapping the patch and gently applying it to his upper arm.

"And if it doesn't work?" Bruce asked.

"We'll just have to try something else."

Bruce turned to face Hayley. "Okay, I'll do this for you, but what are you going to do for me?"

"What do you have in mind?"

He grinned lasciviously. "Let me toss around a few ideas."

And then he kissed her on the lips. She threw her arms around his neck and drew him closer to her. They stood in the bathroom smooching and caressing each other, before Bruce took her by the hand and guided her back into the bedroom. He lowered her down on the bed, a hand cupped behind her neck, and was about to climb on top of her when the police scanner—which Hayley had brought up to the bedroom and plugged in one day while she was cleaning, and had forgotten to take back down to its usual spot in the kitchen—crackled to life. They heard the scratchy voice of a police dispatcher. "Adam Twelve, we have a ten-ninety in progress."

Hayley pulled away from Bruce. "Ten-ninety, what's that?"

"Prowler."

"Resident at Sixty-four Hancock Street has reported a suspicious person loitering outside the home."

Hayley gasped. “Sixty-four Hancock Street? That’s the Garber house!”

A voice that sounded like Chief Sergio himself responded, “On my way. Do you have a description of the person?”

There was some crackling on the scanner before the dispatcher answered, “Uh, yes, Chief, we, uh, actually have a name . . .”

More crackling.

Sergio came on the scanner again. “Dispatch, you still there?”

“Yes, Chief. According to the resident, the person outside her house is a woman by the name of Trudy Lancaster.”

Hayley and Bruce exchanged dumbfounded looks.

A little more crackling.

“Dispatch, could you repeat that?”

“Trudy Lancaster.”

“Dispatch, Trudy Lancaster is dead.”

“Yes, Chief, I know. The woman says it’s her ghost.”

Island Food & Spirits

BY

HAYLEY POWELL

You know by now that I love Halloween! My kids love Halloween, my brother, Randy, loves Halloween, my best friend, Mona, loves Halloween. However, my other best friend, Liddy, well, not so much. She is a dear and does try her best, but mostly she just tolerates it because she knows how much everyone else loves all the traditions of dressing up in costumes, trick-or-treating, and handing out all that delicious candy. I always told her not to worry because I had enough Halloween spirit for the both of us.

When my son, Dustin, was in the fourth grade, I came down with a horrible flu the week before Halloween and was ordered by the doctor to be on strict bed rest to prevent it from turning into anything worse. Well, you can imagine how devastated I was, especially since my calendar was already booked volunteering as a chaperone for the annual Emerson Conners middle school Halloween parade. I had also signed up to provide cupcakes for the party afterward, not to mention I still had costumes to finish sewing and loads of candy to buy. To top it all off, as I was leaving the doctor's office, Dustin called from school in a panic because he had forgotten to bring his bag lunch. For hot lunch they were serving the dreaded American "chop suey," which he detested, so you can imagine the meltdown he was having. "Mommy, you have to do something before I starve to death!"

I called Randy, who was in Bangor buying supplies for his bar, Drinks Like A Fish, and Mona, who was out on her lobster boat with no cell service. I was in a real bind. As they say, desperate times require desperate measures. And I was certainly desperate so I called Liddy. I knew the only thing Liddy hated worse than Halloween was being around little kids with their sticky fingers and snotty noses. Now don't get me wrong. Liddy loved my two cherubs who called her "Aunt Liddy," but she had no time for anybody else's. The idea of setting foot in a school full of them, with all those nasty germs in the air, well, it was just too much for her. But she knew it was an emergency, and she did have some free time in between showing houses to prospective buyers. And so lifesaver that she was, Liddy agreed to run over to my house, fetch Dustin's lunch from the fridge, and deliver it to him personally at the school. Of course, her parting words before hanging up on me were, "I'm sure you hanging around all those germ-infested rug rats was what got you sick in the first place!"

Click.

Anyway, the crisis was mercifully averted. Dustin got his lunch in time, and I went straight home from the doctor's office to bed. Later that evening, when I finally woke up, it was dark outside, and I heard laughter and chatter coming from downstairs. I put on my robe and made my way down to find Randy and his husband, Sergio, having volunteered dinner and bedtime duty, in the living room playing board games with Dustin and Gemma.

Dustin was in the middle of mentioning to his uncles that Aunt Liddy was coming to his class tomorrow to fill in for me until I felt better.

Everyone froze and you could hear a pin drop.

"Liddy volunteered to be class mom? My Liddy?" I gasped as everyone turned to see me standing at the bottom of the staircase.

Dustin nodded, as if it was the most natural thing in the world. "She's going to fill in for the whole week!"

I thought I must be hallucinating and crawled back up the stairs to bed. But sure enough, the next day, when Dustin came home from school and I was lying on the couch watching *NCIS* reruns with my honey Mark Harmon, a thermometer stuck in my mouth, Dustin suddenly announced that Liddy was going to replace me as chaperone in the Halloween parade and make the cupcakes I had promised to provide.

"Are you sure?" I asked, checking the thermometer to make sure my fever hadn't gotten worse.

"Yup! She said she was going to have to buy them at the bakery because she isn't talented in the kitchen like you, but she said if I promised not to say anything, she'd buy me a brand-new Spider-Man costume so you don't have to worry about making me one!"

"She said that?" I asked, incredulous.

Dustin nodded. "And she's going to wear a costume too in the parade!" he declared.

This was just too much.

Maybe this flu had actually put me in a coma and I had awakened in some kind of parallel universe.

Well, the next day I was finally feeling a little better, and I knew I just had to get to the bottom of this. I called Liddy under the guise of thanking her, but slowly guided the conversation toward her distaste for children, and how odd it was that she was getting so involved with Dustin's fourth-grade class.

Liddy scoffed, explaining she was just trying to help me out as my best friend, and found it highly offensive that I would question her motives. I immediately dropped the subject, feeling sufficiently chastised.

The following evening, the night before Halloween, I was feeling much better and eager to rejoin the world. Randy brought over his famous comfort food for all of us: gruyere, fig jam, and bacon grilled cheese sandwiches. With a healthy appetite back in full force, I devoured not one but two of them. Dustin was wiping a glob of cheese off his cheek when he casually mentioned that I shouldn't worry about trick-or-treating because Liddy said she would be more than happy to handle it after the post-parade Halloween party.

Enough was enough.

If anyone was going to take her kids out trick-or-treating, it would be me! Something was up with Liddy and I was determined to find out what! The following day, I arranged with Randy and Sergio to meet in front of the Rite Aid drugstore where we would have a clear view of the parade, and see Liddy herding all the little kids from Dustin's class.

As the children dressed as ghosts, witches, wizards, and superheroes passed us by, we clapped and waved, and cheered on Gemma, who was marching in the middle school band playing her clarinet dressed as a zombie cheerleader.

Randy spotted Mrs. Tripp, Dustin's teacher, and pointed her out as she approached with her class, and as they began marching past us, we quickly spotted Liddy and the big mystery was finally solved.

There was Dustin in his new Spider-Man costume and his best friend, Billy, who recently had moved to town with his family from Brunswick, as Iron Man. Right behind them was Billy's handsome single dad, Eben, dressed as Batman, and next to him, hanging off his arm, was Catwoman played by none other than our very own Liddy Crawford!

Everything came to light in that moment as we watched Liddy, in a slinky black leotard with feline ears on top of her head, staring adoringly up into Batman's eyes. To be fair, Eben looked quite smitten himself. Leave it to Liddy to find the one and only available bachelor in Dustin's class, decide he was the one for her, and change her whole life around in order to catch her man! You had to admire her sheer determination.

A few weeks later, Liddy sadly parted ways with her Batman, something about Eben not being exciting enough for her taste, despite their strong chemistry. I reminded her it was only natural that Batman and Catwoman remain mortal enemies, though enemies with an uncontrollable animal attraction.

Liddy came over later that day after her big breakup for one of her favorite fall cocktails, and I also made her Randy's special comfort grilled cheese sandwich to boot in order to make her feel better!

Liddy's Favorite Fall Cocktail: Apple Martini

Ingredients
1½ ounces vodka
¾ ounce fresh-squeezed lemon
¾ ounce apple liqueur
¼ ounce simple syrup
Green apple slice for garnish (optional)

Pour all your ingredients in a cocktail shaker filled with ice and shake.

Strain into a chilled martini glass and garnish with apple slice if using.

Sit back, relax, and enjoy!

Randy's Comfort Grilled Cheese

Ingredients

4 slices crispy bacon
2 slices sourdough bread (or bread of your choice)
Fig jam
3 ounces sliced gruyere cheese (more if you prefer cheesy goodness)
1 tablespoon chopped green onion
3 tablespoons butter
Salt & pepper to taste

Add 1 tablespoon butter to pan and heat to medium low.

Butter one side of your sourdough bread, then spread fig jam on the other and place butter-side down in heated pan. Add the bacon and cheese. Feel free to add a bit more cheese if you desire, then sprinkle on the green onions. Butter one side of second slice of bread and place it on top of bread in pan butter-side up.

When bread in pan is toasted golden brown carefully flip your sandwich over and toast other side until cheese is melted and bread is golden brown on that side. Remove from heat, place on plate, slice in two, and enjoy!

Chapter 22

"I saw her! She was there! Right outside my bedroom window!" Mary Garber wailed, her whole body shaking, as her husband, Mark, held her hand supportively, glancing nervously at Bruce, not quite sure what to do.

"What was she doing at the time you saw her?" Bruce asked.

"She just sort of stood there, staring at the house! Well, I screamed bloody murder, as you can imagine, and went to get Mark, but when we both came back to the window, she was already gone."

"Are you absolutely sure it was Trudy, honey?" Mark asked quietly, trying to get her to calm down.

Mary nodded vigorously. "Yes, yes, I'm sure." Then she turned on her husband and snapped, "What kind of question is that? I'm not crazy! I know what I saw!"

Hayley and Bruce had jumped in Bruce's car and raced over to the Garber house seconds after hearing the dispatcher on the police scanner. They had even beaten Chief Sergio and Officer Donnie to the scene, who showed up minutes later to investigate. Sergio and his officer were now combing the premises, trying to find any sign of a trespasser on the property, but so far, from what Hayley could tell by peeking out the living room window, they had yet to have any luck or unearth any clues.

Bruce, a born skeptic, couldn't resist remarking, "The thing is, Mary, Trudy Lancaster is, like one hundred percent without a doubt, dead. We all witnessed her burial."

"I am well aware of that fact, Bruce!" Mary cried.

"So are you positive it wasn't someone who just *looked* like Trudy?"

"No, Bruce, it was her! I'd swear on my life!"

Bruce tried one more time. "But that's impossible—"

"I know that! It had to be her ghost! Trudy has come back to haunt me because she blames me for hiring her to cater my Witches Ball and that's why she died! If she hadn't come here with her truck that night, she'd still be alive! It's all my fault!"

Mary broke down in tears and buried her face in Mark's chest. He gave Hayley and Bruce a confused shrug as he patted his sobbing wife gently on the back.

As Mary wailed and Mark comforted her, Hayley and Bruce were left awkwardly standing there until Hayley suggested to Bruce, "Why don't we go outside and see if we can help Sergio search the area?"

"Good idea," Bruce said, jumping at the chance to get the hell out of the house.

They walked out the front door to see Sergio poking around the woods behind the Garber house as Officer Donnie waved a flashlight around near the yard where Mary had claimed to have seen Trudy loitering on the property.

Hayley crossed around to the back of the house

where Mary's bedroom window was located and used her phone's light to illuminate the patchy grass and dirt. She scanned the ground and was about to move on when she flashed over something shiny that was almost completely buried in the dirt. She quickly moved closer and bent down, using her hand to brush away the dirt, revealing a small ruby teardrop birthstone.

Exactly like the one Trudy was wearing at the viewing in the church.

Hayley shuddered at the sight of the piece of jewelry. It appeared as if it was the exact same one. But Hayley distinctly remembered Trudy was wearing it in the casket when she was buried. They had had a conversation with Ted about it. So how on earth did it suddenly wind up here? She reached down, picked it up, and stared at it, dumbfounded.

"What did you find?" Bruce asked, suddenly behind her.

Hayley jumped, startled. "Bruce! Don't sneak up on me like that!"

"I wasn't sneaking. I was walking. Like a normal person. There was no sneaking. What is that you're holding?"

Hayley held out the palm of her hand with the birthstone.

"What is that?" Bruce asked.

"Trudy was wearing this same birthstone in the casket at her funeral. You would recognize it if you had been able to open your eyes!"

"Where on earth did *you* get it?"

"I found it on the ground near the window, the same spot where Mary claimed to have seen Trudy."

"But how did it—?"

"I don't know," Hayley said anxiously.

"It can't be the same one," Bruce said, his mind racing. "Or maybe someone took it off Trudy at the funeral when no one was looking."

"No, I saw with my own eyes Trudy still wearing it when they closed the casket following the service."

"Come on, that can't be the only ruby birthstone around. There must be at least a dozen people in town who own one of those."

"Yes, but how many look exactly like Trudy Lancaster?"

Bruce stared at the birthstone in Hayley's hand, muttering more to himself than to Hayley, "There is no earthly explanation for any of this if Mary is telling us the truth."

"Should we give this to Sergio?"

Bruce nodded. "Yes, but do it quietly. There is no sense in letting Mary see it, at least not yet. She's upset enough as it is."

Hayley and Bruce headed back inside the house. Officer Donnie was sitting outside in the squad car filling out a report.

As they entered the living room, they found Sergio sitting with Mark and Mary, going over all the facts one more time.

"Don't worry, Mary," Sergio said soothingly. "We will get to the butt of this."

"I'm sorry, *what* did you say?" Mary asked, drying her wet eyes with a tissue.

"I said don't worry, we will—"

Hayley interrupted him. "Get to the *bottom* of this."

Sergio threw her an annoyed look. "Yes, that is what I said."

Hayley decided to let it go.

Mark took his wife's hand in his own. "Honey, why don't you go to bed and get some rest? You've been stressed ever since Trudy died at our party. You haven't slept hardly at all. You could be so tired you're seeing things that aren't real."

"I'm telling you, I saw Trudy's ghost! Why won't anyone believe me?" Mary squealed, wrenching her hand free from her husband and shooting up to her feet. She dropped the tissue on the floor and fled to the bedroom.

After a protracted pause, Mark turned to Sergio, who had stood up and was getting ready to leave along with Hayley and Bruce. "Chief, there's something you should know. I didn't want to say anything in front of Mary because I didn't want to get her more riled up than she already is."

"What is it?" Sergio asked curiously.

"Mary has been downing her favorite Bone-Dry Martinis all night long, and whenever she drinks too much and gets too inebriated, she sometimes becomes paranoid and starts imagining all kinds of things. Last week she swore her grandmother, Elsa, called her in the middle of the night."

"And Elsa never called?"

Mark shook his head. "No, sir. Elsa has been dead since 1986."

"I see," Sergio said with a sympathetic smile.

Mark turned to Hayley and Bruce. "What do you two think?"

"Mary's never lied to me about anything," Hayley said before holding up the ruby birthstone. "I also found this outside."

Mark looked at the stone blankly. "What is that?"

"A birthstone. Trudy Lancaster had one just like it. In fact, she was buried with it."

There were several moments of tense silence.

"Are you sure, Hayley?" Sergio asked, disturbed.

"Yes. So unless someone is deliberately trying to gaslight poor Mary, then I believe she did see someone outside the window, and if it wasn't a woman who looks just like Trudy and has the same ruby birthstone as her, then the only other explanation is that Mark and Mary actually got a visit tonight from Trudy Lancaster's ghost."

Chapter 23

The next day during her lunch hour, when Hayley pulled her Kia up in front of the small house on Ledgelawn Avenue that Ted and Trudy had rented shortly after moving to town, she spotted a "For Sale" sign taped to the side of Trudy's food truck, Wicked 'Wiches.

As she got out of her car, Ted emerged from the truck in a loose-fitting dirty T-shirt and scruffy jeans, carrying a box full of sub rolls, deli meats, wrapped cheeses, and wilting vegetables. He promptly tossed the food into a giant rolling trash bin he had borrowed from the Bar Harbor Solid Waste Facility. He turned to head back inside the truck when he noticed Hayley.

"I know what you're going to say," Ted said. "What am I doing wasting all that good food?"

"The thought did cross my mind," Hayley said. "But maybe it's because I'm a little hungry, like always."

Ted wiped the sweat on his forehead away with his arm. "The Food Pantry only accepts canned goods for donations. They don't take perishables, and I have to get this thing cleaned out and washed before I show it to any potential buyers."

Hayley nodded sadly. "Whoever ends up with it will sure have a tough act to follow. Trudy's sandwiches were some of the best I ever tasted."

"She was a real talent," Ted said. "I thought about holding onto the truck, but . . ." His voice cracked. "I don't cook, never have, and I already have a job at the church, so what's the point?"

"I understand," Hayley said. "Can I help?"

"No, thank you," Ted said. "I'm just about finished. I got a potential buyer coming around at two to take a look at it. Fingers crossed he makes an offer."

"Do you know if he's thinking of keeping it as a food truck?"

Ted shrugged. "Beats me. He can strip it down and use it to haul wood for all I care. I just want it out of my sight. I can't look at it anymore."

Hayley stood on the sidewalk awkwardly, not sure how to respond.

Ted suddenly realized how callous he sounded and added, "It's just a constant reminder that she's no longer here. The memories are too painful, I guess." He paused a moment, thinking to himself, and then a lightbulb seemed to go off above his head. "Hey, I hear you're a whiz in the kitchen, why don't you take it off my hands and start your own business? I'll give you a really good deal."

"Oh, no," Hayley said with a laugh. "Not me! I could never do what Trudy did. It's way too much work. And I lack the kind of drive and ambition it would take to make an enterprise like this a success."

"I get that. Sometimes I felt Trudy was more married to this truck than she was to me. Which is probably why I don't mind getting rid of it," Ted said absently.

Hayley waited for him to expound on his last statement but he didn't. He just turned around and went back inside the truck.

After about a minute, he came out carrying another box, this one full of used cooking utensils. "Trudy sure did put a lot of hours into this truck. It must have been hard on you."

"I'd be lying if I said I wasn't sometimes jealous of this truck. Don't get me wrong. We were both devoted to our jobs. Once Reverend Staples officially steps down, I'm going to be at that church pretty much twenty-four seven. And I was thrilled Trudy had something that made her so happy. But like every marriage, things weren't perfect between us," he said casually, almost as an afterthought.

But it was the opening Hayley had been waiting for. "I know, Ted . . ."

Ted tossed the box of utensils in the trash bin and turned back to Hayley. "Did Trudy say anything to you before she died?"

"Oh, no," Hayley said. "I just heard something about her filing for divorce . . ."

Ted froze, stunned that this information was out there. Hayley could see his mind racing for a few seconds as he thought about what he should say. Ultimately he chose to make light of the whole rumor. "Oh that. Yeah, we had a fight over something silly and she threatened to divorce me, but I knew she would never do it."

"But she did put the plan in motion," Hayley said quietly. "She filed papers at the courthouse."

Ted stiffened, struggling to keep up his calm exterior. "Yeah, I know. But we made up pretty quick after that and she told me she was going to withdraw the papers. She just never got the chance."

"What was the fight about?"

Ted sighed, obviously not eager to talk about it, but he was also anxious to put this whole divorce story to bed. "Trudy was keenly aware that Reverend Staples had a crush on her. She showed up at the church with sandwiches for us one day, and she was wearing a tank top because she had been slaving over a hot grill all morning, and I could see the reverend leering at her. I just got all stupid and jealous, and stupidly blamed her for flaunting her sexuality, which of course she wasn't, and it led to a fight between us. I realized later that day I was totally overreacting and I apologized. And Trudy admitted that sometimes she could get too dramatic and do outrageous things like filing those divorce papers. So we kissed and made up. It was completely over by the time she left in her truck for the Garbers' Witches Ball."

"Speaking of the Garbers . . ."

"I already heard," Ted said, chuckling. "Mary Garber saw Trudy's ghost last night. I'm sure she sees a lot of things given how much that woman drinks."

"She was quite shaken up by it. I was there."

"I know you were," Ted said pointedly.

"You do?"

"Chief Alvarez stopped by this morning to ask me about the ruby birthstone you found on the ground outside Mary's bedroom window."

"You have to admit it's kind of a strange coincidence, Mary claiming to have seen Trudy, and then me finding that birthstone," Hayley said.

Ted grabbed a handkerchief from the back pocket of his grimy jeans and started brushing the dust and dirt off his bare arms and face.

"I'll tell you what I told the chief. I have no idea how a similar birthstone found its way to Mary Garber's backyard, but I do know one thing: Trudy was buried with the birthstone that belonged to her. And short of digging my wife up to prove it, which I absolutely refuse to do and said so to the chief, there is no way we'll ever really know for sure how it got there. And frankly, I don't care because solving that little mystery is *not* going to bring my wife back!"

He was done talking. He checked his watch. "This guy's coming to look at the truck in a bit, Hayley, so I need to get it looking presentable."

She knew she had outworn her welcome. "If there is anything you need, please call me."

"Will do," he said gruffly.

Although she knew he wouldn't.

Chapter 24

Hayley stirred awake in bed, her eyes still closed, and she heard Bruce snoring softly next to her.

Or at least at first she thought it was Bruce.

It was odd that he wasn't pressed up against her like he normally would be during the night, one arm slung around her waist, keeping her body close to him. She would always feel the hot air at the nape of her neck as he slowly breathed in and out. But tonight was markedly different. He wasn't touching her and didn't appear to be anywhere near her in the bed, and yet she could hear this unfamiliar whistling sound coming out of him. Usually he was a typical "nasal snorer," which sounded as if he was suffering from congestion, very low and deep and through the nose. But this sounded like someone completely different. Hayley slowly opened her eyes and listened some more. No, this was definitely *not* the Bruce she had been sharing a bed with every night since the day they had gotten married last summer. Which begged the question, who *was* in bed next to her?

Hayley considered jumping out of bed and grabbing the lamp on the night table next to her to use as a weapon. She had seen that famous 1970s horror movie *When a Stranger Calls* when she was a kid where the heroine believes a killer is somewhere in the house and tries to wake up her boyfriend in bed next to her only to realize the boyfriend is gone and it's the *killer* in bed with her! It was shocking and scary and Hayley didn't sleep for weeks after watching that scene! But this was real life, and the odds of a serial killer in bed with her were at best, she hoped, remote.

She slowly, quietly turned her body around to see who it was, and a wave of relief instantly washed over her at the sight of her dog, Leroy, on his back, all fours in the air, his head turned to the side and his tongue halfway out, snoring.

She reached out and scratched his head but he didn't wake up. He just shifted to his side. Hayley looked around for Bruce, but he wasn't in the bedroom. Leroy must have fervently taken his place in the warm bed after he left.

Hayley sat up, her feet touching the cold floor, and padded out of the room into the second-floor hallway. The door to Gemma's room was closed and there was no sound coming from inside so she assumed Gemma and Conner were both in a deep sleep. She was about to head down the stairs to see if Bruce had insomnia and was biding his time watching TV when she stopped suddenly, wrinkling her nose in disgust.

She smelled smoke.

Not the kind of smoke that indicated the house was on fire. No, this was distinctly cigarette smoke. She glanced around and noticed that the door to the bathroom was closed, which was unusual if no one was in there. She could see a light shining through the crack between the door and the floor.

Hayley grimaced, quietly took hold of the handle, and then whipped open the door and charged into the bathroom.

Bruce, in just his boxer shorts, was sitting in the tub, wearing reading glasses, his laptop computer nestled in his lap as he typed, and, as she had suspected, a lit cigarette dangling from his mouth.

Her surprise attack startled him and he dropped his computer and clutched his chest as if he was about to suffer a heart attack. The cigarette also fell out of his mouth and landed in his crotch. He frantically retrieved it before the burning ash caused his boxers to burst into flames.

"Hayley! What the—?"

"Aha!" Hayley cried.

"Why would you do that?" he yelled, still holding onto his chest. "My God, are you *trying* to kill me?"

She turned and closed the bathroom door behind her and locked it from the inside. "Shhh. I don't want to wake up Gemma and Conner."

"Then you shouldn't be sneaking up on me like that," Bruce said as he stamped out his cigarette on the side of the tub.

She noticed Bruce had the bathroom window open in a vain attempt to air out the smell of the cigarette smoke.

"I wanted to catch you in the act."

"Mission accomplished, okay? I came in here to work so I wouldn't disturb you."

"And steal a smoke," Hayley said. "Why aren't you wearing the nicotine patch?"

Bruce sighed as he climbed to his feet and stepped

out of the tub to face his wife. "I tried, I really did, but it was making me nauseous. I couldn't concentrate on anything, which is why I'm up this late trying to finish my column. I got nothing done at the office today. I took the patch off, just for tonight, so I could write, but then after a little while I got a hankering for a smoke, and I remembered I had a pack in the pocket of my leather jacket so I figured I would just sneak one."

Hayley's eyes fell upon an ashtray on top of the bathroom sink that was overflowing with cigarette butts. "Just *one*?"

Bruce followed her gaze, and then with a sheepish look, "I guess I got so engrossed writing my column I lost track of how many I actually—"

"Bruce, I don't want you smoking in the house."

"I know, I'm sorry. I swear I won't do it again. Just cut me a little slack, okay? I'm under a lot of pressure at work. I'll try harder to quit, I promise."

She wanted to berate him some more, but he appeared genuinely contrite and remorseful so she decided to let it go. "What are you working on?"

"I'm writing a special report on Trudy Lancaster's murder. I'm coming at it from the angle of her being a friend of ours. I talk about how the four of us—me, you, Trudy, and Ted—started seeing each other socially right before she died."

"So you definitely agree with me that someone tampered with that propane tank?"

"Not just someone, I think we both know who did it."

"Who?"

"Come on, Hayley, she filed for divorce on the same day someone gassed her to death inside her truck."

"*Ted?*"

"Of course it's Ted!"

"How can you be so certain when there is zero

physical evidence tying him to the alleged crime? You're usually more careful than that, Bruce."

"Look, honey, I've been at this crime-reporting thing for a long, long time. I've written dozens of articles about possessive men who killed their wives when they tried to leave them. Given what we know now, I'm betting this case is no different from at least half the episodes of *48 Hours*."

"Bruce, I know Sal has been on you to write something juicy in order to boost sales and clicks, but I think it's *way* too premature for you to start pointing fingers."

Bruce set his computer down on top of the toilet lid and took Hayley's hand. "Don't worry, I don't name names."

"But you're not shy about *implying* who might have done it? I thought you and Ted were becoming good friends."

"We were. But maybe I never got to know the *real* Ted Lancaster." He just gave her a peck on the cheek. "I better get back to work. I want to file this in the morning. I'll come back to bed soon."

"Forget it. You've been usurped. Good luck kicking Leroy out of your spot."

Bruce smiled as he picked up his laptop.

Hayley turned to go, but stopped in the doorway. She swiveled around, marched back into the bathroom, and snatched the half-empty pack of cigarettes off the sink counter. She lifted the toilet lid and dumped out the contents before flushing.

Bruce's smile slowly faded as she returned his peck on the cheek and went back to bed.

Chapter 25

The following afternoon at the drugstore, Hayley read the installation instructions on the back of the box for her Stealth Smoking Enforcement System, which monitors a house automatically and covertly to protect residents from secondhand smoke. She had stopped by on her lunch hour, knowing Bruce was still at the office. The plan was to have the contraption up and working by bedtime in case Bruce decided to sneak back into the bathroom again in the middle of the night for another secret smoke. He would get a nice, loud surprise.

Hayley checked the price to make sure she had enough cash to pay for it, and then walked it up to the register. She spotted Mona standing in line waiting to check out, holding a package of ZzzQuill, a nighttime sleep aid.

"Struggling with a little insomnia, Mona?" Hayley asked.

"My deadbeat husband's snoring has gotten much

worse lately, although I can't imagine why, he doesn't do anything all day. He can't be that tired. I'm hoping this might knock me out and spare me from tossing and turning all night because of all the noise he makes. I swear, if this doesn't work, my next move is snuffing him out with a pillow over his face! Maybe then I'll finally have some peace and quiet!"

"I may have to pick some of that stuff up for myself."

"Is Bruce keeping you awake with his snoring too?"

"No, Leroy. I can't imagine how that much noise can come out of such a little dog. Bruce is a whole other problem."

Mona checked out the box Hayley was holding. "I thought he quit."

"So did I."

"I've seen those advertised on TV. The alarm is like ear-splitting loud."

"Good because I'm counting on it to scare him straight."

The customer ahead of Mona finished paying for her items and left carrying a bag. Mona stepped up to the counter with her sleep aid, but turned back toward Hayley. "I'm starving. Once we're done here, let's grab some lunch. My treat."

"Sounds good," Hayley said, never one to turn down a free meal.

Once they left the drugstore, Mona led Hayley farther down Cottage Street toward the post office, where Cloris Fennow's truck, Burger She Wrote, was parked out front.

"I know you're not Cloris's biggest fan," Mona said. "But I have a real taste for her Feta Burger."

Unfortunately, when they walked up to the window,

the security gate was locked down and a sign was taped on the outside that read *Closed. Back at 2:00 PM.*

"Now, why on earth would she close during a lunch hour? This has to be her busiest time of the day!" Mona bellowed.

"Six twelve seventy-five," Hayley muttered.

"What did you say?" Mona asked with a confused look.

"The lock combination," Hayley said, circling around to the back of the truck and staring at the padlock. "I just happened to see the numbers when I was here a while back and Cloris was locking up her truck."

"Oh, you just *happened* to see it by accident?"

"Yes."

Mona suddenly appeared nervous. "You're not thinking of breaking in there, are you?"

"It's not really breaking in if I know the combination, right?"

"There may not be any forced entry but it's still a crime, Hayley," Mona said flatly. "And you know it."

Hayley sighed and threw her a dismissive look. She wasn't used to Mona taking the moral high ground. But she just couldn't resist. She had been so certain Cloris was the one who poisoned Trudy. This was her opportunity to prove it was Cloris and not Ted. And she still had a whole hour to search the truck before Cloris was scheduled to return.

"Mona, go across the street and keep watch in your pickup while I slip inside and take a quick look around," Hayley said.

"So not only do you want to break in, you want me to be your accomplice?"

"Just call me if you see her coming back," Hayley said, twirling the wheel on the digital padlock and punching in 6-1-2-7-5. There was a click, and the lock instantly released. Hayley opened the door and hopped up in the back of the truck.

Mona glanced around to make sure no one was watching them. "Just don't take too long, okay? I still haven't eaten and you know how grouchy I get when I have low blood sugar."

"Frankly, I can never tell the difference," Hayley said.

"Oh, aren't you the comedian?" Mona said, scowling before hustling across the street as Hayley disappeared inside the truck and closed the door behind her.

Hayley snooped around the small kitchen area, opening a few drawers, checking the cupboards that were stocked with various spices and condiments. She peered inside a mini-fridge packed with about ten pounds of wrapped hamburger meat. There was a small storage closet that she tried to open, but had trouble with, assuming it was locked. But it turned out she just needed to jiggle the handle a little harder and the door finally popped open revealing an apron hanging from a hook, some boxes filled with folders of paperwork, and tucked in the back corner of the top shelf, a liquid bottle of over-the-counter insecticide. Hayley snatched it up and stared at the label. This had to be it. This had to be what Cloris injected into her candy apple that made Trudy so sick. Not wanting to tamper with potential evidence, Hayley pulled out her phone and snapped a picture of the ingredients on the back of the bottle in order to compare them with whatever was in the toxicology report.

She was about to leave when her eyes fell upon a familiar-looking gadget on a small counter next to the stove. It was a carbon monoxide detector. And it was right next to one that was already plugged in. In Hayley's mind, this meant that either Cloris had a backup detector in case the one she was currently using broke, or this was the one from Trudy's truck, the detector Ted insisted he had bought and installed for Trudy on the day of the Witches Ball. Cloris could have somehow swiped it before fiddling with the propane tank.

All the pieces were suddenly falling into place. It had been Cloris Fennow all along! Cloris was the one who tried poisoning Trudy, and when that effort failed, she decided to silently gas her to death in her own truck, removing anything that might raise an alarm that would alert Trudy before she was overcome by the deadly carbon monoxide!

Hayley's phone buzzed.

It was Mona.

She quickly answered the call. "Hi, Mona, what's up?"

"You have to get out of there right now! I just got a call from the high school principal. One of my juvenile delinquents just set off a stink bomb in his chemistry class and I have to go pick him up!"

"That's fine, Mona. I already found what I'm looking for. I'll be right out."

"No, you don't understand. I got distracted on the phone and didn't see Cloris coming back!"

"What? Well, where is she? How close—"

Suddenly the back door to the truck swung open and Cloris stared, mouth agape, at Hayley, who held the bottle of insecticide in one hand and the carbon monoxide detector in the other.

"Cloris, I can explain . . ."

But Cloris wasn't about to allow Hayley to explain anything. She slammed the door shut and locked it from the outside. Hayley rushed over and banged on the door. "Cloris, open up! Let me out!"

Before Hayley knew what was happening, she could hear Cloris jumping into the driver's seat up front and the truck's engine roaring to life. Then, Cloris hit the gas and the whole truck shot forward. Hayley was thrown about like a rag doll with each sharp turn.

"Cloris, please, stop the truck!" Hayley cried.

She fell against the sink, ducking her head as stainless steel cookware flew from the shelves, crashing to the floor. The cupboard doors banged open and plastic jars of mayonnaise, ketchup, mustard, and relish exploded like grenades as they hit the floor. Hayley tried desperately to make her way toward the front of the truck, but she was separated from Cloris by a wall and small see-through window. She managed to get close enough so that she was able to spot the back of Cloris's head as she gripped the steering wheel, breaking speed records as she headed out of town.

"Cloris, where are you taking me? Would you please slow down before you kill us both?"

Cloris swerved the truck sharply to the right and Hayley lost her balance, slipping on some yellow mustard and falling to the floor, nearly cracking her head against the grill on her way down.

Outside the truck, she could hear a horn honking. It had to be Mona, who was probably driving her pickup and was now in hot pursuit to rescue Hayley.

Hayley snatched up her phone and called Mona.

"I'm right behind you! Can you hear me?" Mona cried.

More horn honking.

"I can hear you, Mona! She won't stop! What are we going to do?"

"I'm going to try and pass her once we hit a long stretch of road, and then I can cut her off and force her off the road!"

"*What*? No, don't do that! It's too dangerous! She could hit a tree or something and kill us!"

Mona had either put the phone down or dropped it because she was no longer talking even though the call was still active.

Hayley could make out the sound of a vehicle speeding up alongside the Burger She Wrote truck, the horn blaring, and then, without warning, Cloris hit the brakes, propelling Hayley forward. She rolled around on the floor, drenching herself in ketchup, mayo, mustard, pickles, and relish. She literally felt like a burger with everything on it.

Hayley thought the truck might tip over, but it didn't, and mercifully it finally came to a screeching halt. In the distance, she could hear the sound of a siren. Hayley sighed with relief, suspecting Mona had called the police.

Up front, she heard the driver's side door open. She assumed Cloris was making a break for it. But the sirens were getting louder, and Hayley knew Cloris would probably not get very far.

Finally, after what felt like an eternity, the back door was pried open and Mona gasped at the sight of Hayley completely covered in multicolored condiments.

"Are you all right? Are you bleeding?" Mona cried.

"No, it's just ketchup. Lots and lots of ketchup."

Mona held out a hand to help her out of the truck. "You're just making me hungrier."

"Where's Cloris?"

"She made a run for the woods, but Sergio caught

her and she's now handcuffed and in the back of his cruiser."

Mona stared at Hayley, a little uncomfortable.

"What?" Hayley asked.

"It's just that I want to give you a ride back to town, but I just had the interior of my truck cleaned."

"Fine, Mona. I can walk!" Hayley said.

"No, I may have some towels in the back of my truck we can use to wipe you down."

Mona hurried off and Hayley, who thought she might have a case of motion sickness after such a violent bumpy ride, bent over to catch her breath.

Sergio suddenly appeared when she stood back up, confident she was not going to pass out or vomit.

"Cloris wants to apologize," Sergio said.

Hayley wanted to scoff, but then realized it might be a good idea to hear what Cloris had to say.

Sergio led Hayley over to the police cruiser where Cloris, her head bowed, sat in the backseat, her hands cuffed behind her back. At the sight of Hayley drenched in her condiments, Cloris almost impulsively laughed out loud, but then thought better of it and adopted a more somber tone.

"Please forgive me, Hayley, I panicked when I saw you in my truck. I didn't even know where I was going to go. I just started driving and figured I'd come up with some kind of plan on the way."

"How did you even get inside her truck?" Sergio asked, turning to Hayley.

"That's not important," Hayley said quickly, not eager to admit to any illegal activity. She held up the bottle of insecticide. "What's important is that I found this!"

Sergio scrunched up his face. "What is it?"

"An insecticide, which I am pretty sure is the exact same kind that was injected in the candy apple that Cloris gave Trudy as a *peace offering*."

Cloris bowed her head again. "She's right. That's exactly what happened."

"You wanted Trudy out of the way so she couldn't work the Garbers' Halloween party and they would be forced to hire you instead at the last minute."

Cloris nodded, then with sad, defeated eyes, she turned to Sergio. "I only used a little bit. Just enough to make her sick. It was an unforgivable thing for me to do. I was just so worried she was going to put me out of business."

"But she recovered, and so you tried again," Hayley said, holding up the carbon monoxide detector. "You sabotaged her propane tank, and then removed this carbon monoxide detector so she would have no idea she was inhaling poisonous gas that would quickly overwhelm her and kill her."

"*What?* No, I did no such thing!" Cloris wailed.

"I found this in your truck!"

"I have no idea where that came from! I only knew of the one that's already plugged into the wall. Someone else must have put that thing in my truck to try and frame me!"

"So you admit you poisoned the apple, but you deny rigging the propane tank?" Sergio asked pointedly.

"Yes! I had nothing to do with that! I didn't kill Trudy!" Cloris cried.

"I'm still arresting you," Sergio said angrily.

Hayley pulled Sergio aside, far enough away from the police cruiser so Cloris couldn't hear them. "Do you believe her?"

"I'm not sure yet," Sergio whispered.

"Why confess to one crime, but not the other?"

"Because assault is one thing, murder is quite another," Sergio said grimly. "She could be put away for the rest of her life."

"So you're saying you believe—?"

"Yes," Sergio said, nodding. "I believe Trudy Lancaster was murdered."

Chapter 26

Hayley stood at her kitchen sink while scrubbing some dirty pots and pans from Gemma's dinner of roast pork, rosemary potatoes, and a veggie medley. She had offered to clean up if Gemma took Leroy out for his nightly walk. In the living room, she could hear Bruce and Conner sitting in recliners, beers in hand, quietly discussing a topic that had been swiftly avoided at dinner.

"So you're still waiting for an answer?" Bruce asked.

"Yes," Conner mumbled.

"What's your gut feeling?"

"I thought she would have said something by now, but she hasn't, which leads me to believe there might be an issue . . ." Conner said, his voice trailing off.

Ever the crack reporter, Bruce was not above prying. "What kind of issue?"

"I don't know. Maybe she feels I'm rushing things. I didn't think I was because I love her and the timing feels right, at least to me. If she doesn't say anything in the next day or two, I'm going to give her a little nudge."

Hayley wanted to run into the living room and warn Conner that the last thing he should be doing is pressuring Gemma, but she was not going to insert herself into this very sensitive situation any further. It was up to Gemma now to decide how she was going to handle this. And if there was one thing she was sure of, her daughter was a calm, thoughtful, reasonable young woman.

Which was why Hayley was so surprised when the back door slammed open and Gemma, wild-eyed, her face a ghostly white, came screaming like a tornado into the kitchen, dragging Leroy by a leash behind her. "Mom! Mom! You just won't believe it!"

She dropped the leash on the floor and a worked-up Leroy ran to Hayley in a panic, as if he was relieved to be free from Gemma's balled-up frantic energy.

"Gemma, good Lord, what is it? What's wrong?"

She stopped, clutched her breast, and tried catching her breath, slowly inhaling and exhaling in order to compose herself. By now, the commotion had drawn Bruce and Conner from the living room and they stood in the kitchen, dumbfounded as to why Gemma was so visibly upset.

"I saw her!" Gemma whispered.

"Who?" Hayley asked.

"Trudy Lancaster."

The kitchen became quiet except for Gemma's labored breathing and Leroy's incessant panting.

Finally, Bruce spoke. "How much wine did you have at dinner?"

Gemma shot him an annoyed look. "I didn't drink any wine. I'm perfectly sober!"

"Where did you see her?" Hayley gulped.

"We were halfway up Ledgelawn, almost to the Episcopal church, and just up ahead I saw a woman crossing the street. I thought she looked vaguely familiar, but then she passed underneath a streetlamp, and I got a good look at her face, and it was Trudy! I swear it was *her*!"

"Trudy's dead, Gemma," Bruce said tacitly.

"Then it was her *ghost*!" Gemma cried.

Hayley studied her daughter's face carefully. Gemma was usually the most sensible and levelheaded person in the room. But right now, she looked genuinely scared, like she had just awakened in her bed to find that creepy evil doll Annabelle rocking in a chair, watching her from across the room.

Gemma had been the first one to scoff at the notion of Mary Garber claiming to have seen Trudy Lancaster's apparition. But now, here she was, swearing she had seen her too.

"Wow, this is becoming an epidemic," Bruce noted.

Hayley spun around and gaped at him. "What are you talking about?"

"It's nothing, really, just something Sal casually mentioned earlier today at the office," Bruce said, trying to brush it off.

"Tell me, Bruce, what did Sal say?"

Bruce sighed. "Okay, I wasn't going to mention it because I know how you get."

"Okay, I'm going to let that one fly by without further comment, but keep going . . ." Hayley insisted.

"Last night, Sal accidentally left the door open when he went to take out the garbage and their cat, Silas, got out. Well, he and Rosana split up to go look for him, and Rosana claims that she saw—"

"*She* saw Trudy too?" Hayley gasped.

"I said she *claimed* to have seen Trudy! But you know how Rosana hates being left out of anything, and always tries to get her fair share of attention. Sal laughed the whole thing off and said Rosana was probably just jealous that Mary Garber saw Trudy's ghost and so she had to get in on the action too!"

Maybe Sal was right.

Maybe his busybody wife was just trying to horn her way into someone else's drama in order to make herself feel more important.

And maybe Mary had just been smashed that night like her husband had confided to Sergio, and through her blurred eyes just saw someone who happened to resemble Trudy poking around her property outside the bedroom window.

Hayley was inclined to believe both likely scenarios.

But she trusted her daughter implicitly. Even as a little girl, Gemma had never suffered from an overactive imagination. That was her brother and budding animator Dustin's department. Gemma had always been the practical and honest one. So if Gemma said she saw Trudy, then Hayley was pretty sure that Gemma saw Trudy.

Which, of course, could only mean one thing.

Trudy Lancaster's ghost was haunting Bar Harbor.

Island Food & Spirits

BY

HAYLEY POWELL

Every year, just a few days before Halloween, I get together with my besties Liddy and Mona at my house and we have a big sandwich supper and prepare all of our homemade Halloween goodies to share with friends and family. It's always a rollicking good time, especially since Mona has made it a Halloween tradition to always try and scare the life out of poor Liddy, who makes no secret of the fact that she hates scary movies, scary books, and trick-or-treating, especially the tricking part. It's something she has in common with my husband, Bruce. Mona, on the other hand, loves the holiday and takes great pride in finding new and creative ways to torture an unsuspecting Liddy. There was the year Liddy arrived at my house and was confronted by a creepy scarecrow sitting lifelessly on my deck. Except it wasn't made of straw, it was Mona dressed as a scarecrow, and when she jumped up and waved her arms at Liddy, the poor thing ran off terrified and hysterical. We had to get in Mona's truck and chase her down.

She was still running, three blocks away, as we drove up alongside her. Then, last year, Mona pretended to slice off her thumb peeling apples. There was a lot of fake blood and a rubber thumb that rolled across my kitchen floor. Liddy nearly fainted dead on the spot.

Every year Liddy swore she would never fall for any more of Mona's childish antics, but of course every year she did.

Until this year.

Mona was supremely disappointed that Liddy couldn't join us for our big sandwich supper this year because of a real estate conference in Portland that she had decided to attend at the last minute. Mona had gone all out this year too, finding a fake horse head and bringing another jar of her fake blood and a set of her own sheets to drench in it. She was all set to "dress up" my bedroom, and couldn't wait to casually ask me to show Liddy the new wallpaper in my room, setting the scene for all of us to walk into my bedroom and stumble upon the grisly scene. But alas, now that Liddy was a no-show, her plan was kaput.

Mona was sulking in my kitchen so I quickly cleared the table after we finished our sandwiches and set up a fun cookie decorating station in order to cheer her up. That's when my cell phone rang. I answered with a cheery "Hello" but all I could hear on the other end of the call was soft spooky music, like the eerie piano score from the *Halloween* movies.

"Hello?" I asked again.

No one said anything so I hung up.

Mona and I started scooping out white frosting for our little ghost cookies when my phone rang again.

"Hello?"

Still nothing.

Just the same soft scary piano music playing on the other end.

I hung up again.

A few minutes later, the phone rang yet again. This time, an annoyed Mona snatched the phone away from me and yelled, "Who the hell is this?"

I could hear someone chattering on the other end before Mona huffed and hung up.

"Who was that?" I asked Mona.

"Liddy, calling from her conference."

"Well, what did she say?"

Mona shrugged. "Beats me. You know I get bored listening to her go on and on . . ."

My phone rang again.

This time I answered the call. "Hello?"

"Why on earth would you allow that lunatic Mona to answer your phone?" Liddy screamed.

I calmly explained that we had received a couple of crank calls from someone playing that creepy music from the *Halloween* movies and Mona had become frustrated and grabbed the phone. I chuckled, adding, "She's also a bit miffed you're not here for her to play a trick on."

"Tell her she should grow up!" Liddy snapped and then hung up.

A half hour later we finished decorating the ghosts and witches and had moved on to the larger haunted house cookies. We had forgotten all about the crank calls when my cell phone rang yet again. When I answered, I heard the soft, spine-chilling music playing except this time it was accompanied by heavy breathing.

"Who is this?" I demanded to know.

I handed the phone to Mona, who slowly put it to her ear, her eyes widening at the sound of the heavy breathing.

Spooked, Mona immediately hung up.

"Maybe it's one of your kids," Mona suggested.

"They're a little old for this kind of stuff," I said.

"Maybe it's one of *my* kids, then."

The phone rang one more time. Mona grabbed it and answered it. "Chet, if this is you, I swear I'm going to wring your neck when I get home! You're supposed to be watching your brothers and sisters to make sure they don't burn the house down!" Mona listened to the music and heavy breathing a bit more and hung up. "I know how to get to the bottom of this!"

Mona punched *69 on the key pad, which would ring back the number calling us so we could finally put this nonsense to rest once and for all. My kitchen landline phone started ringing. Mona and I exchanged horrified glances. The call was coming from inside the house! Just like in that old 1970s horror movie!

Then we heard a bang upstairs that made us both scream.

"Is Bruce home?" Mona cried.

"No! He's having a beer with Sergio at Randy's bar!"

"Let's get out of here!" Mona screeched.

Before Mona could run out, I grabbed her sweatshirt and dragged her toward the staircase. I was not going to be run out of my own home. Quietly creeping up the steps, I could hear the same piano music from the calls playing in my bedroom. The door was closed. I was certain I had left it open earlier because Leroy had been napping at the foot of my bed and I didn't want to trap him inside.

Mona was shaking at this point. She put a finger to her lips and disappeared inside Dustin's bedroom only to emerge a few seconds later with her weapon of choice: a plastic light-up *Star Wars* sword! I almost laughed out loud but clamped a hand over my mouth before any sound could come out.

Finally, Mona steeled herself, raised the plastic sword over her head, and charged into the bedroom, screaming like a banshee. I heard Mona cry, "Good God, it's some kind of monster!"

There was a bright flash from inside the bedroom and then Mona started screaming incoherently. I poked my head inside the bedroom, flipping on the overhead light. There was Mona, sword at her side, staring at her own reflection in a full-length mirror that had been moved in front of the door. Then I saw Liddy, howling with laughter, off to the side holding a camera. She had rolled the mirror in front of the door so Mona would see herself when she flew into the bedroom. She had also gotten the perfect shot of Mona frightened out of her mind, wielding a plastic sword!

"That picture is going to be the cover of this year's Christmas card!" Liddy cooed.

The theme from *Halloween* was coming from her iPhone.

Mona was still a bit confused until Liddy, with a big grin on her face, yelled, "Gotcha!"

Liddy had never gone to the real estate conference. It was all a ruse in order to convince me and Mona she was out of town. Then, she enlisted Bruce's aid in sneaking her in the house when I was busy preparing our sandwiches in the kitchen and before Mona had even arrived.

Ah, sweet revenge.

As for Mona, she vowed to up her game next year.

It was on!

I led everyone back downstairs for more Big Sandwiches, and after a fright like that one, a Frozen Mudslide. There is nothing like a cocktail that tastes like a milkshake to end the evening on a good note.

The Frozen Mudslide

Ingredients

1 ounce Kahlua
1 ounce vodka
1 ounce Irish cream liqueur
2 scoops vanilla ice cream
Crushed ice

Mix all your ingredients, including ice, in a blender until well blended. Pour your mixture into a large glass. Pop in an environmentally friendly straw and enjoy. But please don't drink too fast! No one wants to get a brain freeze!

The Big Sandwich

Ingredients

1 pound sliced ham
1 pound sliced roast beef
1 cup sliced green onion
12 thinly sliced long dill pickles
¼ cup mayonnaise
1 tablespoon Worcestershire sauce
1 8-ounce package cream cheese, room temperature
1 cup shredded cheddar cheese
2 loaves French bread (whole not sliced)

Slice the bread lengthwise and hollow out the top and bottom leaving about a half an inch of bread on both halves.

In a bowl combine the cream cheese, cheddar cheese, onions, mayonnaise, and Worcestershire sauce well and spread over both sides of the bread. Layer the bottom and top halves with ham and roast beef, place the pickles on the bottom, and carefully place your top halves on and gently press down. Wrap in plastic wrap and place in your refrigerator for at least two hours. However, they can be kept overnight for the next day if making ahead.

Cut into serving slices, serve and enjoy!

Chapter 27

"He's going to do *what*?" Mary Garber squealed, as she clutched her glass of lemonade, which Hayley was reasonably sure also had a shot or two of vodka in it.

"Reclassify Trudy's death as a homicide," Hayley explained calmly.

"Well, now it all makes sense!" Mary barked, chugging down the rest of her "lemonade" and slamming the glass down on the plastic table on the deck outside their house.

"What makes sense, dear?" her dutiful husband, Mark, asked calmly.

"Trudy coming back! Don't you see what's happening?" Mary cried.

Mark looked at Hayley and Bruce quizzically. They had unexpectedly shown up at the Garber house a few minutes earlier under the guise of discussing the strange, inexplicable Trudy sightings, but Bruce, the hard-line, facts-are-facts crime reporter, wanted to know exactly where the Garbers were when Trudy was inside her food truck getting gassed to death.

After a brief pause, Mark timidly cleared his throat and asked his near hysterical wife, "Um, what is happening, Mary?"

"It's *so* obvious, Mark! The police think someone *murdered* Trudy! That's why her restless spirit has come back to haunt us! She'll never be able to cross over to the other side until she knows her killer has been brought to justice!"

Another pause as they all digested Mary's otherworldly premise.

"No, I'm sure of it," Mary exclaimed, more confident in her theory now. "I know Mark is a skeptic, and I can't speak for Bruce, but you have to agree with me, don't you, Hayley?"

Not wanting to upset Mary any more than she already was, Hayley hesitantly nodded. "I guess anything is possible."

Bruce, in order not to say anything that might offend Mary, picked up his glass of lemonade and took a big swig and nearly choked on the heavy amount of alcohol in it.

Mary sighed. "I'm just grateful I'm not the only one in town who has seen her. Otherwise people might think I'm some kind of unhinged kook!"

One more awkward pause as everyone silently took a long sip of their spiked lemonade.

Mary turned to Mark. "Remember, this happened to us before about five years ago when my Aunt Reba died in that skiing accident?"

Hayley could tell Mark was wishing his wife was not going to tell this story, but he couldn't do anything to stop her. Mary whipped her head back around to face Hayley and Bruce. "Reba was a beginner and had only taken a few ski lessons when she wiped out and hit her head and died of a traumatic brain injury. Well, for weeks after, I would wake up in the middle of the night and see her standing at the foot of our bed waving at me. I'd scream and wake up Mark and—"

"I never saw a thing," Mark mumbled.

"Well, I did! And guess what? Months later, her awful, rude, arrogant husband, my Uncle Carl whom *nobody* likes, finally admitted under intense questioning from the family that he had pressured Reba to go down a slope reserved for expert skiers called the Black Diamond. She obviously wasn't advanced enough for something like that, so Uncle Carl basically killed poor Reba! Of course we couldn't have him arrested because Reba had agreed to go down the slope on her own, but she *needed* me to know it was Carl's fault she died!"

"Poor Reba . . ."

That was all Hayley could think of to say.

"And then Carl got remarried right away, which also was highly suspicious," Mary snorted.

"Seven years later, Mary," Mark said, shaking his head. "I think he grieved a socially acceptable amount of time."

"Well, I'm curious to see just how long Ted Lancaster waits until he gets hitched again," Mary said, picking up her glass of lemonade to drink more and realizing it was empty. "Anyone else ready for a refill?"

"No, thanks," Bruce said. "So you think it was Ted?"

"Who else could it be?" Mary asked, standing up and heading inside to make herself another cocktail. "It's always the husband. Just ask my Aunt Reba!"

Once she was gone, Mark shifted uncomfortably in his deck chair. "You'll have to excuse Mary. She's been a little on edge lately, especially after what happened at our Witches Ball."

"Perfectly understandable," Hayley said.

Bruce leaned forward with a raised eyebrow. "Now

that the police are treating Trudy's death as a homicide, I'm sure Sergio will be calling us all to come down to the station for an interview."

"Well, he doesn't have to bother with me and Mary," Mark said, almost too quickly. "We're both officially in the clear."

Hayley and Bruce exchanged surprised looks.

"Why is that?" Hayley asked.

"We never left the house for the entire duration of the party, at least until Hayley discovered Trudy's body in the truck. We were too busy entertaining our guests. The chief can ask anyone who was here. Or better yet, he can just see for himself on everybody's Facebook pages. A couple of people even livestreamed the event and you can see us in plain view the whole time."

"I guess it would be hard to miss Mary in that purple muumuu with all those moons and stars, running around waving a wand, or you as Michael Myers from the *Halloween* movies," Hayley said.

But that still left nearly a hundred and fifty guests, more than half of whom were dressed as witches, who did have the opportunity to slip outside the house unnoticed and eliminate the sandwich lady with a rigged propane tank.

Chapter 28

"Either we've all gone mad, or Trudy Lancaster is indeed haunting Bar Harbor!" Gemma cried as she sat with Hayley and Bruce in the living room having coffee after dinner.

Bruce couldn't help but chortle at the dramatic pronouncement, and Hayley, not wanting to offend Gemma, shot him a look of warning to be a little more sensitive, something he wasn't always used to being.

Bruce nodded slightly in Hayley's direction, acknowledging her message had been received, and said, "Or there is another explanation."

"Well, then what is it?" Gemma asked, folding her arms, waiting impatiently.

Bruce shrugged. "I have no idea."

"But you do have to admit, something weird is going on, and it is entirely possible that the explanation could be, I'm just saying, *could be* supernatural," Gemma said.

Bruce smiled and looked down at the floor. "I'm sorry, Gemma, I'm just not there yet."

"Poor Mary Garber, now I see how frustrating it must be for everyone to think you're crazy!" Gemma huffed.

Hayley finally spoke up. "Nobody is calling anyone crazy."

"Conner basically did," Gemma said, sighing. "He thinks I'm letting work stress get to me and that I should perhaps see someone, like a therapist, when we get back to New York. Can you believe that? The only thing stressing me out right now is the fact that he has asked me to marry him!"

"You haven't given him your answer yet?" Hayley asked as gently as she could.

"I'm still waiting for the right moment," Gemma muttered, looking as confused as ever.

Suddenly from upstairs, they heard Conner yelling and banging around.

"What's he doing up there?" Bruce asked.

Gemma shrugged. "Beats me. He just went up to return a call from his manager."

They could hear the door to Gemma's bedroom slam open. Conner came pounding down the stairs, still clutching his phone, trembling with excitement. "You're not going to believe it! You just won't believe it!"

"Why don't you try us," Hayley politely suggested.

Conner turned to Gemma and scooped up her hands in his. "I got it."

"*Dracula?*" Gemma gasped.

Conner nodded. "Yup. I thought I gave a terrible audition and had zero chance of a call back let alone a full-blown offer. But the director loved me, and I guess it was a pretty huge battle with the producers, who wanted to go with a bigger name, but they finally relented and gave it to me!"

Gemma whirled around to Hayley and Bruce. "Conner auditioned for a part in a revival of *Dracula* on Broadway right before we left for Maine! We didn't even bother mentioning it because he thought he did so badly!"

"You'll be great as a vampire!" Bruce said lightheartedly before realizing that might go over as an insult and quickly adding, "I mean, Gemma says you're a *great* actor who can play any role."

Conner seemed to blow right past it. "I'm not playing Count Dracula. Zachary Quinto, the guy from the *Star Trek* movies and a ton of other great stuff, is playing the title role. I play John Harker, the young lawyer whose fiancée, Lucy, has been bitten by a vampire and is in a sanitorium! They're still looking to cast Van Helsing, the guy who drives a stake through Dracula's heart in the end, but there's a rumor going around they're talking to Armie Hammer!"

"I *love* him!" Gemma cried.

"Let's hope my arm is healed and out of this sling by opening night!" Conner exclaimed.

"This is so exciting! Congratulations, Conner," Hayley said.

"Thank you, Hayley," Conner said, still clasping Gemma's hands tightly as he turned back and smiled at her. "Rehearsals start next week so I need to rebook our flights so we can be back in New York on Monday."

"*Monday?* But that's the day after tomorrow," Gemma said, a little taken aback.

"Yes," Conner said. "They just emailed me all the paperwork, and I can docu-sign everything from here tonight, but I have so much to do. Ed wants to sit down with me in his office first thing when I get back and go over all the details. He is planning to put out a press release once all the contracts are signed."

Gemma turned to Hayley and Bruce and said quietly, "Ed Glass is Conner's manager."

They both smiled and nodded as Gemma slowly spun back around and looked Conner directly in the eyes, took a breath, and said, almost too quickly, "So is it really important that we *both* go back on Monday?"

Conner's eyes widened with surprise. "What?"

"It's just that I want to stay in Bar Harbor a little while longer and you're going to be so busy preparing and everything . . ."

Conner frowned. "Why do I get the feeling this isn't about you wanting to stay in Bar Harbor?"

There was an awkward pause.

Hayley finally stood up from the couch. "Maybe Bruce and I should give you two some privacy—"

"No, stay," Gemma said urgently, flicking her eyes toward them, desperate for the two of them not to leave.

Conner couldn't help but notice. A lightbulb finally went off in his head. "You don't want to marry me."

Gemma shifted uncomfortably. "I think the world of you, Conner . . ."

She swallowed the words.

He stared at her painfully. "But . . ."

"But I'm not sure I'm ready for marriage. At least not yet."

"I see . . ." Conner's voice trailed off.

He stared down at the floor. Hayley felt so sorry for him. His shoulders sagged and he looked devastated. Then, he raised his head to face Gemma. "Tell me something. Are you not ready for marriage or are you not ready for marriage *with me*?"

That one caught them all off guard.

Hayley carefully studied her daughter, who was struggling with how to respond.

Finally, Gemma slowly, gingerly withdrew her hands from his and whispered, "I don't know . . ."

"Okay," Conner said, his voice cracking.

"I think it's probably best if I stay here while I sort things out," she said before turning to Hayley and Bruce. "If it's okay with you . . ."

"Of course," Bruce said. "You're welcome here as long as you want."

Hayley could see Conner slightly shaking. He was trying his best to remain in control and not break down.

"Honestly, this is a big deal. You're on your way. I couldn't be prouder of you, and what you've already accomplished, and what lies ahead for you, and I don't want to be a distraction," Gemma said.

"You could never be a distraction, Gemma, that's why I proposed to you in the first place. Because I love you, truly love you . . ." He let the words hang there for a moment. "I better go upstairs and call the airline."

Brokenhearted, Conner turned and trudged up the staircase. He wasn't even halfway to the second floor when Gemma ran to hug her mother and began sobbing.

Chapter 29

Hayley was genuinely happy for Reverend Staples when she arrived at the Congregational church and walked in with Bruce, Gemma, and Conner to find the place packed with mostly just standing room only. Nobody wanted to miss the reverend's final sermon and the official introduction of the new minister, Ted Lancaster.

Hayley scanned the pews for any available space left to take a seat. "Looks like we're not going to be able to all sit together."

"I'll run up and see if there's any room in the balcony," Bruce said, then turned and trotted up a side staircase.

Hayley turned to Gemma and Conner, who were standing stiffly next to each other, avoiding eye contact. They had barely exchanged a word all morning except for Conner to tell her that his travel had been rescheduled for Monday so he was all set to leave Bar Harbor tomorrow, quite possibly for good.

"I'm going to go say hello to Ted. I'll find you before the sermon starts," Hayley said.

"Okay," Gemma said, forcing a smile.

Conner grunted a reply, which was lost on Hayley, but she smiled at him, pretending she had heard what he had said. Then she made her way down the aisle, turned right, and headed toward the small administration office off the reception room. The door was closed but Hayley had been inside the office many times. It was a tiny space with two desks on opposite sides of the room, one for the minister, the other for his secretary/organist. They usually scheduled their office hours separately, his on weekday mornings and hers on weekday afternoons to avoid crowding each other too much.

Hayley knocked on the door.

After a few seconds, the door swung open and a young woman, around twenty-one or twenty-two with straight auburn hair and freckles, appeared. She was rather dressed down for church, squeezed into a tight pair of jeans and wearing a halter top underneath a suede jacket.

She stared at Hayley, disinterested. "My father's not here."

Hayley instantly knew who this was. When she and Bruce had first double-dated with Ted and Trudy, Ted had mentioned having a daughter from a previous marriage, who was in her early twenties.

But Hayley was blanking on her name. "You must be . . ."

The girl wasn't anxious to help her out, but as they both just stood there awkwardly, Hayley struggling to come up with a name, the girl finally got bored waiting for her to take a guess.

"Alyssa."

"That's right! Alyssa! Ted's daughter. I'm Hayley

Powell. I'm a friend of your father and . . ." She stopped short, saddened by the realization that Trudy was truly gone.

"Trudy," Alyssa sighed.

"Yes, I know," Hayley said quietly.

"My father is giving some kind of pep talk to Reverend Staples. He'll be back soon."

"Didn't I hear your father say you're living in New York?"

Alyssa barely offered a nod. "Yup."

Hayley remembered Ted complaining about his daughter dropping out of Boston College in order to move to New York and try to make it as a singer, but she decided against mentioning that part of their discussion.

"My daughter, Gemma, lives in New York also. You two should definitely meet while you're both here. She's currently working for a catering company and studying to be a chef and hopes to one day—"

"Good for her," Alyssa said, cutting her off, not the least bit interested in hearing any more about Gemma.

Hayley could only imagine how much Alyssa must take after her mother because, with the exception of the same nose and chin, she didn't remind her at all of Ted, who was so charming and nice to be around. This girl almost relished her callous, obnoxious, and sullen personality.

Hayley decided to try one more time. "I'm so sorry you were unable to make it up to Maine for your stepmother's memorial service."

"Nobody bothered consulting me about my schedule so I had to blow it off," Alyssa said with a shrug.

"I'm sure it was for something important," Hayley said, though highly doubting it.

"I guess," Alyssa said, scowling. She had no intention of being pressed into admitting her whereabouts.

"It was a lovely service, everything Trudy would have wanted. I felt very lucky that I got the opportunity to get to know your stepmother even if it was for such a brief time—"

"It's nice Trudy made friends here, and I'm sure there were lots of tears shed at her funeral, but you really don't have to recap everything for me because to be honest, Trudy and I didn't get along all that well so I really don't care."

"Oh, okay," Hayley said, fuming.

Ted suddenly appeared in the doorway. "Hayley!"

A wave of relief washed over her at the sight of Ted. She hugged him and said, "I just came by to wish you luck. I heard you're going to say a few words at the end of Reverend Staples's last sermon."

"Nothing that will take away from his big moment," Ted said, chuckling. "Just my own little tribute to him." He then turned to Alyssa. "I see you met my daughter, Alyssa."

"Yes, I did," Hayley said, struggling to refrain from further comment.

"Honey, you better go take a seat out in front. We're about to get started," Ted said to Alyssa.

"Why can't I wait for it to be over here in the office?" Alyssa whined.

"Because I'm just starting here and I don't need my daughter being rude and disrespectful to the church and congregation."

"But it's too crowded out there, there's nowhere to sit." She sighed.

"I told you, sit with the choir. That way, you can sing a few hymns with them and use the vocal talents you quit school for. Didn't Jennifer Hudson start out singing in a church choir?"

"I don't know, I don't care, she's, like, ancient."

"She's still in her thirties," Hayley gasped.

Already bored arguing with her father, Alyssa grabbed her phone and buried her face in it as she pushed past Hayley and skulked out to find somewhere to sit.

Ted gave Hayley an apologetic look. "She's not always that difficult."

"I understand completely. It's been a very rough time for both of you," Hayley said, gently patting his back, although convinced that he was covering for his ill-tempered daughter and she was pretty much *always* that difficult.

"I'm glad she's here. I'm not good at being alone right now. I'm still in a complete state of shock. I wake up in the middle of the night, and I think of something I need to tell Trudy, and then I realize . . ." His voice cracked, and he was about to break down, but then seemed to manage to get his emotions back under control. "Anyway, it's kind of strange. My mind's been playing tricks on me lately. Do you know I actually thought I *saw* her last night?"

Hayley's mouth dropped open. "What?"

"Isn't that silly? I think of her so much I'm starting to believe I'm seeing her ghost."

"Where? Where did you see her?"

"Last night I went to the Shop 'n Save to buy some stuff to make tacos for me and Alyssa, who had just arrived, and when I got back to my car in the Shop 'n Save parking lot, I swear I saw Trudy across the street. Just walking by. It was so weird. I put the grocery bag in the trunk and when I closed it and looked up again, she was gone. Am I starting to go crazy, Hayley?"

"No, Ted, you're not," Hayley sputtered.

He smiled at her, grateful she wasn't treating him like he should be committed. Hayley considered telling him about the others like Mary Garber, Rosana Moretti, and yes, even her own daughter, Gemma, all of whom had sworn they too had seen Trudy. But what good would that do? Especially now when the only plausible explanation was that the spirit of Ted Lancaster's dead wife was haunting half the population of Bar Harbor?

Chapter 30

By the time Hayley had made her way up the stairs into the balcony, Reverend Staples had taken his position behind his lectern, and had already launched into his final sermon at the Bar Harbor Congregational Church. Hayley spotted Bruce, Gemma, and Conner scrunched together, standing behind the last pew along with several others who couldn't find any free space to sit down. What she found odd was that Bruce was between Gemma and Conner, almost as if to separate them and hopefully ease the tension between them. Gemma and Conner both looked miserable as if counting the minutes until the church service was over and they could finally go home.

Hayley made her way through the crowd until she landed next to Conner and offered him a weak smile. Conner tried smiling back, but never made it past a slight upturn of the sides of his mouth, giving up quickly before actually showing any teeth. Then he flicked his eyes back to the reverend, who was at the moment reading down a laundry list of all the people he needed to thank for making his twenty-year run as minister such a resounding success. There were his deeply religious parents, who put him on the path to spiritual enlightenment early on in his life; his mentor, who trained him in a small country church in rural New Hampshire; a litany of teachers and advisors who shared valuable life lessons; his two grown children, their spouses and offspring; the entire congregation for their love and support—and of course generosity every Sunday as the donation plate was passed around. Everyone waited for him to get to his devoted wife, Edie, who had stood by him all these years, his best church spokesperson, the most important part of his life and work besides God. But he never got to her. After a brief pause, he took a sharp turn and started talking about how important it is to forgive those who have sinned against us.

Hayley and Bruce gawked at each other, neither believing he had actually left his wife out of his speech. How could he possibly have forgotten Edie? How could *anyone* forget Edie?

Hayley wanted to run to the front of the balcony and find where Edie was sitting in order to see for herself how the reverend's wife must be reacting to the obvious diss, but she realized that would not be a good look for her, especially during a proper church service. However, Hayley did notice a few parishioners sitting in the pews in front of them, urgently turning and whispering to each other, all of them painfully aware of what had just happened.

Reverend Staples, who at the moment was still blissfully ignorant of his massive faux pas, held a bible to his chest as he spoke. "'For if you forgive others their trespasses, your heavenly Father will also forgive you, but if you do not forgive others their trespasses, neither will your Father forgive your trespasses.' Matthew, Chapter Six, Verses Fourteen to Fifteen." He then paused for dramatic effect.

That's when they heard from the peanut gallery.

"Are you referring to *me*?"

Reverend Staples looked up, surprised, and peered out into the congregation. "I'm sorry, what?"

"What you were saying just now, I assume that was directed toward me?"

It was Edie Staples.

Everyone in the balcony leaned forward to get a better look. Edie was standing on the aisle in the second row from the front. Her back was to them, but Hayley could only imagine the furious look on her face.

"Edie, I-I don't understand—" Reverend Staples stammered.

"Am I supposed to forgive you for neglecting to mention me during the hour it took you to thank everyone else for your success?"

The entire congregation froze, watching the horror show play out in real time.

Reverend Staples picked up a stack of index cards from the lectern and began to frantically rifle through them. "No, I'm sure I didn't forget . . ."

But as he shuffled through to the last card, his face reddening, his hands shaking, he stared at them panic-stricken as the awful truth finally sunk in that he had forgotten to include his wife. He then slowly looked up like a shy child viciously scolded by an intemperate teacher in front of all his friends on the playground. "Edie, I am so sorry . . ."

"I forgive you," Edie said sharply.

Reverend Staples's shoulders seemed to relax just a bit and his hands finally stopped shaking.

"Like the Bible says, if I can forgive your trespasses, then God can forgive me. So I forgive you for forgetting to thank me just now."

"I think everyone here already knows just how important you are to me—"

Edie threw her hands up in the air and addressed the ceiling. "But I'm sorry, Oh Heavenly Father, I can*not* forgive my husband for his shameless behavior, constantly disrespecting me by flirting and fondling with that sandwich lady, the late Trudy Lancaster!"

Gasps from the congregation.

This was taking another sharp unexpected turn.

For the worse.

"Edie, please—" Reverend Staples begged.

"Now I know all about the perils of temptation, and let's face it, we all know Trudy never wore a bra!"

Reverend Staples was in full meltdown mode and clasped his hands together as if he was about to pray. "Edie, you know it's never wise to speak ill of the dead!"

"I'm not speaking ill of the dead! I'm speaking ill of you, and we can all see you are unfortunately very much *alive*!"

Reverend Staples got the shakes again, only this time it was more than just his hands, his whole body was reacting as if he was having a seizure.

Edie pointed a bony finger at her husband. "I woke up this morning, and I said to myself, 'Edie, when you took your wedding vows forty-two years ago, you said for better or worse, and this is about as worse as it can get. Watching your husband embarrass himself, and you, with a girl half his age! And married to his successor, for heaven's sake! It's just inexcusable!' "

"Edie, I'm begging you, please, sit down. We can discuss all this later!"

Edie paused, then shook her head. "No, we can't. Because I'm done. I've had it playing second banana to a man who doesn't deserve me! The thought of traveling around the country in a cramped RV with you for the next five years makes me want to drive that RV right over a cliff on top of Cadillac Mountain!"

"*Edie!*" Reverend Staples cried.

"I want a divorce!" Edie hollered before turning her back on her husband and marching up the aisle of the church and out the door.

Reverend Staples stood still and silent for a moment before suddenly realizing he had to do something, and so he jumped down from behind the lectern and chased after his wife.

Ted Lancaster, who was standing off to the side next to his disagreeable daughter, Alyssa, hurried up the steps to the lectern. After turning to the choir and offering them an apologetic smile, he whipped around to address the congregation. "I think we would all like to thank Reverend Staples for his many years of service to the church . . ."

Hayley couldn't believe it.

Talk about going out with a bang.

Chapter 31

It was no surprise when only a handful of parishioners decided to stay for the social hour immediately following the church service. Many had quickly flocked around the new minister, Ted, to compliment him on his superior oratory skills before deftly slipping out the door to avoid having to hang around and discuss the monumental meltdown of Edie Staples. Even though she was nowhere to be found in the reception room, her presence was keenly felt because of the lingering tension from her earlier explosion, and of course because of her stale cookies that were set out on a cardboard table and barely touched by those who did choose to stick around.

Hayley huddled with Bruce, Gemma, and Conner, sipping coffee from paper cups, in the corner of the room. Ted was making the rounds, shaking hands with the few people brave enough to risk having to talk about what they had just witnessed or try one of Edie's bland sugar cookies.

"I'm starving," Conner said, eyeing the table of sweets.

"Proceed with extreme caution," Hayley warned.

Conner shrugged and walked over to the table.

Ted finally made his way over to them. "I hope I didn't embarrass myself on my first day."

"Trust me," Bruce chortled. "You were the last person who embarrassed themselves today."

"You were great," Hayley piped in.

"I really tried to get things back on track when Reverend Staples's sermon got . . . cut short."

"It was seamless. People hardly noticed," Hayley offered with a forced smile.

Ted raised an eyebrow. "Are you trying to humor me, Hayley? The sinking of the *Titanic* was less dramatic."

Gemma laughed, then her smile quickly faded as something caught her eye. "Who is that woman flirting with my boyfriend?"

They all turned to see Conner standing by the refreshments table, a cookie in hand, chuckling affably as Alyssa coquettishly touched his injured arm in the sling, engrossing him in some small talk by inquiring about how he got hurt.

Ted cleared his throat. "Um, that's my daughter, Alyssa. She just arrived in town."

Conner took a bite of his cookie and Alyssa then reached up to brush a few specs of sugar off one cheek.

Hayley could actually feel Gemma's blood boiling.

"Excuse me," Gemma growled, and marched over to Conner.

Conner reared back, surprised at the sudden appearance of his girlfriend, who stared daggers at Alyssa.

Alyssa, for her part, appeared resoundingly unimpressed, as if the sudden revelation that the handsome young man she was shamelessly flirting with was already taken hardly mattered. And to drive the point home that she simply didn't care, Alyssa went right back to nonchalantly touching Conner's arm not one, not two, but three more times.

After watching his daughter's rather bold and inappropriate behavior for a few more seconds, Ted turned sheepishly back to Hayley and Bruce. "Alyssa can sometimes be a handful."

That was probably the understatement of the year.

Ted shook his head and sighed. "Trudy tried very hard to forge a relationship with Alyssa after we got married, but she could never break through."

"Yes, I remember you and Trudy mentioning it," Hayley said somberly.

Ted sighed. "Even though I had divorced Alyssa's mother years before I met Trudy, Alyssa blamed her for breaking up the family. She can be so bull-headed." He cracked a knowing smile. "I know where she probably gets it from."

Hayley glanced over to see Gemma now physically inserting herself between Conner and Alyssa to keep them safely apart. Alyssa appeared amused by her efforts, not the least bit concerned or intimidated.

After the reception, there were few words exchanged between anyone on the car ride home from the church except for Conner commenting that he needed to check in for his flight soon online, and when Gemma asked what she should make for dinner. But after they arrived home and walked through the front door, the simmering pot of tension finally came to a boil when Conner innocently remarked, "Reverend Ted's daughter seems nice."

Gemma whipped around and sneered. "*Nice?* You think she's *nice*?"

Conner took a step back, confused and suddenly rethinking his comment. "Well, yes. I mean, we didn't talk for very long, but—"

Gemma was totally uninterested in hearing the rest of what he had to say. "She's certainly *not* nice! She's a predator! She knew you were my boyfriend and that just seemed to encourage her even more to flirt with you!"

"I didn't think she was flirting," Conner said, obviously replaying the scene in his head.

"She was definitely flirting!" Gemma cried. "It was plain as day to everyone watching. Right, Mother?"

Hayley's eyes did the deer-in-headlights thing as Bruce hurriedly headed to the kitchen to grab a beer from the fridge to spare himself the agony of being dragged into this conversation as well. "Um, well, of course I didn't hear what Conner and Alyssa were talking about, but . . ." She hesitated as her daughter glared at her. "But from the body language, it looked a little like she might have been flirting."

"So what?" Conner snapped.

Gemma gasped. "You don't think it's rude for a woman to go chasing after someone else's boyfriend?"

"Yes, I absolutely think that's rude, but she wasn't technically doing that because I'm no longer taken."

Gemma's mouth dropped open. "*What?*"

"Yeah, that's right. I'm a free agent now."

Hayley heard the cap on Bruce's beer bottle pop open and land on the counter. But he wasn't about to wander back into the living room. He was finding cover in the kitchen.

"What do you mean you're a free agent?" Gemma growled.

"I proposed to you and you turned me down," Conner argued.

"Just because we're not getting married doesn't mean I want to break up with you," Gemma said evenly, trying to regain her composure, but not doing a very good job of it.

Hayley tentatively took a step toward the kitchen, desperate for a hasty exit. "Maybe I should take Leroy out—"

"No, Mother, please. I want you to stay," Gemma said.

Conner, resigned to being outnumbered, decided to bravely plow ahead. "Listen, Gemma, I want to be with someone who is committed to me and wants to be with me for the long haul. You told me yourself you clearly aren't. At least not yet. And I don't really want to wait around for you to change your mind because maybe you never will be ready to marry me, and I will have wasted a lot of time."

"But Conner—" Gemma whispered.

"No, you've given me a lot of clarity. I'm glad I proposed to you. Because now I know for certain where you stand and it helps me to move on emotionally."

Gemma stared at Conner, distressed. "I just didn't think we were going to break up . . ."

"I better go upstairs and check in for my flight and finish packing," Conner said. "If you decide to go out for dinner, you better count me out. I'm going to turn in early. I have to be up by seven in order to get to Bangor in time for my flight."

And then he bowed out of the room and quietly made his way up the stairs.

Hayley held out her arms, but Gemma stood her ground, defiant, steely eyed. "If that smug little tramp thinks she's going to get her hooks into my Conner, she's sadly mistaken."

Bruce finally strolled back into the living room clutching a now half-empty bottle of beer. "Who's that?"

"Alison or Elaine or whatever that awful girl is called," Gemma sneered. "Reverend Ted's daughter!"

"Alyssa," Hayley reminded her.

"I bet *she* did it," Gemma said under her breath.

Bruce looked at Hayley. "Is it just me who is confused?" He turned to Gemma. "Did what?"

"I bet Alyssa was the one who killed her stepmother! You heard Ted. She *hated* Trudy!"

Bruce scratched his head. "But Alyssa wasn't even in Bar Harbor at the time Trudy died."

"Nobody saw her anyway! That doesn't mean she wasn't! And I'm going to prove it!"

Hayley put an arm around Gemma and said calmly, "Honey, just because you don't like her, I'm afraid that doesn't automatically make her a killer."

"Mark my words, she's going down for the crime," Gemma said, confident and determined.

Bruce took a swig of beer and then said to Hayley, "See how she's thinking? If Alyssa goes to prison, she'll no longer be on the loose in New York to chase after Conner."

Hayley nodded, irritated that he had to state his theory out loud for Gemma to hear. "Yes, I know. I get it, Bruce."

But Gemma didn't hear him. Her mind was too far away ruminating on other topics, like how to salvage a relationship that was now at the moment nothing but smoking ruins.

Chapter 32

Gemma clutched Bruce's phone and stared at the video playing on the screen. A New Orleans jazz band played and a young woman, almost unrecognizable from the grainy image on a tiny stage with bad lighting, sang in front of a microphone. Gemma's mouth was twisted and her nose scrunched up, her whole face emanating a look of complete and utter distaste.

"The place looks familiar. I think I've been there," Gemma said sullenly.

"Mona's. Alphabet City in the East Village," Bruce said. "Small, divey neighborhood bar with live music, mostly jazz, sometimes bluegrass."

"Not to be confused with your Aunt Mona's," Hayley said.

Gemma nodded. "I went with some friends once to hear a band called the Hot Sardines. They were promoting a new album called *French Fries and Champagne*." She glared at the female singer belting out a Diana Krall cover. "And you're sure that's *her*?"

"Yup," Bruce said.

Gemma snorted. "She's not that good."

Hayley and Bruce exchanged a quick look. Actually, in Hayley's opinion, Alyssa was a better singer than she had expected. But she kept mum in order to avoid an unnecessary argument with her daughter.

Gemma, unable to endure the video any longer, handed the phone back to Bruce. "Where did you find this?"

"Her Instagram account," Bruce said. "She posts quite a lot of photos and videos of herself, at least ten or so daily."

"And you're one hundred percent certain that this video was recorded on the night of the Witches Ball?" Gemma asked, still reticent about dismissing Alyssa Lancaster as a suspect in her stepmother's murder just yet.

"Yes, Gemma, she was in New York, performing. There was no way she could have been in two places at once."

Gemma's mind raced. "She could have hired someone to sabotage that propane tank."

"Unlikely," Bruce said gently.

Gemma sighed. "Well, we shouldn't rule her out so fast. She clearly had it out for her stepmother."

Conner came ambling down the stairs. "What are you all listening to?"

"Uh, Alyssa Lancaster, Ted's daughter. Bruce found a video of her doing a show in New York," Hayley said quietly.

"Yeah, after I met her at the church, I started following her on Instagram. She's pretty good, isn't she?" Conner said with a goofy smile.

"Actually I think she's rather pitchy," Gemma snapped.

"Pitchy? No, she's not. That's just something you heard on *American Idol* once," Conner said, laughing.

Gemma fumed but refrained from further comment.

"I just came down to say good night. I finished packing so I'm going to turn in early."

"It's barely eight o'clock," Gemma said.

"I have to be up early and there is a lot to do once I get back to the city," Conner said.

"We completely understand," Hayley said.

Gemma turned to Bruce, who was holding his phone in his hand, the video of Alyssa performing still playing. "Could you please shut that off, Bruce?"

Bruce reacted, surprised, having not even realized they were still listening to it, and clicked out of his Instagram app.

Without missing a beat, Conner said, smiling again, "I'm going to go see her live next weekend."

Gemma whipped around toward him. "*What?*"

"Today at the church she told me she's doing a gig at the Fat Cat this Saturday night and invited me to come."

"*Just* you?" Gemma gasped.

"Well, since you're sticking around here for the foreseeable future, then yeah, I guess just me," Conner said flatly.

"You're seriously going to pay good money to go and hear her . . . *try* to sing?" Gemma asked.

"No," Conner said, waiting a beat before adding, "She's comping me the ticket. I'm going as her personal guest."

Gemma's face flushed with anger.

For his part, Conner beamed from ear to ear, relishing how easily he was stoking Gemma's jealousy. His motive was abundantly clear. He was gleefully seeking revenge on Gemma for rejecting his marriage proposal.

And it was working beautifully.

The tension was stifling.

Bruce had suffered enough. He grabbed his car keys off the kitchen counter and headed for the door.

"Where are you going?" Hayley asked.

"To the office."

Hayley raised an eyebrow. "This late?"

"I'm way behind on my next column. I won't be long."

And then he was out the door. Hayley noticed Leroy perched next to her, tail wagging. She quickly grabbed the leash off the hook next to the door. "I better go walk Leroy. He's been cooped up in the house most of the day."

With Leroy on her heels, Hayley quickly followed Bruce out the door, leaving the young couple to continue their prickly and uncomfortable discussion.

As the door shut behind her, she could hear Gemma shout, "So what, you want to *date* this girl now?"

To which Conner replied calmly, "I don't know, but all options are on the table at this point."

Luckily when the back door shut, their voices were muffled and Hayley couldn't hear anymore.

But she knew this was not going to end well.

Chapter 33

Hayley could not believe her eyes.

It was her.

She was looking at Trudy Lancaster.

Hayley had been lost in thought, worried about Gemma's emotional state following her breakup with Conner, as she walked Leroy all the way from their quiet residential neighborhood to the middle of town, the streets mostly empty at this late hour. But then she spotted someone, a woman, standing on the sidewalk, illuminated underneath the light of a streetlamp, staring at her phone.

She was alive.

In her shock, Hayley let go of Leroy's leash, and the little dog took off running toward Trudy, or what might possibly be Trudy's apparition, because this had to be a ghost. And dogs were known to have some kind of sixth sense when it came to feeling the presence of spirits.

Leroy trotted happily up to the woman, who reacted with a wide smile as she bent down to pat his head.

Hayley squinted, certain she was imagining this whole scene, but as she focused her eyes again, the woman was still there, still playing with Leroy, now scratching him underneath his loose collar as his tags jangled.

"Trudy?" Hayley called out.

The woman suddenly looked up, noticing Hayley for the first time. She offered Hayley a tentative smile before slowly shaking her head. "No, I'm not Trudy."

Hayley stepped forward, cautiously and deliberately, until she was close enough to the woman so that she could reach out and touch her. She resisted the urge, but wanted to know for sure if this woman was actually real. Because if she was, then she was a dead ringer for Trudy Lancaster. "Who are you?"

"I'm Tori," the woman said softly. "Tori Davis. I'm Trudy's sister."

"But you look exactly like—"

"*Twin* sister."

"Ohhh . . ." Hayley moaned, still in shock. "But I don't understand. Trudy never mentioned having a sister, let alone a twin sister."

Tori nodded solemnly. "I know. She probably didn't mention me because the truth is, we hadn't been in contact for a while."

"You two were estranged?"

"Yes, for a very long time," Tori said sadly. "Too long. Because now . . ." Tori's eyes welled up with tears.

"I'm so sorry for your loss," Hayley whispered.

Tori took a moment to regain her composure, wiped the tears from her eyes, and then held out her hand to Hayley. "What's your name?"

"Hayley. Hayley Powell. I was a friend of your sister's."

"It's nice to meet you, Hayley," Tori said, shaking her hand. "Seeing me must have given you quite a scare."

"Your showing up here has frightened half the town. Everyone is convinced they're seeing ghosts."

"I know, I've kept mostly to myself since I arrived, and didn't even think about people mistaking me for Trudy."

"Well, this certainly explains all the ghost sightings that have been reported recently."

"Once I heard what happened, I had to come," Tori said, her voice cracking from grief. "You see, we hadn't spoken for so many years, and recently right after Trudy moved to Bar Harbor, she sent me a letter, an old-fashioned, pen-on-paper letter, if you can believe it, in this day and age. She got my address from an old high school friend, and she wrote about how she wanted to reconnect with me, forget all about what had driven us apart, forge a new, happier relationship. I cried all day after reading it. I had missed her so much for so many years."

Hayley wanted to ask what had caused the rift in the first place, but decided it was probably none of her business.

"So you talked it out and patched things up?"

Tori stared down at the sidewalk. Leroy, panting, smiled up at her. She smiled back. But then, her mind returned to her sister and the smile withered and disappeared. She returned her gaze to Hayley. "No, we didn't. We never had the chance because the next thing I heard was that she had passed away unexpectedly."

"Oh, Tori . . ." Hayley whispered.

Tori held up a hand. "No, it's okay. At least I know

we were on the path to reconciliation. If she had died and we were still mad at each other, I'm not sure I could have handled that."

Her tone was strong, but Hayley could tell Tori was breaking up inside. She felt terrible for her. So close to reuniting with her twin sister, but then tragedy had cruelly kept them from a truly happy ending.

"What brought you here to Bar Harbor?" Hayley asked.

"I want to know what happened to my sister. How she died was no accident. Trudy was always the meticulous, careful one. She never would have allowed something like that to happen. Someone obviously tampered with that propane tank, and she was overcome by those noxious, poisonous fumes before she had a chance to get out of that truck."

Foul play.

At least Tori and Hayley were both on the same page.

Now if they could just find out who did it.

It suddenly made perfect sense why Mary Garber had spotted "Trudy's ghost" outside her window because Tori wanted to investigate the scene of the crime.

"Does Ted know you're in town?" Hayley asked.

"No," Tori said, pausing before adding, "We've never met. I don't believe Ted even knows I exist."

Hayley's eyes widened. "What?"

"When Trudy and I stopped talking, almost fifteen years ago now, Trudy refused to even admit she had a twin sister. She cut me out of her life and pretended she was basically an only child. To be fair, we both did. So I'm not sure she ever told Ted about me when they got married."

"Perhaps when she reached out to you, she finally let him know about you . . ."

"Maybe, but I can't be sure."

Hayley was certain of one thing. If Ted didn't know about Tori, he was about to be in for the surprise of his life.

Island Food & Spirits

BY

HAYLEY POWELL

About five years ago, after a hearty blueberry pancake breakfast at Jordan's Restaurant, Liddy, Mona, and I piled into Mona's truck, '90s rock blasting, and headed up to Levant to go apple picking at an orchard owned by an old friend of Mona's family, Fred Malcolm. It was very late in the season, the last weekend of October, and so we knew this would be our last chance to stock up on some delicious apples for homemade muffins, apple sauce, and of course my favorite, chicken salad with fresh diced apples.

Once we hit the town limits of Levant, Mona pulled off the long, winding country road and pointed up to an old, faded, paint-chipped sign that was only being held up by one side with a rusted chain. I squinted to see the name on the sign, but sure enough I was able to make out "Malcolm Orchard." At least we were in the right place.

Mona told us her father, Sid, who was an old Vietnam war buddy of Fred Malcolm's, would bring her here to pick apples every fall and Fred was always kind enough to let her take home her entire haul. He had told her at the time she was welcome to come by anytime. Well, that was admittedly over twenty years ago, but Mona was reasonably confident that the invitation was still open.

Mona turned down another dusty dirt road that appeared as if it hadn't been used in years because it was so overgrown with weeds. Lined on both sides of the road were towering apple trees so overgrown they created a tunnel effect as we slowly navigated the potholes and dead branches strewn everywhere.

I began to suspect the ominous "No Trespassing" sign we zipped past might be something we should pay attention to, but Mona dismissed me with a wave of her hand and told me to stop being such a worrywart. So I kept my mouth shut as we drove past a second, third, and fourth "No Trespassing" sign.

Mona hit the brakes and we squealed to a stop at the side of the road. "I guess this is as good a place as any to start!"

Mona hopped out of her pickup, grabbed her basket from the flatbed, and began picking fresh, juicy apples off the ground underneath the endless rows of towering trees. Liddy and I both shrugged and followed suit. I had to admit, we were going to go home with a huge haul, and we both excitedly started filling our reusable shopping bags, dumping the apples in the back of Mona's truck, and then went about filling the bags up all over again.

After an hour, we had a huge pile of apples

in Mona's flatbed and were about to call it a day, when suddenly we were distracted by the sound of a motor chugging in the distance. We all turned to see—and I'm not making this up—a nun steering a four-wheeler with one hand while waving what looked like a stick at us with the other! We could see her mouth moving but couldn't hear what she was saying because of the deafening roar of the motor of the four-wheeler approaching.

The three of us looked at each other, dumbfounded.

"Is there a Catholic church nearby?" Liddy asked.

When the four-wheeler was close enough for us to see the nun's face, Mona started laughing and told us it was only Fred, dressed as a nun.

"Whatever floats your boat," Liddy cracked.

"It's almost Halloween," Mona reminded her. "He's probably dressed to go to a costume party!"

Mona started smiling and waving at Fred the nun, who was obviously not at all happy to see her. That's when it dawned on me that he hadn't seen Mona in twenty years and might not recognize or even remember her.

Mona was yelling, "Hi, Fred! It's me! Mona Butler!"

Unfortunately he didn't hear her over the loud motor of the four-wheeler. It was around that time that I noticed the stick he was holding was actually a rifle!

What happened next was a big blur. But it involved the angry nun firing off a couple of warning shots, and the three of us turning and hightailing into the thicket of apple trees desperately in search of cover!

I whipped my head around to see the nun hop off the four-wheeler, brandishing the rifle, and chase after us. We managed to hide behind the trunk of a massive apple tree, holding hands, trying to stay as quiet as we possibly could, although I was convinced Liddy's whimpering would give us away.

We heard Fred shout, "Come on out, or be ready to say your final prayers!"

We weren't sure if Fred was self-aware enough to realize he was dressed as a nun as he shouted that warning.

We knew there was no escape, so with our hands held high in the air, we stepped out of hiding. Fred was close enough to get a good look at us, and growled, "This is private property! Didn't you see the 'No Trespassing' signs?"

"Mona, say something!" I hissed.

But Mona was pretty much struck dumb at this point, a first in her life. We weren't sure if she was more afraid of the loaded rifle pointed at her or her father's war buddy dressed as a nun.

The one thought that crossed my mind was that not one person knew we were here because we decided to drive to Levant on a whim. And there were so many apple trees around, Fred could bury our bodies anywhere and no one would be the wiser!

The three of us just stood there, quaking,

ready to drop to our knees and pray for a miracle when Fred looked straight at Mona for what felt like an eternity, then broke out into a big grin and said, "Little Mona Butler, is that you?"

"Little?" Liddy asked incredulously.

That snapped Mona out of her paralysis of fear and she swatted Liddy's arm before turning back to Fred. "Yes, Fred!"

"Lordy, I didn't recognize you!" Fred cried.

"I didn't recognize you!" Mona replied, giving him the once-over.

Fred laughed. "Oh, this? The wife and I are on our way to the Masonic hall for the annual Halloween fund-raiser for the children's hospital. We decided to shake things up this year and have me dress as the nun and her as the priest. Give the folks a good laugh!"

Fred dropped his rifle and gave Mona a big bear hug while Liddy and I lowered our hands, immensely relieved we were going to live to see another day.

Fred had us all come back to his house where his wife, Vera, served us apple cider and Fred and Mona reminisced about old times. Fred and Vera both could not have been nicer.

We were homeward bound about an hour later with a bounty of apples and a great story to tell.

On a side note, ever since that day, we always make a point to give Fred a call before we come to the Malcolms' place to pick apples in order to avoid a repeat of our first meeting. And we always make sure to bring Fred and Vera a homemade treat from the apples we pick. This year I took them my favorite chicken salad and Fred made us some delicious Appletinis, and we all gave both a big thumbs-up!

APPLETINI

INGREDIENTS
1½ ounce vodka
1½ ounce apple pucker
½ ounce sweet and sour mix

Fill your shaker with ice and add all the ingredients. Shake until ingredients are well blended then pour into a chilled martini glass and enjoy!

Hayley's Favorite Chicken Salad

Ingredients
4 cups cooked chicken
2 tablespoons oil
1 cup diced apple
1 cup thinly sliced almonds
4 green onions sliced, white and green parts
2 celery stalks sliced
2 tablespoons fresh dill
1 tablespoon fresh parsley
1 cup mayonnaise
1 tablespoon Dijon mustard
Kosher salt and ground pepper to taste

In a large bowl, add your chicken, apple, almonds, celery, dill, and parsley.

In another bowl, mix together your mayonnaise and Dijon mustard and add it to the chicken mixture and mix well.
Salt and pepper to taste.

I love this chicken salad on a nice fresh croissant but feel free to use your favorite roll or bread.

Chapter 34

Ted Lancaster stood in the doorway of his single-story house, face pale and his mouth agape, as if he too was seeing a ghost. He was speechless and couldn't take his eyes off the woman standing next to Hayley.

"I don't understand, Hayley, what's happening?" Ted croaked.

"This is Tori. Trudy's twin sister," Hayley said slowly, gently, hoping to ease him into it.

Tori smiled and slowly offered her hand.

After a moment more of simply gawking at her, trying to comprehend her uncanny resemblance to his late wife, Ted finally took her hand. As they touched, he jolted upright, as if a light socket had just given him an electrical shock.

"Please, come in," Ted said shakily, keeping his eyes fixed on Tori, fighting the urge to believe his wife had suddenly come back to life.

Tori nodded and entered the house first, fidgeting uncomfortably, knowing how awkward this moment had to be.

"I know this must come as a complete surprise to you, Ted . . ." Hayley said after Ted ushered her inside behind Tori and shut the door.

"No, Trudy did mention she had a twin when we first started dating, but she didn't talk about her much because . . ." His voice trailed off.

"We hadn't seen each other in so many years," Tori said sadly.

"Yes," Ted muttered.

After offering them something to drink, which they both politely declined, Ted led them into the living room to sit down and talk. Tori told Ted what she had already related to Hayley about Trudy recently reaching out to her, how a reunion was in the early planning stages, and how she felt compelled to come to Bar Harbor and find out for herself how and why her twin sister had died.

As she spoke, something dawned on Hayley. "Tori, I found a birthstone in the dirt outside the Garber house right after Mary claimed to have seen Trudy's ghost."

"It belongs to me. My parents gave it to me for my birthday, same as Trudy since we were obviously born on the same day."

"Trudy was buried with hers," Ted said, his bottom lip quivering.

Tori nodded solemnly. "The clasp of my necklace broke as I was poking around the Garber house looking for any clues near the area where Trudy died. The birthstone must have fallen to the ground. I didn't even notice it was missing until I got back to my motel."

Hayley turned to Ted, who continued studying Tori, completely discombobulated by this living, breathing, spitting image of his beloved wife. "Ted, Tori also believes Trudy's death was no accident."

"I think we all know Trudy well enough to know she would never, ever be so careless," Tori emphatically stated.

"I couldn't agree more," Ted chimed in.

"That's why I've come here. To uncover the truth," Tori said, a renewed determination on her face.

There was a moment of silence before Ted finally spoke. "Tori, I've always been curious, ever since Trudy first mentioned you in passing . . ."

He was starting to lose his nerve so Tori decided to help him out. "What it was that drove us apart?"

Ted nodded slowly.

Tori took a deep breath. "Many years ago, back when we were teenagers in fact, even though Trudy and I were identical twins, we were very different people. In fact, we could not have been more opposite. Trudy was outgoing and popular and thrived in high school. I was withdrawn, shy, and according to the long list of therapists my parents hired to fix me, emotionally unstable. I don't know what caused it, I just never fit in like Trudy did, never excelled at academics or athletics or anything. I just kept to myself and hoped high school would just be over soon."

"This was in South Portland?" Hayley asked, remembering Trudy talking to her about growing up in that area.

"Yes. Toward the end of our senior year, a fire broke out in our high school. It nearly burned the whole place down before the fire department managed to arrive on the scene and put the blaze out. I had been alone in the library, it was after school hours, and because I was considered this kooky freak, a lot of people started blaming me for starting it. The kids began calling me Carrie and Firestarter."

"Kids can be so cruel," Hayley said.

Tori shrugged. "We were in Maine and Stephen King was a really big deal at the time so it kind of made sense, I guess. But I didn't do it. I was deathly afraid of fire, ever since some kids at summer camp pushed me and I fell into a fire pit and burned my whole backside."

"Was it just the kids at the high school or did the staff think you set the fire too?" Ted asked.

"Everybody assumed I did it. Troubled Tori. Psycho Tori. It was the easiest theory to believe. The principal questioned me, the police questioned me, but the more I denied it, the more people just thought I was lying. The pressure got so bad I had a mental breakdown and my parents finally had to take me out of school and enroll me in a facility dedicated to helping disturbed children. I was stuck there until the winter after my graduation."

Hayley leaned forward. "Did they ever find out who it was who did start the fire?"

Tori shook her head. "No, but there was a gang of kids seen hanging around the hallways after school that day, and I saw one flicking a lighter as they passed by the library. But there was never any proof. I think they let everyone believe I did it to cover up their own culpability." Tori paused, gazed glumly at the floor, and murmured, "Anyway, after I became a pariah, Trudy distanced herself from me as much as she could. In a way, I don't blame her. It was self-preservation. She didn't want my sordid reputation rubbing off on her and ruining her future."

Hayley and Ted exchanged glances. They both pitied this poor woman, but Ted's mind appeared to wander for a second before he suddenly sat up straight. "That's so strange."

Hayley snapped to attention. "What is, Ted?"

"Well, Trudy literally told me the same story about the high school fire recently, out of the blue, like just a few days before she died."

"That is an odd coincidence," Hayley said. "I wonder what made her feel the need to bring it up at that particular time?"

"I asked her," Ted said. "She said that she had met someone here in town who kind of reminded her of a boy she knew back in high school, who she always thought might have been involved in setting the fire, but he had another name back then and looked totally different now so she didn't think it could be him."

"Wait," Tori gasped, clasping her hands together. "Are you saying Trudy didn't think I was responsible for the fire?"

Ted nodded. "I guess so."

"I always assumed she did," Tori whispered, a wave of relief seeming to wash over her.

"Whomever she saw, whomever she suspected might have been one of the real culprits, maybe that's what triggered her to try and get back in contact with you," Hayley said. She then turned to Ted. "Did Trudy ever say the name of the boy or the man here in town who reminded her of the boy?" Hayley asked.

"I'm afraid not. She ultimately dismissed the idea that they were one and the same, and so she dropped the whole subject and never brought it up again."

A jolt of excitement shot through Hayley as her mind began to race. "Is there a yearbook we can look at?"

Tori regretfully shook her head. "I don't have one. Since I left school early, I wasn't around to collect one. And my memories of high school were so painful, I didn't want any kind of reminder of those awful years."

"What about Trudy?" Hayley asked, spinning around to Ted.

"I'm not sure. I haven't gone through all of Trudy's things yet, but I can certainly take a look and see if I can find it."

Hayley could sense that discussing her late sister was taking an emotional toll on Tori, and so she stood up to leave. "Tori, can I give you a ride back to your motel?"

"That would be lovely, thank you," she said.

"You are welcome to stay here," Ted said. "My daughter, Alyssa, is staying here with me, but we have plenty of room."

It was a genuine gesture to be sure, but Hayley could not help but think Ted was desperate to have someone who reminded him so deeply of his late wife he loved so much around.

Tori sensed it as well.

"It's probably best if I go back to my motel," she said. "But thank you, Ted."

Ted nodded soberly, realizing he had probably just crossed a line.

As Hayley led Tori out to her car, she couldn't ignore the distinct feeling that she was on the road to cracking this case wide open. It was just a feeling, but it was strong enough to propel her forward to her final destination: Trudy's killer.

Chapter 35

Reverend Staples grabbed his wife by the arms and smooched her firmly on the lips as she came rambling out of the RV in search of another box to pack inside. Hayley, who was walking up the pathway to the Congregational church, stopped suddenly at the sight, surprised.

After Edie Staples's very loud and public announcement that she wanted a divorce, and that her cross-country trek with her lout of a husband was officially cancelled, a loving kiss shared between the two of them was the last thing Hayley had expected to see this early morning.

But there they were, in the church parking lot, in front of their monstrosity of a recreational vehicle, getting frisky with each other. Edie playfully pretended to try and get away from him and the gleeful reverend lightly swatted her behind as she giggled and cooed and scurried back to the side door to the church where Hayley stood, frozen in place.

"Good morning, Hayley, looks like it's going to be a

gorgeous Monday!" Edie chirped as she hurried up the steps and disappeared inside.

"Uh, yes," Hayley mumbled.

After a moment of watching Reverend Staples head back into the RV, a definite spring in his step, Hayley entered the church through the side door. She wandered down to Ted's office where she found him pouring over some paperwork.

"Ted, I'm not sure I believe my own eyes, but outside just now I saw—"

Ted didn't have to wait for her to finish. He laughed and said, "Yes, the reverend and his wife have reconciled. I don't mean to toot my own horn, but as my first official business as the new minister of the Congregational church, I made it my personal mission to make sure the outgoing one left happy."

"How on earth did you manage that?"

"Part of the job for us men and women of the cloth is to know how to counsel and guide our parishioners, and so I just explained to them that all marriages have bumps in the road, and there's plenty ahead for them both literally and figuratively, but it would be a shame to let a little midlife crisis on his part and a little jealousy on her part prevent them from sharing and enjoying what promises to be the most joyful years of their lives, or something to that effect."

"Well, it certainly worked. Those love birds can't keep their hands off each other," Hayley said, chuckling. "You're very good at your job."

"I wish I could be more helpful with what you needed from me," Ted said.

"Oh," Hayley groaned. "You couldn't find Trudy's yearbook?"

"No, and there is very little information about her graduating class on Facebook, Twitter, Instagram, or any other social media sites I looked at. I found a few posts here and there, but nothing significant."

"The high school must have a hard copy of the yearbook in a filing cabinet somewhere," Hayley said.

"I called, but the woman I spoke to said I would have to come down there in person to look at it. They don't give out copies to anyone."

"Looks like I'm going to have to take a little road trip down to Portland."

"That's a three-hour trip!"

"But worth it if we find out more about this mysterious classmate of Trudy's who she thought she recognized here in Bar Harbor."

"You really think that story Tori told us about the fire is somehow connected to Trudy's death?"

"I'd be willing to bet on it."

Hayley raced out of the church to her car that was parked out on the street just in time to see Reverend Staples and Edie pawing each other again outside their RV. She turned her head to avoid witnessing anything too lurid, hopped in her car, and drove straight to the *Island Times* office.

As she entered the front office, Sal was at the coffeemaker pouring himself a cup.

"What is this, a national holiday I didn't know about?" Sal bellowed. "Where the hell is everybody?"

"Bruce is driving Gemma's boyfriend, Conner, to the Bangor Airport. Didn't he tell you?"

"He sent me an email. I'm not talking about him. I'm talking about *you*!"

Hayley glanced up at the wall clock.

It was after nine.

She was usually at her desk before eight thirty, but had lost track of time stopping by the church before work.

"I'm sorry I'm late, Sal. It won't happen again," Hayley promised.

"Good. Now we're out of coffee and you know I don't know how to operate this damn thing—"

"I was wondering. It's going to be kind of slow today and I've already filed my column for tomorrow and—"

Sal raised an eyebrow. "Kind of slow today? What are you, some kind of psychic? So now you can predict that no big stories are going to break today that will require all hands on deck?"

"Well, no, but—"

"But you're going to ask for a personal day anyway, am I right?"

"Yes, that was the plan."

"I guess I'm psychic too, then!"

"It's just that I need to drive down to Portland—"

"Portland? What is so important that you have to drive all the way down there? If you need some kind of retail therapy, can't you just drive up to Walmart in Ellsworth?"

Hayley quickly explained the errand she needed to run, how Trudy Lancaster's yearbook might be able to shed some light on the facts surrounding her mysterious death. Sal listened patiently, for a change, and when she was finished, he exhaled, drawing out his breath long enough for her to be in a little suspense as to what his final decision would be, and then he waved an arm at her and barked, "Go!"

"Seriously?"

"I'm always serious, Hayley."

"Thank you, Sal. Who knows? I might come back with a big scoop!"

"If you do, then I might kick your husband to the curb and just have you write the crime column."

"*Please* don't do that! I want a happy marriage."

Hayley spun around and headed for the door.

"Wait!" Sal screamed.

Hayley stopped in her tracks. When she turned back around, Sal was scribbling something down on a piece of paper with a ballpoint pen. When he was done, he crumpled it up and shoved the paper in her hand.

Hayley unfolded the paper to see a name and number written on it. "Who's Sandra Wallage?"

"An old friend of mine and my wife's. I was in the press pool when her husband ran for Congress back in the day."

"Congress? Wait, Wallage? You mean you know Senator Stephen Wallage and his wife?"

"Yes, it may come as a surprise to you, Hayley, but I do happen to know a few important people. Anyway, Sandra is—or was—the PTA president at South Portland High School. I'm sure she can help you get your hands on a yearbook. Tell her I told you to give her a call."

"Thank you, Sal," Hayley said, clutching the piece of paper to her chest.

"I also heard through the grapevine Sandra is working part-time with a private detective so they may be able to provide some additional information."

Hayley was so excited by these new key contacts she raced across the room and pecked Sal on the cheek.

He immediately stiffened. "Now don't go getting all mushy on me. I gave you the day off. Isn't that enough? Now get the hell out of here before I change my mind!"

Without saying another word, Hayley scooted out of the office. She swung by her house first, and when she pulled into the driveway, she noticed Bruce's car was already gone. Gemma stood on the deck attached to the side of the house, lost in thought. She had not even noticed Hayley arriving. Only when Hayley jumped out of the car and slammed the door shut did Gemma turn her head in Hayley's direction and see her for the first time.

"They just left," Gemma said quietly.

"How did you leave it with Conner?"

Gemma shrugged. "I don't know. Awkward. Sad. Like it might be the last time we ever see each other."

Hayley could see Gemma's emotions rising to the surface, as if she was about to burst into tears. "Come on, get in the car."

"Where are we going?"

"I'll explain on the way."

"Should I pack a bag or anything?"

"If we need something, we'll pick it up there. I'm not leaving you here on your own all day. I'll call Mona and have her drop by to feed and walk Leroy. Let's go."

Gemma decided not to argue, and just got in the passenger's side of Hayley's Kia and strapped in. Hayley jumped back behind the wheel, backed out of the driveway, and drove straight for Route 3 and out of town.

Their mother-daughter road trip to find some answers was officially underway.

Chapter 36

In Hayley's opinion, the photos she had seen on the internet or in the newspaper did not do Sandra Wallage justice. The blond wife of the junior senator from Maine was simply stunning to look at in person, and her colleague, Maya Kendrick, with her long raven hair, big brown eyes, and gorgeous caramel skin, was just as beautiful. The two of them together resembled a fashion ad in *Vanity Fair*.

Gemma, who was sitting on the couch in their office next to Hayley, was also visibly taken aback by the two women. What was most curious to Hayley, however, was how this pair had happened to come together. Sandra had spent most of her time hosting luncheons and running in political circles while Maya, an ex-cop, had a much more streetwise way about her. But from the moment Hayley and Gemma had arrived at the office at the appointed time, Hayley had immediately sensed an easy rapport between them, a familiarity, like they had been working together for years, even though Sandra was quick to point out that she was a newcomer to the whole private investigation world and was learning on the job from her partner, Maya.

When Gemma inquired as to how they met, Maya seemed to brush off the question, answering with a curt "We met while I was working on a case, became friends, and it just sort of developed from there." Neither seemed anxious to get any more detailed, so Gemma decided not to ask further follow-up questions.

Hayley had read a few gossip columns about the shaky state of Sandra's marriage, and all the rumors that she and her senator husband had separated, but the couple was keeping any hints of trouble under wraps and had not put out any public statements. Whether Sandra's new career as a private eye had anything to do with her leaving her husband and starting a new life was not something Hayley was going to find out, at least not today.

Instead, Sandra was laser-focused on why Hayley and Gemma had come all the way down to Portland, and was definitely eager to help. "Sal said you wanted to know about the fire that happened at the South Portland high school way back in the mid-2000s."

"Yes," Hayley said. "Sal thought you might be able to fill in a few details for us."

Maya, who was behind her desk, leaned back in her chair and put her feet up. "I was a rookie with the Portland Police Department at the time. They caught the girl who set the fire, if I remember correctly?"

"Yes, but I met her in Bar Harbor recently and she claims she didn't do it, even after all these years. She told me that because she had a history of emotional problems at the time, everyone was anxious to pin the blame on her, close the case, and move on," Hayley said.

Sandra folded her arms, lost in thought. "I was a

stay-at-home mom when that happened. I had just given birth to my son, Jack. My husband, Stephen, was running for state attorney general at the time. That story was such a big deal and got so much press coverage. I remember thinking at the time how lucky it was no one died or got seriously hurt. If the fire department hadn't raced to the scene as fast as they did, the whole school would have burned down. Parents were outraged and wanted answers fast. It didn't take long for them to find that girl . . ."

"Tori," Hayley said.

"That's right. Tori something. When I heard they had found the culprit, like everyone else, I was so relieved and disgusted she would do something so stupid and dangerous. But then I saw her picture in the paper, and I thought, I don't know, I just had this gut feeling that she didn't do it."

"You were pretty much the only one," Maya said.

"I know. Maybe I'm a sucker for a troubled, lonely girl. I wanted to believe her, I really did."

"As I said, I've met Tori and I am absolutely convinced she had nothing to do with setting that fire," Hayley said. "I guess that's why we came to you. To find out if there are more facts than what's generally known."

Maya swung her feet down to the floor and stood up. "Well, we can't exactly take you on as a client right now—"

"Good, because we can't afford to hire you," Hayley said, smirking.

Maya returned her smile and then picked up a book off the desk and handed it to Hayley. "But we did manage to get our hands on this."

It was the South Portland High School yearbook from the time of the fire.

Hayley flipped open the book excitedly as Gemma scooted closer to her mother so they could both pour over it. The graduating students were listed with their photos alphabetically, and Hayley found Trudy's picture in a matter of seconds. Next to her, Tori was listed but there was no photo. She had already been sent away and her family probably felt they shouldn't submit a picture of the girl who nearly destroyed the entire school. They thumbed through a few more pages, and Gemma suddenly gasped.

Hayley turned to her, puzzled. "What?"

Gemma pointed to a picture. "Look at that boy."

Hayley studied the picture Gemma had picked out and the name listed underneath it. "Erik Henderson. What about him?"

"Doesn't he remind you of someone?" Gemma asked.

Hayley scrunched up her face as she stared at the photo. "I don't know, he seems familiar to me, but I can't quite place him, and I'm pretty certain I've never heard of an Erik Henderson."

"It's Mark Garber," Gemma said confidently.

"*What?*" Hayley choked, fixing her eyes on the picture again.

Gemma snatched the yearbook from her mother and raised it up to inspect it closer. "Mom! Look at the nose, the chin, that crooked smile, it's Mark Garber! I'm sure of it!"

"But the hair color is different and it's hard to tell what color his eyes are behind those thick glasses."

"People can change their hair color and get Lasik surgery to correct their eyesight, Mother!"

Hayley was skeptical at first, but the longer she studied the photo and imagined what the boy might look like now, as a grown man, she slowly became more and more convinced her daughter might be right.

Maya circled around the desk and handed some papers stapled together to Hayley. "After Sal told us you were coming down, I called an old buddy at the police department I used to work with and he got me a copy of the original police report. I skimmed it while we were waiting for you to show up, and I remember that name. Erik Henderson. It's in the report."

Hayley shuffled through the pages and stopped when she came to the name. She read through the section quickly, and then looked up, surprised. "He was questioned by the police the next day."

Maya nodded. "A janitor had seen him and a few of his buddies in the vicinity of the school the night of the fire, and brought them down to the station to ask them a few questions. If you look at the officer's notes, he clearly states the Henderson kid was acting suspicious. But then, very quickly, evidence started mounting against Tori, and he was discarded as a suspect."

"Why would he change his name if people didn't think he was responsible for the fire?" Gemma asked.

Hayley stared at his picture again. "I have no idea . . ."

Gemma scanned a few more pages of the yearbook. "Here is another picture of him. He was on the track team with Trudy."

The track team was lined up for their official photo with Trudy front and center, obviously a star runner. Erik was in the second row on the far left, gazing longingly at her.

"Look at that. He's the only one on the team not looking at the camera. He's too distracted staring at Trudy. He must have had a huge crush on her," Gemma said.

"Excuse me." Hayley reached into her bag for her phone and made a call. After a few rings, Tori answered. "Tori, it's Hayley. I'm in Portland with a couple of private detectives."

Sandra beamed and turned to Maya. "I love being called a private detective."

"Private detective *in training*," Maya snapped, not quite ready to consider her an equal just yet.

"Tori, do you remember an Erik Henderson?" Hayley asked.

"Of course. He was in my class. He had a huge crush on Trudy. But Trudy never gave him the time of day, so unfortunately for him it went unrequited."

"Were you friends with him?" Hayley asked.

"No, not really," Tori said. "I remember once he tried to get me to talk to Trudy and try to convince her that she should give him a chance, that they should be a couple, but I refused. I was going through my own turmoil at the time and didn't want to play matchmaker for my twin sister, so I just told him to get over it."

Hayley lowered the phone, her mind racing.

So Erik Henderson, aka Mark Garber, was in the vicinity of the high school the night of the fire. He was questioned by police shortly thereafter. And then he ultimately changed his look and name when he became an adult for some still-unknown reason and eventually got hitched to Mary and moved to Bar Harbor. Then, years later, Trudy and Ted moved to town and when Trudy met Mark at the restaurant, the night of their double date with Hayley and Bruce, Trudy later told Ted that someone reminded her of a boy she knew long ago in high school. And then, very soon after that, Trudy Lancaster was dead.

Chapter 37

It was already dark outside when Hayley and Gemma finished indulging in crabmeat rolls, haddock chowder, and a couple of cocktails at J's Oyster Bar in the Old Port. Not wanting to drive all the way back to Bar Harbor late at night, Hayley suggested they check into a roadside motel off Interstate 295 and hit the road at dawn so Hayley could be in the office on time for her normal work day.

Gemma, who was yawning throughout dinner, quickly agreed, and so they left the restaurant after paying the bill, hopped in the car, and after stopping at a convenience store to stock up on some toiletries, arrived at the motel within ten minutes.

Although Hayley considered a more expensive hotel with robes and room service like the Regency or the Westin, they were both tired and just needed a bed to collapse in, and so it was more practical to go with a cheaper option.

After checking in and receiving their key card from the bored-looking college-age kid at the reception desk, Hayley and Gemma walked down to their room, on the bottom level of the two-story establishment, at the far end near the trash bin. Hayley was already missing her white robe and all-night dining menu she could have had if they had stayed right in downtown. Neither of them had bothered to pack an overnight bag because they had assumed they would just drive home after meeting with Sandra Wallage and Maya Kendrick, and they were way too exhausted to race to the Portland Mall before it closed to pick up some sleep wear, so it looked like they would both be going to bed in their street clothes tonight.

Hayley calculated enough time in their return trip so she would have a chance to go home and take a quick shower and put on some fresh clothes before reporting for work.

"Did you text Bruce and tell him we decided to spend the night?" Gemma asked.

"Yes, right after we left Maya and Sandra's office. I thought I would have heard back from him by now."

Gemma yawned again. "I'm going to go brush my teeth."

"All right, I'll try calling Sergio again," Hayley said, grabbing her phone from her jacket pocket as Gemma padded into the tiny but relatively clean bathroom.

Hayley sat down on one of the two beds separated by a scuffed and dingy nightstand and put the phone to her ear. She had already left two messages, one as they had left Sandra and Maya's office and another during dinner at J's.

"*Hello, this is Sergio, I can't take your call right now so leave a message after the beep.*"

Beep.

"Hi, Sergio, this is Hayley again. I've been trying to reach you because I'm in Portland with Gemma, and we got our hands on some important information involving Mark Garber and the Trudy Lancaster case. Please call me the minute you get this."

She ended the call and set her phone down on the nightstand. She assumed Sergio had other police business to attend to and would get back to her as soon as possible. Perhaps somebody plowed into another rare bird.

Hayley was drowsy from all the food and drinks she and Gemma had gorged on during dinner and stretched out on the bed. She closed her eyes and started to doze off, on the verge of slipping into a deep sleep, when Gemma wandered in from the bathroom and announced in a sad voice, "Conner must be back in New York by now. It feels weird not getting a text from him telling me he got home safely."

Hayley opened her eyes to see her daughter sitting on the edge of the bed across from her, wringing her hands, clearly distraught. "Gemma . . ."

"I know, I know," Gemma groaned with a wave of her hand. "I need to get over him."

"That's not what I was going to say."

"Well, I do. We broke up. End of story. It's time for me to move on and just forget about him."

"What I was going to say was, if you can't stop thinking about him, which clearly from my point of view you can't, then maybe you should call him."

"No, he broke up with me. I'm not going to humiliate myself and beg him to take me back. That would be pathetic."

"No one is suggesting you beg. But you seem to be forgetting that the only reason he ended your relationship is because you turned down his marriage proposal, and you had every right to do that, especially if you believe things were moving too fast."

"I was scared."

"Believe me, I get it. Marriage is a big step. You want to make sure you get it right the first time. I should know!"

Gemma chuckled.

"But why were you scared? Was it because you're not ready for that kind of a commitment or do you honestly believe Conner is not the one for you?"

Gemma sat up, suddenly more certain and self-assured. "No, of course I love Conner, more than even I realized before all this happened—"

"Then maybe he needs to know that."

Gemma slumped over again. "It's too late. I've made such a mess of things. And he's already looking around for someone else obviously."

"Oh, Gemma, I don't think Ted's daughter, Alyssa, has anything to do with this. Conner was hurt, he needed to lash out somehow, and Alyssa was the perfect excuse. Do you honestly believe Conner is interested in Alyssa, other than as a way to make you jealous?"

Gemma looked down at the floor. "No."

"Call him."

Gemma, eyes still fixed downward, slowly nodded. "Let me sleep on it. Maybe I'll do it in the morning. He must be so busy right now, getting ready for his first rehearsal."

"Don't put it off too long," Hayley warned.

Gemma looked up and smiled at her mother. "Yes, Mother. Good night." She then crawled under the covers and switched off the light.

Hayley closed her eyes and heard her daughter ask

through the darkness, "Is your mattress as hard as a rock too?"

"It's like something out of *The Flintstones*," Hayley said, rolling over, trying to get comfortable.

"I pray there are no bedbugs," Gemma moaned.

"Try not to think about it."

As hard as the bed was, Hayley managed to drift off to sleep for perhaps a minute or two before Gemma's bloodcurdling scream startled her awake again and she bolted up in bed.

She reached over and turned on the lamp to see Gemma sitting upright, the covers pulled up to her neck, a wide-eyed, frightened look on her face.

"Gemma, what is it?"

"Someone was staring at us through the window!"

"What?"

"I couldn't get to sleep because the streetlight was shining through the window because we forgot to close the curtains, and when I started to get up to close them I saw someone right there, standing at the window, looking in here at us!"

"Are you sure you weren't dreaming?"

"No, Mother! I know what I saw!"

"Okay, calm down," Hayley said, jumping out of bed and crossing to the door.

"No, don't open it! He might still be there!" Gemma cried.

"Well, we'll never get any sleep if we don't check for ourselves," Hayley said, unlocking the door and stepping outside. It was eerily quiet with no signs of anyone around. After scanning the entire parking lot and surrounding area, Hayley walked back into the room and fetched her bag. "There's no one out there. I'm going to go get us some bottled water from the vending machine."

"And leave me here alone?" Gemma gasped.

"You can come with me, if you want," Hayley said, fishing for some change.

Gemma decided to stay put, huddled in her bed, the cheap covers with their minimum thread count still pulled up to her neck.

Hayley padded to the vending machine next to the main office. The clerk was gone but the light was on inside. She inserted enough coins for two bottles of water, glanced around to make sure she was still alone, and returned to the room where Gemma waited for her, still anxious and shaken by what she had claimed to have just seen.

Hayley handed a water to Gemma and plopped back down on her bed. "Are you going to be able to get any sleep tonight?"

"I'll try," Gemma said, popping the cap off the bottle and taking a swig. "But let's leave as early as possible in the morning. I don't want to hang around here too long. This place gives me the creeps."

"Agreed," Hayley said, setting her bottle down on the nightstand next to her and swinging her feet back up on the bed. She closed her eyes, but had a harder time falling asleep again.

Not two minutes had passed by when they heard a loud smashing sound, like glass shattering.

Gemma snapped on the light again. "What was that?"

"Someone broke a window," Hayley said, trying not to panic.

"Where is it coming from?" Gemma cried.

As more glass crashed to the floor, they heard a thumping sound as if someone was right on top of them. Gemma turned to the bathroom door, which she had closed. "Someone's breaking into our room through the bathroom window!"

"Gemma, run!"

They both leaped out of bed and shot out the door, screaming. Hayley instantly collided with someone who wrapped his arms around her in a bear hug. She pounded her fists against her assailant's chest in a desperate attempt to get him to let her go so she could run away.

"Hayley! Hayley!"

She immediately stopped fighting her attacker because she instantly recognized his voice. Hayley pushed away from him. "Bruce, you scared me half to death!"

Hayley turned to find Gemma, who to her surprise had fallen into the waiting arms of Conner, who was hugging her tightly, quietly comforting her.

"What's going on?"

Hayley pointed back toward the room. "Someone's trying to break into our room!"

Bruce dashed off toward the motel room.

"Bruce, no! He could have a weapon!" Hayley cried.

But Bruce didn't listen. He disappeared inside the room and emerged a few moments later. "You're right. The bathroom window is smashed to bits but there's no sign of anyone. Your screaming might have spooked him and he ran off."

"How . . . did you find us?" Hayley gasped.

"You texted me where you were going to stay when you were at dinner," Bruce said calmly.

"But what are you doing here?" Hayley asked.

Bruce threw Conner a knowing look before returning his gaze to Hayley. "Go back in the room. I'm going to search the area to make sure this guy is really gone."

"I'll come with you," Conner said bravely, stepping back from Gemma, who was still in a state of shock.

After a brief sweep of the area, Bruce and Conner joined Hayley and Gemma back inside the motel room, where both women were still visibly upset by what had just happened.

"I went to the main office but no one is there. The clerk must be on his break or something," Bruce said.

"We should call the police," Conner said.

Gemma was less interested in reporting the crime than finding out what Conner was still doing in Maine. "Did you miss your flight?"

"What? Oh, uh, yes," Conner mumbled.

"I don't understand," Gemma said. "You left in plenty of time. What happened?"

Conner hesitated in answering her question. He just fidgeted with the sling on his arm.

"Are you going to tell her or should I?" Bruce asked, losing patience. When Conner still didn't respond, Bruce turned to Gemma and sighed. "We were on our way to Bangor, and the whole way there I had to listen to Conner drone on about how he hated leaving you in Maine, how he didn't want to end things the way you did, how he felt like he had made the biggest mistake of his life, but then we got to the airport and he checked in and we had some time for a drink at the bar, and when it came time to board, he couldn't do it. He couldn't get on the plane. And so instead of going home, after I got the text from Hayley that you were staying in Portland for the night, we just got in my car and kept driving all the way down to Portland. You said you were going to have dinner at J's Oyster Bar so we swung by there first, but the hostess said we just missed you, and so here we are."

"But what about the play? Don't you start rehearsals tomorrow?" Gemma asked.

Conner sat down on the bed next to Gemma. "You're a whole lot more important to me than some stupid play."

Gemma's eyes welled up with tears and her head dropped down on his shoulder as she quietly sobbed. He caressed her hair with his hand. "Listen to me, Gemma, you don't have to marry me. But you need to know just how much I love you. I love you with all my heart. Look, I know nothing is guaranteed in life. We may break up and go our separate ways, no one can ever predict what might happen one day, but I would never be able to live with myself if I didn't tell you how I truly feel about you."

Gemma wrapped her arms around his neck and pulled him closer to her, being careful not to lean in and crush his injured arm in the sling. She finally raised her head from his shoulder and turned so she could whisper in his ear, "I love you too."

Now it was Hayley's turn to cry.

Island Food & Spirits
by
Hayley Powell

Starting from when I was in high school, when something good or exciting happened in my life, my mother would make me one of her mouthwatering club sandwiches to celebrate. Come to think of it, when something bad happened and I was in desperate need of cheering up, she'd, well, make me one of her mouthwatering club sandwiches. I guess club sandwiches can do it all!

I happily carried on the tradition with my own children, even now that they're fully grown. I will always remember the time the club sandwich cure-all had gotten started. I was fourteen, a freshman in high school, and I had a huge crush on a boy in my class. Don't all high school stories start out like that?

It was around Halloween and Beth Sanborn was having a huge Halloween party for all the kids in our class at her house. Well, you can imagine my excitement when I learned Calvin, my crush, had been invited to the party too. This was my chance to finally make my move!

Calvin and I had hit it off the first day of the school year in English class with our shared love of movies, especially *Jurassic Park* since Calvin was an unapologetic fanatic about everything dinosaurs, and wanted to study to one day become a paleontologist.

Truth be told, I didn't give one whit about dinosaurs. I was more of a *Fugitive* kind of gal when it came to big summer blockbuster movies mostly because I thought Harrison Ford was adorably cute for an old guy. But that didn't stop me from gushing to Calvin about how much I worshipped *Jurassic Park,* which, to be honest, I had not even seen.

Calvin was exceedingly good-looking and there was always a swarm of girls around him in the cafeteria during lunch, so I knew I had my work cut out for me. I had to stand out at that Halloween party so he would notice me and all those other girls would just melt away, unable to compete. I already had a home field advantage because Calvin thought I was funny and liked dinosaurs so he would always want to walk together to class and sit with me at lunch. Finally, it dawned on me how I could win his affections over all those other smitten girls who were so much prettier than me: I would get him by wearing the perfect Halloween costume!

I would literally transform into his true love: a dinosaur!

The night of the party arrived, and I could barely contain my excitement as I stepped into my blow-up dinosaur costume in the living room so my mother could inflate it with the plug-in air pump that came in the packaging.

My first clue that this might not have been the perfect costume for me was when it was inflated, and I could barely see out of the mouth of the dinosaur. It was also a lot harder to walk in than I had expected. But if it caught Calvin's attention, then it would be well worth the discomfort and all my babysitting money I had spent on it, not to mention the expedited shipping expense.

My second clue was when Mona and her dad arrived to pick me up for the party. I wouldn't fit in the cab of the truck, even with Mona pushing me from inside and her father, Sid, outside throwing his shoulder into the dinosaur's inflated butt. So that's how I wound up sitting in the flatbed, bouncing around while we drove to the party.

After we finally arrived at Beth Sanborn's house, I thanked my lucky stars no one was outside to see Mona and her dad roll me out of the back and struggle to get me in an upright position. Sid wiped the sweat from his forehead from the effort and told us to have fun before jumping back in his truck and speeding away, promising to be back to pick us up by eleven.

Once we were inside, I needed Mona to guide me since I couldn't see where I was going. I could hear the party in full swing, but couldn't see much unless I stood up on my tippy-toes. I managed to get a partial view of the room and immediately spotted all those adoring girls who had their eyes on Calvin in various sexy Halloween costumes. One was a vintage '80s Madonna from *Desperately Seeking Susan*, another a sexy cheerleader, a sexy nurse, a sexy witch. No matter what they came as, they made sure it was sexy! There was no way I could sell the idea that I was a sexy dinosaur, that was for sure!

I finally saw Calvin, dressed as some kind of explorer, sitting across the room on a couch chatting up a very beautiful foreign exchange student who was dressed as sexy Jasmine from *Aladdin*. I was devastated. In my mind, it looked like world adventurer Calvin was definitely exploring her!

I decided in that moment that my best course of action was to just retreat. Unfortunately before I could, someone bumped into me from behind and I lost my balance in the bulky blow-up costume and down I went! I yelled as I fell, which of course drew the attention of all the party guests, and I bounced—yes, bounced—before landing on my back, dinosaur arms and legs flailing in the air!

As if that wasn't humiliating enough, Calvin, along with four other guys, rushed over to hoist me up off the ground. It took three tries, but they managed to get me on my feet where I could steady myself.

I had pretty much had enough. I ran out of there, knocking over two lamps and breaking a vase before I squeezed out the front door and called my mother to come pick me up early. As I waited for her on the front lawn, I was totally deflated, both literally and figuratively, because I stepped on a sharp rock that tore a hole in the costume and let all the air out.

When we got home, Mom made me one of her club sandwiches (along with some tasty hot chocolate), which did the trick and managed to calm down my hysterics. And that's how the club sandwich cure for the blues began.

The story did have a happy ending. The next day in English class, Calvin told me he thought my dinosaur costume was, in his words, "awesome" and he invited me over to watch an old movie he had on VHS called *The Land That Time Forgot,* which, you guessed it, featured dinosaurs! I forgot what the movie was about but I will always remember the time Calvin first kissed me while we were watching it.

Adult Hot Chocolate

Ingredients
½ teaspoon vanilla extract
1 cup semisweet chocolate chips
2 cups milk (whatever you like to use)
3½ ounces Godiva chocolate liqueur
3 ounces whipped cream vodka
Whipped cream and chocolate syrup for garnish

In a saucepan on medium heat add the chocolate chips.

As they start to melt add your milk, whisking until it is melted and smooth.

Bring the chocolate and milk to a low boil, stirring often, and add the vanilla, chocolate liqueur, and vodka. Cook together for about a minute.

Pour your mixture into mugs and garnish with whipped cream and chocolate syrup. You will love this yummy treat!

SHEILA'S CLASSIC CLUB SANDWICH

INGREDIENTS

4 slices cooked bacon (You can use less, but you know how I love my bacon!)
3 ounces thinly sliced deli ham
3 ounces thinly sliced deli turkey
3 slices whole wheat bread
Lettuce
Tomato slices
2 tablespoons mayonnaise or more to taste
1 slice Colby Jack cheese
Salt and pepper to taste

First, toast your bread and set your 3 slices to the side.

Spread your mayonnaise on all three slices.

Add your lettuce and tomato to bottom slice. Add some salt and pepper. Take the second piece of toast and place mayonnaise-side down on lettuce and tomato.

Spread more mayonnaise on dry side of toast, then add your meats and cheese.

Add your last piece of toast mayonnaise-side down on top of cheese and meats, then cut into triangles using toothpicks to hold everything together. Place on a plate and enjoy because there is nothing better than a classic club sandwich.

Chapter 38

Hayley stood at the checkout counter in the drugstore as the clerk behind the register rang up her items. She was drained and dead tired after the attempted break-in at the motel in Portland. Not only did she and Gemma drive straight home behind Bruce and Conner in the middle of the night so they could feel safe sleeping in their own beds, but Hayley had put in a full work day at the office. Now as the time crept toward six o'clock in the evening, and she still had to make dinner before she could plop facedown in bed for a proper night's sleep, Hayley had swung by the drugstore to restock on some toothpaste, paper towels, trash bags, and a few other household necessities that she was running low on at the house.

Jenny—the hefty, apple-cheeked girl whose light blue store uniform was two sizes too small for her, the sleeves so tight they threatened to cut off blood circulation to her arms—tapped the keys on the register as Hayley provided a reusable bag to pack up her purchases.

"That'll be twenty-six dollars and forty-nine cents, Hayley," Jenny said, bored, checking her watch to see how much time was left on her shift.

Hayley inserted her card in the machine, typed in her phone number for her rewards points, and waited for the transaction to be complete.

Jenny suddenly remembered something. "Oh, by the way, and I'm sorry because the manager is making me say this to everyone, all our Halloween costumes are half price so you might want to think about picking one up now and not wait until next year when the prices will be much higher."

"I can never think that far ahead, Jenny. I don't even know what I'm making for dinner tonight," Hayley said, laughing.

"I understand. Like I said, the manager wants me to really push the leftover costumes."

"I'm curious, what was your biggest seller this year?"

"Well, obviously we always sell a lot of witches because of the Garber shindig every year, although I'm not sure about next year given what happened at the party this year."

Hayley nodded solemnly.

Jenny grimaced briefly, but then quickly moved on. "Superheroes always do well. Any Avenger or Justice League character. We sold a lot of Wonder Woman and Spider-Man costumes this year. And of course, the scary characters are perennial favorites. Freddy Krueger, the crazy clown from those *It* movies, the killer dolls like Chucky and Annabelle. Lord, those really creep me out."

"I hear you," Hayley said, shuddering. "And I know you sold at least one Michael Myers because I was with Mark Garber when he bought it."

"That's right. We only had two in stock and he bought both of them," Jenny said as she ripped off the receipt and handed it to Hayley.

Hayley was knocked back on her heels. "What do you mean he bought *both* of them?"

"I remember about a half hour after you two were in here buying the one mask, he came back and they picked up the other one."

Hayley remembered that when they were perusing all the Halloween costumes in the drugstore and she had suggested Mark go to the ball as Michael Myers, there were two masks on the shelf for sale. He was going to buy both to make sure no one could show up to his party in the same costume, but she had discouraged him and they had left the store after just buying the one.

"Jenny, you said '*they* picked up the other one.' Was Mark with his wife, Mary?"

Jenny shook her head. "No, he was with Ethan Dudley."

"Ethan Dudley?"

"You know, the kid who works in the ticket booth at the Criterion Theatre across the street?"

"Yes, I know Ethan. But I didn't know he and Mark were friends."

Jenny shrugged. "I guess so."

The clerk was not nearly as interested in this development as Hayley was. But Hayley knew this new information was a game changer because Mark Garber's airtight alibi on the night of the Witches Ball was suddenly on shaky ground.

"Thanks, Jenny," Hayley said, snatching her bag before racing out of the drugstore. She swiveled her head in both directions to check for oncoming traffic and then bolted across the street to the Criterion Theatre.

The lights on the historical landmark's marquee flashed brightly as a few people lined up to buy tickets for the seven o'clock showing of *Double Indemnity* starring Barbara Stanwyck and Fred MacMurray, part of a series of Hollywood classics presented every week.

Hayley waited patiently to reach the head of the line and, as she had hoped, behind the ticket booth's glass window was Ethan Dudley, a self-conscious, fidgety young man in his early twenties who quite notably was about the same height and weight as Mark Garber.

"Hi, Ethan, I don't know if you remember me, but I'm Hayley, I work at the *Island Times* and I'm friends with your parents."

"Yeah, my mom likes your recipes. She made your slow-cooker Cuban sandwiches for our Sunday family dinner a couple of weeks ago and they were awesome."

"Thank you."

"Would you like to buy a ticket for the show?"

"Uh, no, I just have a couple of questions I'd like to ask you."

"Okay," Ethan said warily, glancing to see if anyone was waiting in line behind her.

Luckily there was no one.

"Did you attend the Witches Ball at the Garber house this year?" Hayley asked.

Ethan hesitated, his eyes darting back and forth.

"It's a simple yes-or-no question, Ethan."

"Yes . . . ?"

"And did you dress up in a Halloween costume?"

"Didn't everybody?"

"Did you go as Michael Myers?"

"Is that the guy from all those *Halloween* movies?"

Hayley nodded. "Yes, that's him."

Ethan hesitated again, not sure where this was going, wondering if he should just keep his mouth shut, but Hayley was on a mission and she was not about to give up until she got what she wanted out of him.

"Did someone help you pick out your costume?" Hayley asked.

An elderly man suddenly appeared behind Hayley, clearing his throat as he checked his watch to make sure the movie had not started yet.

"I'm sorry, I have to get back to work, Mrs. Powell," Ethan said.

Hayley stepped out of the way so Ethan could sell a ticket to the old man, but the moment the man sauntered into the theater, she was back in front of Ethan, her face almost pressed up against the glass, confronting him. "Was it Mark Garber? Did he suggest you go to the ball as Michael Myers?"

Wanting this third degree to be over, Ethan nodded slightly, but didn't elaborate any further.

"Did he *pay* you to go to the Witches Ball as Michael Myers?"

"Am I in some kind of trouble here?" Ethan asked, his voice wobbly, an uneasy look on his face.

"No, not at all. I just need to know the truth. Please, Ethan, it's important."

"Yeah, he paid me. I barely make minimum wage here. And I'm saving to buy a new Harley."

"Did you ever ask why he was willing to pay you to wear the same costume as him at the party?"

"It was two hundred dollars. I didn't care to ask any questions."

He had a point.

Hayley sighed. "Thank you, Ethan."

He stared at her, unsettled, as she dashed off.

It was all becoming crystal clear now.

If Ethan Dudley was walking around the Garbers' party wearing a Michael Myers mask, then everyone there would have assumed he was Mark, which would have allowed Mark to sneak out unnoticed if he wanted to kill Trudy!

Chapter 39

By the time Hayley reached her car, which was parked in front of the drugstore across the street from the Criterion Theatre, she was already on the phone with Sergio.

"Slow down, Hayley," Sergio said with an exasperated tone. "You know English is my second language."

"I'm sorry, but it's Mark Garber! He did it! He killed Trudy!"

"Yes, I got all your phone messages last night when you called me from Portland," Sergio said calmly.

"But now I know *how* he did it! His alibi is collapsing like a house of cards in a stiff wind!"

Hayley briefly recounted all the information she had gathered that pointed the finger at Mark Garber.

"The thing is, Hayley, I went over to his house last night after I got your messages, and Mary said he hadn't come home from work yet. And today, she told me he had to go out of town on business. I just haven't been able to track him down yet."

Hayley was in the driver's seat with the engine running. She gripped the steering wheel with one hand as she held the phone up with the other. "Mary may have tipped him off that you were looking for him and he fled town. If he's on the run, you may never catch him."

"Don't worry, I'll find him," Sergio assured her. "He could just be hiding out somewhere locally, figuring out his next move."

"What should we do now?" Hayley asked.

"*You* don't do anything. This is a police matter. I'm going to head back over to the Garber house and press Mary some more, confront her with this new information and find out how much she knows. Maybe she'll slip and give me a clue to his whereabouts. You go home. I will call you as soon as I can." Sergio ended the call.

Hayley took a deep breath, dropped her phone in the cup holder next to her, and clenched both fists around the steering wheel. Sergio was right. She had taken this about as far as she possibly could. Her job was done. She had given Sergio everything he needed to arrest Mark Garber for Trudy's murder.

Now it was a matter of waiting.

She reached down and picked up her phone again and called Bruce, but it went directly to voicemail. Bruce had a habit of turning off his phone when he was in the middle of writing one of his crime columns. She assumed she would just see him at home when he finally finished. Conner had called his theater director in New York after they had arrived home from Portland earlier that morning, and begged him to give him an extra day in Maine before he was to report for rehearsals. After getting an earful about professionalism, the director, who luckily was still determined to see Conner in the role, reluctantly relented and agreed he could be late one day. Conner had rebooked his flight again and was now scheduled to return the following afternoon. So he and Gemma had driven up to Ellsworth to do a little shopping.

Hayley had received a text earlier from Gemma telling her they would be home by seven thirty. It was almost six thirty now so that left her an hour to whip up something for supper. Hayley stopped at the Shop ’n Save, picked up a package of pasta and some fresh tomatoes and tomato paste for a simple marinara sauce she could quickly prepare with spices she had at home, and drove straight to the house.

When she entered through the back door with her bag of groceries, the house was eerily quiet. She found it odd that Leroy wasn’t waiting for her by the door since he could always hear her car pull into the driveway from anywhere in the house. She bent down and pulled out a pot from the bottom cupboard, filled it with water, and set it on the stovetop, cranking the heat up to high. Then she pulled some oregano, salt, pepper, and parsley from the spice rack and went to the refrigerator for her jar of minced garlic. She was cranking the tomato paste open with a can opener when she stopped suddenly, hearing a faint scratching sound.

She looked around, perplexed, but the scratching soon stopped. She resumed opening the can of paste and dumping it into her food processor when the scratching started up again.

This time it was accompanied by soft whimpering.

She certainly recognized that sound.

“Leroy?”

Her eyes flew to the door to the basement.

The scratching and whimpering were coming from the other side of the door.

“What the—?”

Hayley was confused.

Who locked her dog in the basement?

She crossed the kitchen and tried to open the door to the basement but it was locked. She turned to the ceramic bowl on the kitchen counter where she kept all the keys, but instantly noticed that the key to the basement was gone.

"Looking for this?" a man's voice asked.

Hayley jumped back, startled, and whipped around to see Mark Garber standing in the doorway to the dining room where he had been hiding, the key to the basement dangling from one hand while he gripped a small pistol with the other.

"Mark . . . ?"

"Looks like I beat you home. With just a few seconds to spare. I barely had time to toss that flea-infested mongrel down the stairs into the basement and shut the door before you pulled into the driveway," Mark sneered.

"My dog does *not* have fleas," Hayley seethed.

"I bet you're wondering why I'm here."

"The thought had crossed my mind."

"Ethan texted me the second you left him and told me everything. You should have paid him something. He would have been more loyal. With me, he knows I'll keep shelling out cash until he's riding atop that big, beautiful, brand-new Harley Davidson," Mark said with a crooked smile.

"Sergio knows everything, Mark. He's on his way here for dinner right now. He should be pulling into the driveway any second," Hayley lied.

Mark chortled. "I don't think so. I just got a text from Mary. The chief just called her and told her he was heading over to our house to ask her some more questions."

Hayley's heart sank.

But she was not about to show him any fear.

"You started that fire in your high school, didn't you, Mark?"

Mark nodded, a pained look on his face as his memory returned to that obviously harrowing time in his life. "Yes, it was me. I loved Trudy so much, I'd never felt that way about any girl in my whole life. But she never took me seriously. She rejected me in front of all my friends. It was so humiliating. So I set a small fire inside her locker one night after school. I just wanted to teach her a lesson, but the fire got out of control and it spread so fast I couldn't put it out. I got the hell out of there as fast as I could and didn't look back. The school sustained major damage. It was going to take all summer to repair. I was so scared everyone was going to find out it was me and my life would be ruined."

Hayley averted her eyes to the pot of water on the stove as it came to a boil, and then returned her gaze to Mark's gun, which was pointed right at her.

"But then a miracle happened," Mark continued. "Once the fire department traced the origin of the fire to Trudy's locker, people started to whisper that it was probably her whacko twin sister, Tori, who set it because she was so jealous that Trudy was much more popular than her. The rumor somehow took hold and before I knew it everyone was just assuming Tori was responsible. All I had to do was keep my mouth shut and let her take the fall, and I would get away with it scot-free."

The boiling pot of water was heating up the whole kitchen. Mark tossed the basement key onto the counter and used his now free hand to wipe some sweat off his brow.

"So Tori got sent away and you were able to go on

with your life as if nothing happened, like you didn't destroy a troubled young girl's life," Hayley spit out.

"That's where you're wrong," Mark hissed. "I actually felt a little guilty . . ." He scowled as he caught a decidedly skeptical look on Hayley's face. "I did! And there was a janitor who saw me running away from the school that night who was telling anyone who would listen, but nobody did because it was easier and more convenient to just keep thinking it was Tori so nobody would have to deal with the fact they sent her away for no good reason. Living with all of that and fearing the truth would eventually come out, my life took a horrible turn. Maybe it was karma, who knows, but I got into drugs and was arrested a few times. I couldn't get any kind of decent job with my rap sheet. I needed a fresh start."

"So you decided to change your name and appearance and Mark Garber was born," Hayley said.

"Funny thing is, it worked," Mark said, almost not believing it himself. "I met Mary, we got married, moved to Bar Harbor. Things really took a turn for the better. We're both happy living here, content, despite the brutal winters. I even managed to let go of the past, like it was all just a bad dream."

"Until Trudy showed up in town," Hayley said.

Mark's face darkened as he glared at her and muttered, "Yes."

"When Mary met Trudy, she couldn't wait to hire her for your Witches Ball, but you couldn't say anything for fear of giving up everything. But when you were with her, all those raging, bitter feelings came flooding back, didn't they?" Hayley snapped accusingly.

He didn't answer her.

He didn't have to.

The hurt and fury and resentment were written all over his face.

"And to add insult to injury," Hayley said, "Trudy didn't even recognize you."

Mark gripped the gun so hard his knuckles were white. "I had spent so much of my teenage years thinking about her, obsessing over her, even as an adult, wondering what had happened to her. When I saw her, my heart nearly stopped. But she just introduced herself to me with this blank look on her face, like I was a complete stranger she had never seen before. She *should* have seen me, even with a new hair color and no glasses and all the cosmetic changes I made. She should have known it was *me*!"

"But she didn't and that just set you off again! You wanted her to pay for her rejection, the pain she caused, your life going so spectacularly off the rails when you were still just a teenager! You just had to get justice once and for all," Hayley barked.

The steam from the boiling water was now blasting Mark in the face to the point where he had to keep wiping off the perspiration while simultaneously steadying the gun in his shaky hand as Hayley confronted him with his grievous past.

"And so you set an insidious plan in motion. You were the one who stole the carbon monoxide detector out of Trudy's food truck earlier in the evening, before the party."

Mark sniffed. "She was there and didn't even see me do it because she was so busy making sure she had enough food for all the guests."

"Then, when Ethan Dudley showed up dressed in the exact same costume as you, you changed out of your own Michael Myers getup and into a witch costume so you would look exactly like half the party guests.

You slipped away, leaving Ethan—whom everyone would assume was you—and then you rigged the propane tank so it would leak gas inside the food truck while Trudy was busy cooking meat for her hot subs she was planning to serve."

"We told the guests the food truck wouldn't be open until eight so everyone was still inside getting drinks at the bar, giving me enough time to rig the propane tank and lock the back door of the truck from the outside with the padlock. It was her fastest way to escape. She didn't even have time to try and climb into the front and get out that way because she was overcome with the poisonous fumes before she even realized what was happening. I heard a thud inside the truck and knew she was gone."

"It was you who my husband, Bruce, saw running away in a witch costume when he went outside to sneak a cigarette. Later, you planted the carbon monoxide detector in Cloris Fennow's food truck in order to point the finger at her."

"It worked beautifully," Mark said proudly. "Cloris was the perfect patsy. Everyone knew she was upset because there wasn't enough business in town to support two food trucks so why wouldn't everyone think she did it, just like with Tori?"

"I have one question. How come no one saw two Michael Myers at the party once you came back inside?" Hayley asked.

"Because I prearranged with Ethan that he should leave the house precisely at eight fifteen, ditch the mask, and go home where his money would be waiting in an envelope underneath his front door, allowing me to take his place as if I had been in there the whole time."

"It was a brilliant plan if it had worked. But it didn't. The police chief knows everything now," Hayley reminded him.

"I'll deal with the chief later! You, I can take care of right now," Mark growled, the gun now aimed at her chest.

Leroy, sensing danger from the other side of the basement door, barked wildly, frantically, annoying Mark.

"Shut up!" Mark barked, trying to think.

Hayley knew she had to act fast or she was a dead woman.

The problem was she hadn't the faintest idea what to do.

Chapter 40

As Mark advanced upon Hayley, pushing her toward the back door, Hayley knew if she made any sudden moves she was a goner.

"Come on, let's go!" Mark yelled, jamming the gun in her side, his eyes darting back and forth, desperate to come up with some kind of plan to get rid of her. "We're going to take a little ride."

Suddenly, a deafening, blaring sound startled them and they both froze in their tracks.

What on earth was that?

It was coming from upstairs.

And then it dawned on Hayley.

It was the smoke detector she had secretly installed in the bathroom in order to surprise Bruce if he tried to sneak a smoke inside the house. Which meant he had been upstairs this entire time, puffing on a cigarette, completely unaware of what was happening down in the kitchen.

Mark looked up at the ceiling, trying to locate the

source of the ear-splitting, screeching sound, momentarily distracted.

It was all Hayley needed.

Mark's eyes were off her for just a few seconds, but it was enough time for her to reach out and grab the handle of the stainless steel pot on the stovetop filled with the boiling water. She flung the pot at Mark and the scalding water spilled all over his hand that was holding the gun.

Mark howled in pain, dropped the gun to the floor, and grabbed ahold of his scorched hand.

"Bruce! Help!" Hayley cried as she dove to the floor and scooped up the gun. Mark, who had snapped back into the moment, realizing he was about to lose control of the situation, seized Hayley in a bear hug, grappling with her for possession of the gun. Hayley held on tight, determined not to allow Mark to get the upper hand again. They struggled with each other mightily, banging into the kitchen counter, and then falling back down to the floor, rolling across the floor and slamming into the refrigerator.

Leroy continued loudly barking from behind the basement door, in a frenzied state, scratching at the door furiously.

Hayley heard the bathroom door upstairs fly open and whack against the wall and then pounding footsteps as Bruce hurried downstairs to find out what was going on in the kitchen.

When Bruce reached the hallway, he stopped suddenly. His mouth dropped open in shock at the sight of Mark Garber writhing on the floor, wincing in pain as he nursed his reddened, blistered hand.

Hayley was sitting upright, her back against the oven, pointing a gun at him.

She hadn't needed her husband's help after all.

Hayley had managed to take care of it all on her own.

The shrieking wail of the smoke detector finally, mercifully shut off.

"What the hell happened here?" Bruce cried.

"I'll tell you what happened," Hayley whispered, still trying to catch her breath. "I caught you smoking again, that's what happened. Now do me a favor and call Sergio. He needs to get over here right away."

Bruce nodded, still stunned, and obediently reached for the phone.

Chapter 41

Mary Garber stared out her living room window, her elbow resting on the arm of the chair she was sitting in and her hand cupped underneath her chin. Her eyes were wet and she sniffed a couple of times during the silence as Hayley sat respectfully across from her. On the coffee table between them was a Styrofoam cup of hot coffee and a lemon danish in a small brown paper bag Hayley had thought to pick up for her on the way over. It was still early, not even eight in the morning, but Hayley knew Mary would be up after a sleepless night, processing the news that her husband, Mark, had been arrested for the murder of Trudy Lancaster, not to mention assault with a deadly weapon against Hayley herself. Hayley had not been sure she would be welcomed into the Garber home given her personal role in the whole ugly matter, but Mary had seemed genuinely pleased to see her when she had shown up on her doorstep.

Hayley glanced over at the TV and Savannah Guthrie was interviewing some actor promoting his new movie on the *Today Show*, but there was no sound since Mary had pressed the mute button before they sat down.

Finally, after what seemed like an eternity, Mary dropped her hand from the bottom of her chin to her lap and turned back toward Hayley. "I want you to know, I *need* you to know, that I had no idea . . ."

"About Mark's secret past?"

"Yes, I've been totally in the dark, all these years. It's just so unfathomable to think about. All this time, he was lying to me. How could I not see it? Why was I so stupid?"

"You can't blame yourself Mary. Mark legally changed his name before he even met you. There was no way for you to know. You had absolutely no reason to be suspicious."

Mary nodded, accepting that fact, but not willing to completely let herself off the hook. "But we've been married for so long. You would think I would eventually pick up on something, some clue that would have driven me to find out the truth. But I didn't. I just stayed so blissfully, so frustratingly ignorant to who he really was."

Hayley hated seeing Mary beat up on herself.

After Sergio had shown up at Hayley's house and slapped the handcuffs on Mark, reading him his rights and quickly frog-marching him out the door, Hayley had immediately picked up the phone and called Mary. Sergio had never reached Mary's house to confront her with the new information regarding Mark, and so at the time she was innocently baking a glazed ham and whipping up some mashed potatoes for dinner.

Hayley had felt obligated to at least give her a heads-up that Mark had been arrested. Hayley had known in that moment that Mary was utterly blindsided. Mary at first had assumed Mark had swung by Drinks Like A

Fish and perhaps had one too many beers, and had been pulled over by the police for erratic driving, which would have been bad enough in her mind, a public scandal splashed all over the court page of the *Island Times*. But when Hayley had quietly explained that she was not calling from her brother's bar, but from her own house, where Mark had shown up brandishing a gun, it was hard to hear Mary gasp and wail, "Gun? What was Mark doing with a gun?"

Hayley had tried to fill in a few of the blanks, but it was difficult. Mark's identity change, his connection to Trudy, stalking Hayley and Gemma all the way down in South Portland fearing what they might discover—it was all too much for Mary to bear.

Finally, Hayley stopped and advised Mary to head straight for the police station where Mark could explain the rest himself.

Hayley had been up all night worrying about Mary and what she must be going through.

It had been a risk showing up with a danish and coffee since she had assumed Mary would be too upset to think about eating some breakfast, and she had been right. The danish was left untouched as they sat down in the living room and Mary unspooled the events of the previous evening: her husband's ghastly confession; the details of his false identity, and years of cover up to escape paying for a crime he had committed; the ugly truth of allowing an innocent bystander with a few emotional issues to take the fall; and most disturbingly, taking a woman's life because of a dark years-long obsession.

"I just want to jump in my car and drive off this island, back to my family in Rhode Island, and never come back here ever again so I don't have to deal with the constant whispering behind my back and all the judgmental looks," Mary said, sniffing again and wiping her nose with a tissue.

"No one will judge you, Mary," Hayley tried assuring her. "You did nothing wrong."

"This is a small town, Hayley. We both know what happens in small towns."

"Yes, every town has a few annoying gossips. But you've been here a long time. You have friends, a support system."

"Who?"

"Me, for starters. And I am pretty confident I can speak for Liddy and Mona too. That's three people, and I bet there will be a lot more."

Mary smiled weakly, at least grateful for Hayley's rousing pep talk, but she was still wary of truly believing it.

Hayley glanced at the wall clock.

It was five minutes past eight.

She was already late for work.

Hayley stood up. "I better go. I'll call and check in on you later. Would that be okay?"

Mary nodded. "Thank you, Hayley."

Hayley felt the urge to hug her, but Mary made no move to stand up and see her out. She just gazed back out the window, and so Hayley noiselessly backed away and slipped out the front door.

Outside, Bruce waited for her in the car as she circled around and hopped in the passenger's side.

He turned to her as she shut the door. "How did it go?"

"She's devastated. It's going to be tough coming back from something like this."

"Mary's strong. She can do it."

"I hope so," Hayley sighed.

"By the way, so are you."

"What are you talking about?"

"My wife, the badass. Tackling a man like a running back on the Patriots, saving the day. It's like I'm married to Wonder Woman."

"Truth be told, I was scared out of my mind."

"I would be too. But promise me you won't try anything risky like that ever again," Bruce demanded as he pulled away from the curb and headed for the office. "I've waited too many years to marry you, I certainly don't want to lose you now."

"That depends."

"On what?"

"If you promise me—"

Bruce sighed. "Yes! Okay! I'll quit smoking!"

"Thank you!"

"But technically, it was my smoking habit that kind of saved your life. If I hadn't been upstairs sneaking one in the bathroom that detector never would have gone off—"

"Bruce!"

"All right! I promise!"

Chapter 42

After leaving Mary Garber's house, Bruce swung by the *Island Times* office and dropped Hayley off before heading back home. He had taken the day off so he could drive Conner up to Bangor for his flight back to New York. This time, Conner promised, he would actually get on the plane. Gemma was planning on saying her goodbyes at the house and then joining some longtime friends for lunch.

Hayley had barely sat down behind her desk and begun scrolling through her dozens of emails when the door to the office burst open and Tori blew in, a shy smile on her face.

"Good morning," she said, closing the door behind her.

"Tori! It's lovely to see you! I didn't know you were still in town. Can I get you a cup of coffee?"

"That would be nice, thanks," she said softly.

Hayley shot up, circled around her desk, and walked over to the coffee station in the corner of the reception area to pour Tori a cup.

"I wanted to stop by and thank you personally," Tori said.

"Thank me?" Hayley asked, confused. "Whatever for?"

"You got justice for Trudy, and for that I will be forever grateful," Tori said, her bottom lip quivering, trying to fight back her emotions.

Hayley set the coffeepot down and sauntered over to Tori, whose arms were folded as she looked down at the floor, embarrassed that she was on the verge of crying.

Hayley set the cup of coffee down on her desk and gave Tori a warm hug, whispering in her ear, "I didn't know your sister for very long, but I thought the world of her."

Tori nodded and rested her head on Hayley's shoulder for a few moments before finally pulling away and picking up the coffee cup from Hayley's desk to take a sip. "I promised myself on the way over here I wouldn't get all emotional, but here I go . . ."

"It's obvious how much you loved your sister even after such a long time apart," Hayley noted.

Tori managed to keep the tears from flowing and remain in control, and then she smiled. "I also wanted you to know that I've decided to stay in town for a little while."

Hayley lit up. "That's wonderful news!"

"Ted is understandably lost right now. It's been tough working through the grieving process while starting his new job as the local pastor at the Congregational church, so he asked me to stick around and help him out for a few weeks. I didn't know if it was a good idea at first, me being Trudy's twin sister and all, constantly reminding him of her, but I have a strong feeling about him, that he's a good man . . ."

"He is, I can assure you of that."

"A good man who is feeling very overwhelmed right now and quite frankly I don't have a lot else going on . . ."

"I think it's a fantastic idea, Tori. What about Alyssa? Is she going to stay to be with her father too?"

Tori cracked a knowing smile. "Um, no. Actually I drove her to the Bangor airport last night. She caught a late flight back to New York. The good news is, apparently she's booked another gig singing at some club."

"She must have been very excited."

"If she was, she didn't show it," Tori said, shaking her head. "I volunteered to drive her since Ted needed to work on his sermon for Sunday. She barely spoke to me the whole way. At first I thought it was because I reminded her of Trudy, who she never liked, but then I kept glancing over to see her staring at a text on her phone and I realized it was the text that had put her in such a sour mood."

"Did you ask who it was from?"

"Conner," Tori answered.

Hayley's heart began racing. "Oh? What did he say?"

"She didn't tell me too much, and she refused to show me the text, but apparently they were supposed to see each other when they both got back to New York, but he had texted her to tell her that it was not going to happen."

Hayley heard her phone buzzing in her bag. "Excuse me just a moment, Tori."

"Certainly," Tori said, taking another sip of her coffee.

Hayley rounded her desk, picked up her bag, and fished for her phone. She scooped it out and pressed the home button.

"It's a text from my daughter," Hayley said, reading the message.

Mom, can you come home? It's urgent!

Hayley's heart was practically pounding through her chest.

Her first thought was, *Did something happen to Leroy?*

Her second thought, *Did something happen to Bruce?*

Her third thought was, *Should I feel guilty for worrying about them in that order?*

It suddenly didn't matter.

She just had to get home.

Hayley glanced up at Tori. "I'm sorry, Tori. I have to go."

"Of course. I should be on my way anyway!"

Hayley whipped her head around and called in the direction of the back bullpen where her boss Sal's office was located. "Sal, I have to go home! I'll be back when I can!"

Sal angrily barked, "Sure! Why not? It's not like you just took a personal day to drive all the way down to Portland so you could play detective—"

She didn't hear the rest of his rant because she was already out the door.

Chapter 43

Bruce's car was still parked in front of the house when Hayley frantically pulled her Kia in behind him, nearly colliding with his rear bumper because she was in such a panic.

She leaped out of her Kia and dashed up the front steps, barreling through the front door. She instantly spotted Bruce in the kitchen, scarfing down one of her ginger snap cookies she had made for the library bake sale and had strictly forbade him to eat.

He looked at her guiltily. "Wow, that was like record time. You must have broken the sound barrier getting home so fast."

"How many cookies have you eaten?"

"This is the only one, I swear."

He was lying.

His neck was turning red, which was a telltale sign he wasn't being honest with her. But him sneaking one of her ginger snaps was hardly the topic in the forefront of her mind.

"Where's Leroy?"

As if on cue, her adorable off-white Shih Tzu bounded down the stairs, tongue panting, tail wagging, looking healthy and happy. She suddenly noticed Conner sitting in the living room, a packed suitcase next to him, his face buried in his phone. Hayley checked her watch.

"You guys better get going soon or Conner is going to miss his flight," Hayley said.

"We're just waiting for Gemma," Conner said, not looking up from his phone's screen, two fingers apparently tapping out a text to someone.

Hayley raised an eyebrow. "Gemma's driving to Bangor with you? I thought she had other plans."

Gemma suddenly appeared at the top of the staircase, bright-eyed and beaming. She carried her suitcase in one hand. As she descended the stairs, Hayley couldn't help but notice her waving her free arm around as if she was having muscle spasms or some kind of seizure.

"Gemma, what's wrong? What's happened? Where are you going?"

"Nothing's wrong. I just wanted you to come home so I could say goodbye. I'm going back to New York with Conner."

This surprised Hayley. She looked at Bruce, confused, wondering if he had any idea what was going on. But he just stared at her with a big, dumb grin on his face.

Gemma was now waving her hand so violently in front of Hayley's face, Hayley reached out to grab her by the wrist out of fear Gemma might accidentally smack her in the face.

"Gemma, what is this? Why can't you control your body movements?"

Gemma sighed, then held up her left hand directly in front of Hayley's eyes, wiggling the ring finger, which had a simple silver band on it. "We're engaged."

Hayley was struck dumb as she finally realized Gemma had been waving her arm around to draw her mother's attention to the engagement ring on her finger. It took her a few seconds before she could say anything, but finally Hayley managed to spit out, "Who?"

"Me and Zac Efron," Gemma snapped sarcastically. "Who do you think? Me and Conner! He proposed to me again late last night—and this time I accepted!"

The moment finally began to sink in, and then Hayley let out an excited squeal and hugged her daughter, who was now jumping up and down, unable to contain herself.

When they finally pulled apart, Hayley had to steady herself because she was still reeling from the news. "I can't believe it . . . My baby's getting married . . ."

"After I said yes, Conner jumped on the phone and rebooked my flight so we can go back to the city together," Gemma said.

"There are so many thoughts swimming around in my head right now," Hayley gasped. "But the biggest one is, I feel so old . . ."

Conner finally finished texting and joined them in the hallway. "Sorry, that was my director. He had a few notes on the script he wanted me to keep in mind as I prepare for my first rehearsal tomorrow."

Hayley grabbed Conner by the shoulders and gave him a tight squeeze. "I just heard. Congratulations. This is wonderful news."

"I want you to know, the engagement ring is just a temporary place holder. I wanted to make it official before we left Maine, and so I didn't have a lot of time to pick something out . . ."

"Conner, the ring doesn't matter. It's the love that you two share, that will always be the strongest symbol of your relationship," Hayley said solemnly, gently taking Gemma's ring finger to inspect it.

"No, seriously. My grandmother has this really beautiful French-set halo diamond ring my grandfather gave her back in the 1950s that she's been waiting to give me for when I got married."

"Oh, thank God!" Hayley cried with relief. "I mean, simple can be elegant sometimes, but that looks like something out of a Cracker Jack box."

They all laughed, but Hayley still felt the need to add, "I'm kidding."

Even though she wasn't.

Bruce stepped up behind her and kissed her on the neck. "Sure, dear. We believe you." Of course, his comment was laden with his usual sarcasm. Then he turned to Gemma and Conner. "We really need to hit the road."

"Call me the minute you get home so we can start discussing wedding plans. We need to reserve the church and a reception venue. We can bring Liddy in to help because, well, as you know, her own wedding blew up in her face last June, but she knows all the best florists and dressmakers, and she can really help us with all the details . . ."

Gemma smiled, shaking her head, and then glanced over at Conner. "I told you she'd be like this." She turned back to Hayley. "We haven't even set a date yet. Maybe sometime next summer."

"It's never too early to start planning. You know how busy it gets around here. Places book up fast," Hayley insisted.

"Conner's parents live in upstate New York, so we shouldn't automatically assume we'll be having the wedding here in Bar Harbor."

"It's the most beautiful spot in the United States!" Hayley insisted.

"But you're not biased or anything," Bruce cracked.

Again with that sometimes annoying sarcasm.

She did love him, though.

He was just so darn cute.

"Come on, let's get out of here before she has me trying on dresses," Gemma said, heading for the door.

"We already know you fit into Liddy's wedding dress, the one you wore for the Witches Ball. You looked so lovely in that," Hayley said.

Bruce reached the front door first and opened it, ushering Gemma and Conner, who were carrying their suitcases, out of the house and to his car parked.

"Take care of that arm, Conner! I don't want it still in a sling come your wedding day!" Hayley yelled.

Bruce finally stopped her with a hard kiss on the lips. He was such a good kisser it left her swooning for a second, her thoughts a muddled mess.

"I'll be home in time for dinner," Bruce said and then hustled out, leaving Hayley standing in the front doorway.

"I'm serious, Conner, your parents will love Maine!"

They loaded the trunk, hopped in Bruce's car, and tore off down the street, probably happy to finally escape the overly excited mother of the bride.

As Hayley watched them disappear around the corner, she couldn't stop smiling.

Finally, she stepped back inside the house, closed the door, and leaned up against it, closing her eyes.

And that's when she broke down in tears.

Tears of absolute, unbridled joy.

Island Food & Spirits
BY
HAYLEY POWELL

As many of you already know, I was recently blindsided by my daughter's sudden engagement. Quite frankly, the news sent me over the moon, and I have already been busy with all the wedding plans. That distraction, however, caused me to ignore keeping up with my housekeeping and yard work duties. So finally, last Saturday, I decided enough was enough. Enough putting things off. My husband, Bruce, and I would spend the weekend sweeping inside and trimming outside. He could tackle the yard on Saturday and I would hit the bedrooms and bathrooms with my arsenal of cleaning products on Sunday.

Of course, the challenge was getting Bruce to join the cleanup effort. He had declared the night before that he was planning to spend his Saturday stretched out on the couch, reading the sports page and just relaxing until the big football game on Sunday he was excited to watch.

This certainly did not fit into my plans, and

so I knew he was going to need a good kick in the . . . I mean, a little extra motivation.

When Bruce came down for his morning coffee on Saturday morning, I told him I was going to run errands with Liddy in Ellsworth and wanted to make a deal with him. If he raked the entire yard, which was blanketed with fall leaves from our trees and what looked like most of our neighbors' trees, and trimmed the hedges for winter, and got it all done by three that afternoon when I planned to arrive home, I would make his favorite Philly Cheesesteak Patty Melt sandwich for the next four Sundays, and he could watch his beloved football games with absolutely no complaining from me.

Well, I had never seen him put down a newspaper so fast as he jumped up, and with a twinkle in his eye and his mouth already watering, blurted out, "You got yourself a deal!" The idea of four blissful Sundays of uninterrupted football, my delicious patty melts washed down with beer, and no nagging from me was just too enticing to pass up.

Before Bruce had the chance to grab his rake and get started, I told him the catch. If he wasn't done by three when I got home, he would agree to spend the next four Sundays accompanying me out for a day of my choosing, no matter what it was.

This gave him pause as his mind must have contemplated the agonizing activities I might cook up for the two of us. Clothes shopping, an arts and craft show, or, God forbid, helping me plan my daughter's wedding. But he was determined to watch football so we shook hands on our little wager.

I kissed him goodbye and off I went to Ellsworth with Liddy. I was reasonably confident I was going to win our bet because Bruce was notorious for getting distracted by a neighbor or phone call or even a *Law & Order* rerun on TV. I was already planning our first outing for next Sunday: apple picking in Levant.

But when Liddy dropped me off at the house at three o'clock on the dot later that afternoon, I was utterly speechless. The yard had been completely cleared of leaves, the trees and hedges perfectly trimmed, and all the debris disposed of at the town dump.

And there was Bruce sitting idly on the porch with a beer in hand and a big satisfied grin on his face.

Bruce informed me that now he was free to watch football on Sunday. He had already invited his friend Reverend Ted Lancaster over to join him as well as his sister-in-law, Tori, who could hang out with me while I prepared his Philly Cheesesteak Patty Melts and served cocktails. Spending the afternoon with Ted and Tori would certainly take the sting out of losing the bet.

The following day, while the boys were yelling and cheering for the Patriots on TV, downing their beers and sandwiches, Tori and I sat in the kitchen gossiping and sipping my delicious Pumpkin White Russians.

There was a knock at the back door, and when I got up to answer it, I found Shawn

Cooper, a nice local boy who owned a lawn and yard service. He told me he had been up all night worrying that he hadn't been able to take care of the large limb hanging over the back of the garage yesterday in the time frame he was given to complete the job of cleaning our yard. Given the generous amount of money Bruce had paid him, it only felt right that he come back, cut it down, and haul it away today so it wouldn't collapse and cause any damage.

I smiled and invited Shawn in, and promptly led him to the living room where I picked up the TV remote and shut off the game. Bruce and Ted sat up, confused.

Well, Bruce's face went completely white at the sight of Shawn because he knew that he was totally busted. Shawn apologized in advance if the sound of his electric saw might drown out the game.

I happily told Shawn not to worry about getting it done today because he could come back next Sunday since we wouldn't even be home. We would be apple picking up in Levant, and so he could saw that tree to his heart's content. I also promised to bake him an apple pie for being so thoughtful with the haul Bruce and I planned on picking *all day long.*

"Right, Bruce?" I asked, my arms folded across my chest.

Bruce nodded and took a big bite of his Philly Cheesesteak Patty Melt, knowing it would be the last one he would be getting for a long time.

Pumpkin White Russian

Ingredients
2 ounces vodka
1 ounce Kahlua
1 ounce heavy cream
1½ tablespoons pumpkin puree

Add all the ingredients to a shaker with ice and shake until well mixed.

Pour over ice in a cocktail glass and enjoy!

Bruce's Favorite Philly Cheesesteak Melt

Ingredients
1 medium onion, diced
1 green pepper diced
8 ounces mushrooms your favorite
8 slices provolone cheese (2 per sandwich)
1 16-ounce steak
1 tablespoon Worcestershire sauce
Texas toast (or your favorite bread)
½ teaspoon kosher salt
½ teaspoon ground black pepper
Butter
2 tablespoons olive oil

Slice your steak as thin as possible against the grain and marinate in the Worcestershire sauce, salt, and pepper for 1 hour at least.

In a sauté pan add your olive oil, onions, peppers, and mushrooms and sauté until soft. Salt and pepper to taste.

Remove the veggies and set aside. Add the sliced meat to the pan and cook until your desired doneness. Do not crowd the pan, so cook in batches if you must.

Heat a nonstick griddle on medium heat. Butter four slices of Texas toast and place two butter-side down on the heated griddle.

Add a slice of provolone cheese to each slice of bread, then steak, veggies, and the second slice of provolone cheese and top with bread butter-side up.

Press down with a spatula to compress sandwich. When golden dark brown, flip over and press again. Cook until cheese is melted and sandwich is golden brown.

A quick note: I like to spread mayonnaise inside my bread before layering the ingredients, but this is just a personal preference! But honestly, it's yummy!

Index of Recipes